Maybe Murder
A Kalico Cat Detective Agency Mystery

by

Penny S. Weibly

This book is fiction. All characters, events, and organizations portrayed in this novel are the product of the author's imagination or are used fictitiously. Any resemblance to actual persons—living or dead—is entirely coincidental.

Copyright © 2019 by Penny S. Weibly

All rights reserved. No parts of this book may be reproduced or transmitted in any form or by any means, electronic or mechanical, including photocopying, recording or by any information storage and retrieval system, without written permission from the author, except for the inclusion of brief quotations in a review.

For information, email Cozy Cat Press, cozycatpress@aol.com or visit our website at: www.cozycatpress.com

COZY CAT PRESS

ISBN: 978-1-946063-74-8
Printed in the United States of America

10 9 8 7 6 5 4 3 2 1

To Eileen and Deb who were my first gentle readers and are my dear friends. Thank you also to Roshan and Ryan for their feedback and encouragement. You are the daughters of my heart. Also to Zoe and Riley, my good dogs, who inspire me daily to live in the present and to discover joy in small things.

Chapter One

Benjamin Kalico grabbed his car keys, bolted out of his office, down three flights of concrete stairs, and ran across a side street to his car. In thirty seconds he had maneuvered his ten-year-old silver Honda Civic into the busy Austin traffic.

"Talk to me, M's," he said to his assistant, placing his iPhone into a hands-free holder.

"Tweets report a sighting of Sunny Bono at Live Oak and Alameda. That's Stacy Park."

"Right." He merged onto Congress Avenue heading south. If he timed the lights right, he would be at Stacy Park in six minutes. "What's his profile?"

"Sunny Bono is an eight-year-old, long-aired orange tabby with golden eyes. White chest. Distinguishing mark: white left paw. Not declawed. Indoor cat only. Escaped through a sliding glass door left open by a cable repairman. Missing since March 7 at approximately 7 p.m."

Kalico zigged into the right lane to pass a sightseeing Subaru, then swerved back into the left lane, just making it through a yellow light at Riverside. "The boy's probably hungry; he's been missing nearly forty-eight hours."

"Favorite food: Fancy Feast Savory Salmon."

Kalico pulled into the left turn lane at Live Oak. He tapped his steering wheel, willing the light to change. "Anything else?"

"You won't believe it."

"What?"

"Sunny B has a favorite song. Owner sings it to him often."

"Don't tell me."

"Yep. Apparently the cat loves *I Got You Babe.*" M's suppressed a chuckle. "Last sighting was in the 1700 block of Alta Vista."

Kalico entered the Travis Heights neighborhood, found the correct block, and slowly cruised the length of the street, scanning each yard to his left for a flash of orange. He turned the car around and scanned the opposite side of the street before parking under a tall live oak. No sign of Sunny Bono.

He rolled down his window, letting a warm March breeze fill the car, and brought up Sunny B's mug shot from Kalico's Pet Capture webpage. Deep golden eyes stared out from a tiger-striped face. He was a big guy at approximately twelve pounds. His owner, Miss Cheryl Adams, was pictured holding a petite black cat. Her caption read: "Cher and I miss our Sunny. $300 reward for his safe return."

Kalico opened his trunk to reveal neatly stacked plastic bins labeled with various missing pets' names. He pulled out Sunny B's bin and transferred a small, blue cat food bowl, a can of Savory Salmon, a feathered cat toy, and a gray sweater covered with orange and white fur into his backpack. He also grabbed a cat carrier, leather jacket, gloves, and a cat catching noose. Although the noose looked ominous, looped at the end of a long, hollow pole, he knew from experience the kind of damage a frightened or angry cat could do to unprotected skin. He absentmindedly rubbed his thumb against a jagged scar on the back of his right hand.

Alta Vista was quiet. At 10 o'clock in the morning most people were at work, and Travis Heights Elementary was in session. Kalico walked slowly down the shady street, admiring the beautifully restored upscale homes with their deep front porches and groomed front yards. Lavender wisteria covered a tall trellis beside a dark gray and white house. He scanned the shrubs—no Sunny B. Kalico's nose caught the unmistakable scent of Grape Kool Aid emanating from a mature mountain laurel.

Five houses down, he caught a flicker of moving orange out of the corner of his eye. Kalico froze. "Here, kitty. Kitty, kitty, kitty," he called in a high-pitched falsetto. "Come on: show yourself. Let me see a white left (right?) paw. Come here, kitty."

Nothing. Perhaps he had imagined the movement. He stood still, slowed his breathing, and stared into the shadows. Yes. Just there, under a dense elaeagnus shrub, an orange tabby stood like a statue, only the flicking tip of its tail indicating its displeasure. Silently, Kalico commanded: "Don't run!"

He surveyed the compact blue and white house: shades drawn and no cars in the drive. Good. In slow motion he placed the cat carrier down, edging it partially under a shrub about five feet away from the crouched feline. He set his backpack down and removed the gray sweater, cat dish and Fancy Feast. He placed the sweater in the carrier. "Good kitty-boy," he crooned. "I bet you're hungry. Come on, Sunny Bono and get some dinner." He inched back the lid of the Savory Salmon, emptied it into the cat dish, and pushed it to within two feet of the tense tabby. "Doesn't that smell wonderful? Come and get it. Come on, Sunny."

Kalico stood up and stepped back, holding his breath. The cat was still crouched, ears down, and tail flicking. Obviously it was too scared to come out of hiding. Patience is a detective's most important tool. Kalico sat down on the warm grass, never letting his gaze waiver from the cat. He thought he perceived a white front paw and certainly the cat had a white chest.

It had to be Sunny B. Although the temperature had risen to 82 degrees—unusually warm for March—he donned his leather jacket and gloves. Sweat trickled down his spine.

Minutes passed. The cat did not relax, but he did not run away. Kalico looked at the houses to left and right to insure that he was alone, then in a rusty tenor he began to sing "I Got You Babe" softly to the shrub.

As Kalico began the chorus, he heard a distinct meow that mimicked "Babe." Sonny Bono had emerged half-way from the shrub and seemed to be rocking in time to the song.

Kalico continued, making up new words to the Sonny and Cher classic as he willed the tabby forward.

Just a few steps more and I'll get you home
Your adventure is over and no more will you roam

"Mister, what ya doin…?"

Kalico's song jerked to a stop, the cat retreated to the deep shadows, and the detective turned to see a little blonde girl in jean shorts, a red tee shirt, and pink flip flops standing beside him. *Damn.*

Flushing, Kalico whispered, "Just trying to retrieve a lost cat."

"Were you singing to the kitty? I love, love, love kitty cats," the child squealed. "Where is it?"

"Shhhhhh. Quiet. We don't want to scare him. Isn't that your mommy calling you?"

"Nah. Mommy sent me to get the mail out of the mailbox because I'm a big girl. Oh! Is that the cat under there?"

Kalico held out an arm to keep the child from tackling Sunny B. "Listen. If you ask your mother's permission, I'll let you help me capture the cat. But you must be quiet."

"*Okay!*" she said in a stage whisper, then ran next door, shouting, "Mommy! Mommy!"

Kalico returned his attention to Sunny Bono, half expecting the boy to have vanished. To the detective's surprise, he was still sitting beneath the elaeagnus, eyes fixed on his cat food. He took a step forward.

"I know you want it, kid. Come get it, Sunny Bono."

He began Sunny's song again softly.

"Excuse me, but you're on private property."

Kalico swore under his breath as he watched Sunny retreat again. He turned to see a young woman staring at him suspiciously, holding the little blonde girl's hand.

"I know. Sorry," he whispered. "You see, I'm trying to retrieve that cat." He gestured toward the shrubbery.

"See the orange kitty, Mommy? He's lost and needs to get back to his mommy," the child whispered. "The man said that I could help."

"Quiet, Meggie." The mother narrowed her eyes looking first at Kalico and then at the frightened tabby. Then, she smiled. "Why you're that cat detective, aren't you? It's great work that you're doing. I lost my dog, Freckles, when I was ten, and we never found him. I was devastated." She sighed. "How can we help?"

Kalico flinched at the woman's nomenclature. He was, after all, a serious private investigator who for now just happened to find lost pets. He shrugged off his annoyance. Sunny B was still in his place. "Just stand back and be still. If he runs towards you, block him and herd him toward the carrier. Okay?"

"Okay," Meggie and her mom said.

The waiting game began again. Gradually, Sunny's tail stopped its frenetic dance and his ears pointed forward, nose twitching. He relaxed into the shade and the mulch.

"Come on, Sunny B. Here kitty."

"Here kitty," Meggie echoed.

Minutes passed. A garbage truck passed, putting Sunny back on alert. Sweating profusely now, Kalico cleared his throat, looked apologetically at Meggie's mom, and sang his song again.

Behind him, a light soprano joined in, singing the harmony. At the chorus, Sunny B joined in. By the time they were through the song once, the cat had emerged from the shadows and was eyeing his cat dish. Kalico could sense Meggie vibrating behind him, and signaled her to keep still as he and her mother kept singing softly to the cat. As they reached the chorus again, Sunny seemed to sigh. He moved to the bowl of food, sighing and purring simultaneously. Meggie squeaked softly.

Kalico placed his gloved hand on the cat catching pole with its looped noose dangling from the far end. He hated the pole—he knew logically that it would not hurt the animal and that it protected him from teeth and claws—yet it felt cruel.

Decision time.

He set the pole back down and removed the glove from his right hand. Humming softly, he approached Sunny Bono and gently placed his bare hand on his back, stroking it gently. Sunny tensed, but did not stop eating. Kalico continued to pet his back and sing. Supper done, the cat turned his golden gaze to Kalico's face, seemed to like what he saw, and, purring, rubbed his cheek against the detective's knee. "*Okay?*" Kalico asked politely. Sunny seemed to nod his acquiescence, so he was lifted into the detective's arms. Meggie and her mom held the cat carrier up so that Sunny could be placed safely inside.

"Hurray!" Meggie and her mother cheered and applauded.

"Nice kitty! I helped," Meggie shouted.

"That was amazing. How did you know that he wouldn't fight or run?" asked Meggie's mother.

"I didn't. It was just a feeling." Kalico flushed.

An hour later, Sunny Bono was safely home and in the arms of his delighted owner, Kalico had a check for $300 in his pocket, and was feeling satisfied as he sat behind his desk and dug into a hamburger and fries. People could make fun of his pet retrievals, but at least his work made his clients happy. As an intern, his job had consisted mostly of trailing unfaithful spouses to gather evidence for divorce: a process that broke hearts, leaving behind sadness and bitterness.

"Send the picture, and I'll update our pages," M's called from the reception area.

"Will do."

In an instant M's saw a beautiful orange tabby cradled in the arms of a tearfully smiling woman. She posted it on the agency's webpage and Facebook accounts with the caption: *"Sunny and Cher reunited! We got you, Babe. Sunny Bono joyfully returned to his grateful owner, Cheryl Adams."*

Chapter Two

As Miss Emelia Winterjoy entered Suite 305, the dilapidated home of The Kalico Detective Agency, her nose was assaulted by the smell of onions, French fries, and mustard. The young woman behind the reception desk did not bother to look up from her iPhone; she just waved her toward the detective's office.

Detective? The young man who rose hastily to greet her looked more like one of her recalcitrant high school seniors. Ignoring his extended hand and quelling his greeting with a look, she declared, "My neighbor is a murderer."

"Good afternoo...Please, won't you... What?" Benjamin Kalico's pulse raced. *Murder?*

"Young man, are you hard of hearing? I have come to hire you to solve a murder."

"Terrific! Who's the victim? When did the killing occur? Where? How? Ms....?" Grinning, Kalico grabbed his tablet, prepared to take a statement.

Miss Winterjoy settled herself onto a cold, metal chair and inspected the Private Detective's license framed behind the young man. "*Miss* Winterjoy," she corrected him. "I should be more specific. The murder has not yet occurred. I want to hire you to prevent it."

Kalico's grin vanished, and his right hand pushed through his shock of red hair that was already standing on end. *Damn.*

"I am neither delusional nor wanting attention." She fixed her blue eyes on his brown ones. "And I am prepared to pay you a retainer as well as cover your expenses—provided they are reasonable."

At the word, *retainer*, his grin reappeared. "All right, Ms., I mean, Miss Winterjoy. Tell me about this perspective murder."

"Prospective," she corrected. "Perspective signals your point of view."

Forty-three minutes later, Benjamin Kalico ushered Miss Winterjoy out of his office.

"Remember, I expect detailed daily reports and an itemized list of expenses."

"Yes, Miss Winterjoy. Not to worry. I will get right on the case." He closed the door behind her and faced his receptionist.

"Lost tabby?" Melissa Moon, "M's" to her friends, yawned.

"Murder." He watched as her dark brown eyes outlined with black charcoal registered his news. Then he continued. "And look!" He flashed a check for $1000.00 in front of her surprised gaze before waltzing it around the room.

"Pay day is this Friday," she reminded him. "Sign it, and I'll deposit it." She held out a hand tipped with black nail polish.

"And you will be paid on time. Did you ever doubt it?" Kalico signed and handed over the check, then two-stepped back into his office, still grinning.

"But who was murdered...?"

Kalico stretched his 6' 2" frame out, placed his feet on top of his desk and gazed at a diagonal crack that ran through his ceiling. So what if the old woman was fanciful, imagining murderers behind each rose bush? At least he was investigating a possible murder and not another lost pet. Since he had recovered Diva, a show quality Persian cat, for its socialite owner three months ago, he'd had nothing but lost pet cases. A video of

Kalico handing the beautiful feline over to her equally beautiful owner had gone viral, earning him the media-induced name of the "Cat Detective." At least business had been steady if not particularly profitable....

Kalico sat down in front of his computer. Miss Winterjoy suspected that her friend and neighbor, Mrs. Nancy MacLeod was in danger. Several accidents, including a fall downstairs and a fender bender, had convinced Miss Winterjoy that someone was trying to murder her friend. And that someone was none other than Connor MacLeod, the intended victim's twenty-two year old grandson who had moved in with her just weeks prior to the first accident. Miss Winterjoy seemed to feel that young MacLeod was a villain based on the facts that he had plagiarized his senior English thesis, slouched, and rarely made eye contact.

First step: background checks. His new client had saved him time—he would not need to do an extensive search for her history.

"You will want to check my credentials," she had said, handing him a neatly typed, two-page resume. "My full name is Emelia Rose Winterjoy. I was born on March 16, 1944 in Austin, Texas." Noting Kalico's attempt to do the math in his head, she said, "That makes me seventy-four years old. I earned a bachelor's degree in Education from the University of Texas as well as a Texas teaching certificate. I began teaching English at Travis High School in 1967, where I remained until I retired in 2012."

Glancing down at her resume, he noted that in her long career she had served as Department Chair for ten years, earned a Masters degree in Victorian literature, and was honored by the Texas Professional English Educators Association."

"You are welcome to search that Internet contraption for me," Miss Winterjoy had said, scowling at his laptop. "You will find no criminal history or…" her blue eyes had glinted with amusement, "stints in a mental hospital—although you may question the sanity of someone who spent her life wrangling teenagers. I live in a house that I inherited from my mother in 1988, enjoy gardening, my book club, and long walks with my dogs."

Kalico set her resume aside and Googled her. Not surprisingly, Miss Winterjoy did not engage in social media. She did not have a Facebook or Twitter account, and her email seemed to be lightly used.

Kalico retrieved the bag of French fries he had stashed in his desk drawer and crammed cold, greasy potatoes into his mouth. Miss Winterjoy was exactly who she appeared to be: a concerned old woman who wanted to protect a friend. She was probably lonely, bored in retirement, so she needed to imagine murder to fill the time. As long as she was willing to pay, he was willing to indulge her fancies.

A booming voice in the reception area interrupted his thoughts.

"Hello, M's, my love. When are you going to give up this glamorous life and get a real job? Is the Cat Detective in?"

"This is as real as it gets, Officer Carrillo." Melissa Moon smiled at the burly cop who filled her reception area. "He's in the office—a big case."

"Benjamin, my man, another catnapping? A felonious feline, perhaps? Or have you graduated to the pooch patrol?" Victor Carrillo chuckled and leaned against the office door.

"Laugh all you want, Victor, but those pets pay the bills."

Victor looked at the shabby office. "Not very well. When are you going to give this up and join the force? So what's the big case you're working on?"

"Possible homicide." Kalico watched his friend's eyes narrow.

"Best not to interfere in an ongoing police investigation."

"It's not ongoing."

"Did you pick up a cold case?"

"Not exactly. Look, I've got to get back to work."

"Let's go catch a burger at Dirty's, and you can tell me all about it."

"Can't, Vic. Besides, I already ate."

"Okay. I get it: big time private dick at work."

Frowning, Kalico shrugged and purposefully returned his attention to his computer.

"See you for hoops Saturday morning?"

"Sure."

As Victor strode out of the office, Kalico smiled at his long time friend's back. They'd met in middle school, played ball together in high school, and shared a keen interest in law enforcement. Vic had gone straight into the Police Academy after graduation, while Kalico had gone to UT, majoring in criminal justice, then interning at The Lone Star Detective Agency, before opening his own office six months ago. It had been a rough start to the business, and Vic constantly advocated for his friend to join the force and work his way up to detective. But Kalico had a dream: he may be under capitalized and under paid; he may be behind on his rent and worried about paying M's salary—let alone his own; he may be the "cat" detective for now, but, by God, he had his own agency, a possible, if unlikely, murder to prevent, and a big check in his pocket.

He turned his attention to Miss Winterjoy's neighbor, and began a background check. Nancy MacLeod, née Simmons. Born: 1945. Married James Dulson in 1965. Married Gareth MacLeod in 1966.

Graduated from UT with a degree in library science in 1967. One son, Patrick, a lawyer, now living in California, born 1968. One grandson, Connor, age 22. Widowed in 2001. Profession: children's librarian....

Kalico sighed. Nancy MacLeod was an unlikely target for murder. Maybe she'd fined a toddler one too many times for an overdue book? He clicked on the Texas Library Association's website to review her professional associations: a member since 1979, she had worked downtown at the Austin Central Library, the Faulk Central Branch, for eighteen years, transferring to the Hampton Branch in 1997.

At 4:30, M's poked her head into Kalico's office, announcing that she was off to the bank to deposit the checks before heading home.

Kalico looked up from his computer screen. "Did you make the calls?"

"Of course. No new reports from any of the rescue groups. No tweets. No postings."

"But did you call Animal Control?"

M's frowned and glanced away from Kalico. Ben knew she loved her role in tracking missing pets—everything except calling Animal Control. She didn't want to know if one of their clients' pets had become road kill. The loss of a miniature poodle, named Puddles, had been shattering. She shuddered. "Well, no," she admitted.

Kalico studied his assistant for a moment. "Not to worry. I'll make the call today."

"Thanks. See you tomorrow. Don't work too late."

Kalico listened as M's gathered her stuff and left the office. He'd finished his notes on Sunny Bono's capture, completing and closing his file. Tomorrow M's would turn his notes into a clever narrative for their blog. He'd listed his mileage and expenses. It was almost time to pay his quarterly self-employment taxes. Thank goodness for Sunny B and Miss Winterjoy.

Kalico returned to researching Nancy MacLeod, finding nothing in the life of the librarian that would make her a target for murder. With increased interest, he turned his attention to Connor MacLeod, Miss Winterjoy's prime suspect. He pulled up the young man's Facebook page. An exasperated chuckle escaped him: Kalico did not know what he had expected—certainly, not the face or profile that appeared before him. Instead of the dead eyes of a Dylan Klebold, he saw a fresh, freckle-faced kid in a cowboy hat mugging for the camera. A junior at UT, majoring in mechanical engineering, his profile indicated that he loved indie rock, living in the Live Music Capital of the World, and brown-eyed girls. A quick background check indicated that he worked part time as a waiter at Truluck's, had no outstanding warrants or any past run-ins with the law, and had a single unpaid parking ticket.

Well, shoot. It appeared that his new client was indeed fanciful. Kalico pondered whether or not he would have to refund her retainer. He sighed. He would.

His stomach growled: 6:30. Time to call it quits for the night. He pulled up his open case files—an end of the daily ritual—and studied the faces of four cats and seven dogs who were missing. The number was down from the thirty cases he'd compiled after the publicity frenzy surrounding Diva, and no new missing pet investigations had opened this week. *That's okay*, he thought. *I don't want to be boxed into being the pet detective*. But the money had kept him afloat. Aside from the dead end provided by Miss Winterjoy, his only other case was a subcontracted insurance fraud investigation—a bone from a colleague at the Lone Star Agency.

Kalico put his laptop in its case, locked his desk, and turned off the lights. His phone vibrated.

"Hi, Mom."

"Hello, Benjy dear. I called to congratulate you on finding Sunny Bono. Such a beautiful boy."

"Ben," he corrected automatically. "Thanks. You must be my most avid Twitter follower."

"I am. Your father is hungry for enchiladas, so we wondered if you would like to join us at Maudie's on Slaughter at 7?"

"Mom, you guys don't need to feed me," Kalico grumbled.

"We know that, but we're your parents, and we worry. You're too thin. Come on, you know you love chicken enchiladas in tomatillo sauce. We'll even spring for a margarita. And you can tell us all about the exciting capture."

"Okay," he acquiesced, somewhat ungraciously. "But please ask Dad not to bring up my giving up the agency for a real job, and, Mom, no asking me to move back home."

"We promise."

Two hours later, Kalico entered his sparse one-bedroom apartment, kicked off his shoes, and sank into his couch as he turned on his TV to catch the end of *Law and Order*. True to their word, his parents had not discussed his finances; instead, his mother delicately asked whether or not he had met a nice girl—a sore topic, since Kalico had no time to date and a sense that women around his age were looking for someone more professionally established. "After all, son, you're almost thirty…" was the evening's refrain.

At 11 p.m. just as he was heading for bed, his phone buzzed. Kalico read the message, grabbed his tablet and raced out the door. Ghost, a white Siberian husky, missing since March 6th, had been spotted running along the frontage road near Mo-Pac and Loop 360.

Chapter Three

Wednesday, six a.m. found Kalico parked across the street from a modest three-bedroom home in the Dove Springs neighborhood of East Austin. The tan and brown house was dark, its shades drawn. It belonged to Carson Bolter, who lived there with his wife and two school-aged children. A forty-one year old roofer for a small business, he had been off the job since January, filing a Workman's Compensation claim for a back injury. The roofing company had called in Lone Star to investigate possible fraud, and Lone Star had subcontracted with Kalico on a case that promised little monetary remuneration for the firm.

Kalico bit into his Egg McMuffin, washing it down with strong, black coffee. It had been a long night. He'd cruised the Mo-Pac frontage road, Loop 360, and the surrounding area for two hours, catching only a flash of the white dog in a sliver of moonlight. Then Ghost had vanished into the Barton Creek Greenbelt. If time allowed this evening, the detective planned to don hiking boots and walk the trail. Not only did Ghost have the honor of longest escapee on Kalico's missing pet list, but he also carried a bonus of $2000.00.

Keeping one eye on the house, Kalico opened his email. Early morning surveillance provided quiet time for documentation and planning. He updated Ghost's file, making a note to M's to canvas the Travis Country subdivision. He suspected that Ghost would move from the greenbelt into a neighborhood in search of food.

The March sky was brightening, and mourning doves were cooing.

A message blinked.

From: *Miss Emelia Winterjoy*
To: *Mr. Benjamin Kalico*
Subject: *Daily report*

"I expect your first report today by noon. Time is of the essence."—E.W.

And the game's afoot, Kalico thought in his best British accent. Last night he had determined to give up Miss Winterjoy's "case," let the woman down as gently as possible, and return the retainer, minus one day's hourly rate and expenses. Too bad. It was a nice check.

Somewhat gloomily, he began his report, noting that nothing in Connor MacLeod's initial background check indicated anything unusual or even hinted at possible criminal intent. By all accounts, he was a good student, earning a "B" average, worked approximately thirty hours a week waiting tables, and had no outstanding warrants and no criminal record. He placed the last fact in bold and underlined it. He closed his report, promising to submit a full transcript of the background check, an itemized account of his time and expenses, and a refund of most of his retainer.

6:45 a.m. Lights came on in the corner bedroom of the Bolter house. Ten minutes later, light appeared from the kids' rooms and then in the kitchen. The family was up. Kalico peered through his digital camera binoculars. No sign of Carson. At 7:15 the family gathered at the kitchen table for breakfast. There. He could just make out Carson, who stood at the head of table to eat his breakfast. Was he wearing his black back brace? Hard to tell. At 7:40 Mrs. Bolter, a nine-year-old boy, and a thirteen-year-old girl exited the house. Each hugged Carson who stood stiffly in the doorway and waved them on. He was, indeed, wearing his brace.

Kalico waited and watched the house for another twenty minutes. A television flickered through the living room curtains, but he could not see Carson. If his suspect held true to the pattern Kalico had documented over the past ten days, he would remain prone until his wife came home to fix lunch. He had not left the house in the last week except to visit his doctor and a physical therapist.

Kalico placed a red and blue Round Rock *Express* baseball cap over his red hair, grabbed a missing pet flyer, and walked across the street to knock on Carson's door. A minute passed, and he knocked again, a little more loudly. He heard shuffling and mumbling from inside. Then Carson inched open the door, not lifting the chain lock.

"We don't want anything," he growled.

"Not selling anything," Kalico responded cheerfully. "I am sorry to bother you, but I'm looking for a lost Bichon Frise puppy, named Pippa. Have you seen this little gal?" He held up the flyer several feet from the door at eye level.

Carson released the chain, and his door swung open. He took a small step forward to look more closely at the flyer.

"My niece is frantic. The puppy pulled the leash out of her hand on their walk last night. We hope someone in the neighborhood has seen her or taken her in," Kalico prevaricated. (Pippa was missing, but not from Dove Springs; she belonged to a UT student, and she had been gone for nearly a week.)

He observed Carson closely: he was barefoot, wearing flannel pajama bottoms and a white t-shirt. The back brace was cinched around his waist and extended from just below his armpits to his hips. Deep frown lines were etched between his brows, and pain lines framed his mouth.

"No. Sorry. I haven't seen her," Carson said. "And, believe me, my kids would've mentioned finding a puppy. We bought my son, Ryan, a turtle, but it didn't cut it."

"Thanks. And, man, I'm sorry to have disturbed you. I didn't know you were injured." He looked pointedly at the brace.

"Yeah. Strained my back on the job."

"Back pain is the worst," murmured Kalico, sympathetically.

"It's a bitch. The doctor said I'd be back to work in four to six weeks, and it's been nearly ten."

"Sorry to hear it. But it must be kind of nice to have such an extended time off; that is, if things are okay financially." Kalico looked down. "I can hardly imagine a full week off without going into the office." He sighed and smiled innocently.

"That's okay. Insurance is taking care of us. As for the time off, that's what I thought—at first. But I can't sit, so I can't drive. The meds make me foggy, so I can't read. I can't work, and, if I never see another daytime talk show in my life, it will be fine with me." Carson shuffled back a step. "Hope you find the pup."

"Thanks, again. Our number is on the flyer." Kalico turned to go, then paused. "Say, do you need anything, before I go?"

In the middle of shaking his head, "No," Carson stopped and pointed to his front lawn. "Yes. Would you mind grabbing the newspaper for me? I can't manage the front steps yet, and Susan, my wife, forgot to bring it in this morning."

Kalico picked up the *Austin American-Statesman*. As he handed it to Carson, he had an instant to note a disheveled couch covered with blankets and pillows, a television turned to *Good Morning America*, and a tray table with four medicine containers, a bottle of water, and a *Sports Illustrated*. "Hope your back gets better real soon."

***

As Kalico endured the stop and go rush hour traffic on I35, he decided that Carson Bolter was the real deal, a genuine guy who was benefitting from Worker's Comp, a guy who was not attempting to defraud his company. He'd observe him for three more days per his contract with Lone Star, but did not anticipate finding out otherwise.

"Good morning, M's." Kalico rushed into the office, dropped his backpack on the floor, and smiled at his assistant. "There's been another Ghost sighting. Please get his owner, Mr. Skifford, on the phone so that I can give him an update. I think we'll need to canvas…"

M's cleared her throat loudly. "Ben. Mr. Kalico, you have a client waiting." She directed her gaze to his office door and mouthed, "Miss Winterjoy."

Kalico shrugged and walked into his office. Miss Winterjoy, dressed in a dusty rose pantsuit, stood before him, blue eyes narrowed, unsmiling. This look had quelled hundreds of unruly high school students. Kalico suddenly felt awkward and could feel himself blushing.

"Miss, Miss Winterjoy," he stammered. "Hello. What can I do for you this morning?"

The elderly woman remained silent. She appeared much taller than her 5' 4" frame. Kalico stopped himself from squirming. He picked up a chair and brought it to her, holding it out for her to sit down.

Miss Winterjoy inclined her head in acknowledgment as she lowered herself onto the metal office chair and sat, ramrod straight, hands folded in her lap. She continued to stare at Kalico.

"Can I get you some coffee?
"May I."
"I beg your pardon?"
"*May I*. May I get you some coffee."
"No, thanks," Kalico quipped. "I've already had three cups."

Miss Winterjoy did not smile. "Mr. Kalico," she began.

"Please, call me Ben."

"Mister Kalico," she continued, "I do not accept your report." She handed him a print out of his email, marked copiously in red ink. "I have hired you to stop a murder, and I expect you to live up to your commitment."

"But, Miss Winterjoy," Kalico began, "There's nothing to indicate in Connor MacLeod's background that he's capable of violence, and certainly, your friend, Mrs. MacLeod, is not a someone who has made enemies. We need to be practical: I don't want you to waste your money."

"It is my money, young man, and I do not consider looking after my friend a waste of resources. Besides, people are rarely who they seem to be. For example, your profile would suggest that you are more qualified to find lost pets than to, say, solve more serious crimes."

"Touché."

"I have reported two serious incidents…"

"Incidents that appear to be simply accidents!" Kalico interrupted.

"*Incidents* that endangered Mrs. MacLeod and could have killed her. I expect you to follow up and to dig deeper. Or do I need to find another investigator?"

Kalico studied Miss Winterjoy for a moment, brown eyes meeting blue ones. Behind her assertions, he saw real concern and something else—could it be fear?

"Okay. I will continue the investigation, but it will most likely lead to nothing."

"Let's hope so." Miss. Winterjoy rose to leave. "And take more time on your reports. I expect proper English usage with correct punctuation."

"Yes, ma'am."

Kalico ushered Miss Winterjoy out of his office, then turned and flopped down on the royal blue love seat in his cramped reception area, muttering something that sounded to M's like, "Damn all cats and dogs and English teachers." He sank into the love seat with his longs legs sprawled over an armrest and groaned. He glanced at M's who was just lifting a Starbuck's cup to her lips.

"I'd kill for coffee," Kalico offered, looking pointedly at the empty coffee pot behind her desk.

"I don't do coffee." M's gazed thoughtfully at her boss. "She ambushed me when I arrived at 8:00 this morning. Sorry. I tried to tell her that she needed an appointment, but she said that she would wait."

"Okay. Look what she did to my report!" He handed M's the printout marked in red.

Laughing, she said, "Looks like you need to review where to place commas. And, oh my," she read from the markings, "correct your passive and awkward sentences structures."

Kalico groaned. "It's like being back in Freshman English."

"Well, she greeted me by saying that she thought that this was a business and not a night club."

Kalico looked at his assistant. Today her dyed black hair was tipped with electric blue and tied up in pigtails. She wore a camouflage man's shirt tucked into a full, blue print skirt, and ruffled white socks peeped over the edge of her black boots. No fewer than twelve silver rings adorned her left ear.

"She has a point."

"You should talk. Have you looked in a mirror lately?"

Kalico rubbed the reddish stubble on his chin and his coffee-stained Longhorn tee-shirt. "I chased Ghost all night and had an early morning surveillance."

"Poor Ben." M's turned her attention back to her computer screen. "I'll get Ghost's owner on the phone for you, but come check this map out first."

Kalico came over and looked at her screen: he saw an Austin city map littered with red *x*'s, seemingly placed at random. "What am I looking at?"

"At what am I looking? Don't end a sentence with a preposition." M's smirked.

"Stop!"

"Couldn't resist." M's clicked, and an image of Ghost filled the screen with his profile. The husky was stunning: deep blue eyes, rich white coat with only a touch of blue-gray around the eyes and on his right side. "Ghost has been missing since the 6th—that's four days." M's switched back to the map. "This is the husky's home just outside of Dripping Springs. The *x*'s represent reported sightings—over twenty."

Kalico studied the map. If all the reports were accurate, the beautiful white dog had been spotted in Oak Hill, and near the Nutty Brown Café, and last night, in the Barton Creek Greenbelt. If even half of the sighting were accurate, Ghost had traveled at least twenty miles in his wanderings.

"Excellent work, M's. Give me thirty minutes to study this map—there's a pattern, but I can't quite see it. Then, get Mr. Skifford on the phone—I need to update him on Ghost's progress. And I want you to canvass the Travis Country neighborhood above the greenbelt. The boy has to be hungry, so I bet he's headed into a neighborhood."

"Will do. Remember, I have an Econ exam, so I won't be in this afternoon. I'll check the rescue websites before I leave and go straight to class after I canvas for Ghost. Be sure to check your messages."

"Great. Good luck on your exam, and again, great job on that map."

Hiring Melissa Montgomery had been a good move. He'd agreed reluctantly to give her the job because his youngest sister, Katie, had asked him to as a special favor—and he could never refuse her anything. Also, M's had accepted minimum wage, did not need or expect health insurance, and appreciated flexible hours. Kalico had not recognized the serious, black-haired Goth who showed up for work on that first day. Where was the giggly, little, fair-haired girl he recalled playing in his sister's room? "Call me 'M's,'" she'd said. "And I changed my last name to Moon. Don't ask me about my family, and we'll be fine." And they had been fine, but he wondered what had happened in the Montgomery household.

Kalico rubbed his chin and walked into the small bathroom beside his office to shave. Ten minutes later, clean-shaved and wearing a sky blue Polo shirt and sharply pressed khakis, Kalico turned to the work on his desk. It was going to be a busy day—so much better than the first long weeks in business when he had waited for clients, had tried to network, and had devised multiple marketing plans. He needed to revisit his marketing strategies, but not today.

Today he had a dog to track, Carson Bolter to monitor, and a retired English teacher to pacify. He needed to observe the MacLeod household and interview Mrs. MacLeod about her accidents.

His email pinged:
From: *Miss Emelia Winterjoy*
To: *Mr. Benjamin Kalico*

Subject: *N.M.'s Schedule*
Mr. Kalico:
I assume that you will want to interview Mrs. MacLeod as soon as possible. She will be at the Hampton Branch Library from 9-12 this morning and will be home the rest of the day. (Connor has classes today, so he will not be present until suppertime). I trust you will be discreet. –E.W.

Chapter Four

Emelia Winterjoy marched out of the Kalico Detective Agency, feeling triumphant. Perhaps she had bullied the young man a bit—she smothered a twinge of guilt. *Such a useless emotion,* she thought. *Guilt assuages our conscience so that we may repeat the shameful behavior. Guilt stops nothing.* But at least he was still on the case, and, if the danger to Nancy proved to be an old woman's over-active imagination, so much the better. But Emelia had a bad feeling, and she had learned not to ignore her notions.

"Trust your woman's intuition" was a directive that her mother and grandmother had repeated often. As a twenty-year-old budding feminist, Emelia had scoffed, "Women are rational beings. We can trust logic, not fall prey to unsubstantiated hunches." Fifty years later, she heeded their advice and trusted her intuition. "The unconscious knows things before our conscious minds can process or prove them," she affirmed.

As she merged her red Honda Fit with the southbound Mo Pac traffic, she recalled January 6, the night of Nancy's first accident. She had awakened at 2:47 a.m.—perhaps disturbed by the distant siren's song, still too far off to hear consciously. Her calico cat, Perdita, meowed in protest at her change in position before settling onto her chest, purring softly. Usually, Perdita's presence was sleep-inducing, but not that night. Emelia remembered pulling her soft, white comforter up because the room was chilly. A norther had dropped the temperature into the 20's. Her mind had switched onto ideas for her spring garden. She wanted to establish a new perennial flowerbed that would eat up another piece of her thirsty St. Augustine lawn. She was picturing a showcase planting of Esperanza, locally known as Yellow Bells, when sirens screamed onto her street and red and blue lights flashed.

For an instant she'd thought the ambulance had pulled into her drive; she could feel the rumbling of its engine in her bones. But no. It was parked in front of Nancy MacLeod's house next door. Emelia jumped out of bed, sending Perdita flying; her corgis, Trey and Snowdon, scrambled toward the front door. She grabbed a robe, neglected slippers, ordered her boys to stay, and ran next door.

A series of images flashed before her: EMT's, serious and efficient and comforting, moving through the pulsating lights. Nancy, pale and so small under a navy blue blanket, carried out on a stretcher, calling out reassurances to Connor as the men lifted her into the ambulance. Nancy stretching out a hand to Emelia. And Connor, fully dressed, standing silently, backlit by the open doorway, his expression unreadable.

"Which hospital?" Emelia demanded.

"South Austin."

"Nancy, we will follow you. Breathe, dear. You're going to be all right."

"Get my purse! My insurance. Take care of Connor…And Moody. She must be frantic."

Emelia watched the ambulance pull out, then she turned to Connor. "Give me five minutes, and we'll go to the hospital. You drive. What happened?"

"She fell. In the kitchen." The young man did not move.

Emelia recalled with a shiver rushing into Nancy's home, calming her terrier-mix, Moody, finding Nancy's purse, grabbing her plush lavender robe and fuzzy slippers. She'd glimpsed broken glass in the kitchen and, she thought, something shiny on the floor. Then she'd run home, pulled on black pants and shoes, and joined Connor on the never ending, fifteen minute drive to South Austin Hospital.

Shaking off the memory, Emelia exited MoPac at William Cannon. 10 a.m. Nancy was now safely at work in the library. She had been lucky. She had sprained her left wrist, bruised her hip, and received a nasty bump on the head, but no concussion. Although a vague worry had nagged Emelia at the time, she had accepted the idea that Nancy had slipped when she had gotten up in the middle of the night for a glass of orange juice. Then three weeks later, accident number two had occurred.

When she pulled into her driveway, Emelia surveyed the tidy tan brick house next door. All was quiet. Nancy was at work, and Connor must be in class. She greeted Perdita and the boys, then sat down to email Kalico. The young man needed direction.

***

M's poked her head into Kalico's office. "Hey, Ben. I just got a text from Andy, one of the volunteers at Town Lake, and he's reported the intake of a dog that may be Mr. Chips. I'll stop by there on my way to campus."

Kalico looked up from his computer screen. His red hair stood on end, and his eyes looked bleary. "Thanks, M's. Fingers crossed—that little guy has been missing for almost a week." He opened their rescue webpage. The soft, brown eyes of a tiny, long-haired Chihuahua gazed at him. The dog owner's five-year-old son, Billy, had decided to walk the dog by himself. Apparently Chips had startled a sleeping cat, slipped his collar, and disappeared around a corner in yapping pursuit. An exhaustive search of the neighborhood had not uncovered the pet. Frantic, the family had called Kalico. "Text me, if you find him," he called to M's. "And good luck on your exam. English, is it?"

"I wish," she grimaced. "Econ. Anyway, I sent out alerts on Ghost and updated our site. I'll check our accounts after the test and again this evening."

"You're the best. See you tomorrow."

Kalico watched as she grabbed her backpack, a file of Ghost flyers, and left, closing his office door behind her. The eighteen-year-old was a godsend. She had designed the agency's pet-rescue website, linked it to all of the rescue organizations in the Texas hill country, kept his calendar, and even helped furnish the small office. He knew that she had taken the job reluctantly—not wanting to work for her friend's nerdy older brother. Initially, she had been efficient, but stone-faced and monosyllabic. But recently, he had glimpsed vestiges of the old Melissa.

An hour later, his phone chimed, revealing a broadly grinning M's, her face being thoroughly washed by an ecstatic Mr. Chips. Her message read simply: *Found! Family is on the way.*

"Hey, Benj. What her name?" Katie Kalico, his youngest sister, walked quickly to his desk and peered over his shoulder.

"It's *Ben*, Kit Kat."

"Whatever." She grabbed his phone and pinched the screen to enlarge the photo. "She looks almost like the old Melissa."

He took back his phone. "What are you doing here?"

Katie dropped her book bag, pulled her long, red hair into a messy ponytail, and leaned her elbows on his desk. "Came to see if you wanted to take me out to lunch. Dorm food sucks."

"Can't." He purposely returned his attention to his monitor. "Go home. Mom has left over lasagna."

"I don't dare." Katie sighed hugely. "Dad is starting to ask why he's paying for the dorm's meal plan."

Ten minutes later, Kalico looked up, aware of his sister's gaze. "Haven't you left yet?"

"Ben, has Melissa said anything to you? She's shut me out—and I'm her best friend."

"Not really. I gather things are rough at home. Mr. and Mrs. Montgomery require check-ins. They call to make sure M's is where she's supposed to be."

Kalico had been interning full time at Lone Star, had his own apartment, and had been too busy to be all but tangentially aware of what was going on with his sister and her friend. He recalled giggling girls, always in motion, always talking. He conjured a picture of the Melissa of a year ago: long, silvery blonde hair, laughing brown eyes, thrilled with her parents' gift of a butter yellow Volkswagen Beetle. (She now referred to the car as the vomit mobile.) Like Katie, M's had been a straight A student, college-bound, a star on the high school's volleyball team.

"We were supposed to attend the University of Texas together."

"What happened senior year, Kat?" He pushed back from his desk and focused his attention on her. After all, this was a mystery worthy of his detecting skills.

"I don't know."

"Try. Go slowly and tell me what you recall."

Katie arched her brows. "Are you interviewing me, Mr. Private Eye?" She shrugged. "Fall semester was such fun: we ruled the school. Of course, college applications, AP classes, sports, and trying to get Bobby Martin to notice us meant serious sleep deprivation. But we figured we could sleep when we got old—like you."

"When did things change?"

"First quarter of spring semester. I remember that Melissa missed several days of school and did not respond to my texts. When she returned, she had not completed her essay for AP English." Katie shook her head as though failing to turn in an important assignment was inconceivable. "She stopped participating in class, dropped off the team, and received demerits for being out of dress code." Katie's eyes filled with tears. "And the worst: she would not talk to me."

Kalico was aware that the girl had had a fight with her parents, packed a bag, and appeared at his parents' front door.

"She looked like a zombie—no emotion. *Nada*. Zip. Nothing. Melissa just said that she'd left home, was dropping out of high school, and would not be applying to college. She didn't even want the Fudge Brownie ice cream that I offered her."

"But she did return home."

"Yes. Mom acted, I think, as a mediator. Melissa agreed to get her diploma, find a job, and pay her parents rent. The next time I saw her, she'd cut her hair, dyed it flat black, and changed her name."

Kalico rose and enfolded his sister in a bear hug. "Don't give up on her, Katie. Give her time and space."

"I just want the old Melissa back." She sniffled. "Guess I'll go home for lunch."

***

Stomach growling, Kalico stared dejectedly at the spreadsheet. He habitually caught up with paperwork at the end of each day, but he needed to kill some time before he interviewed Nancy MacLeod. He completed notes on Ghost and on Bolter, and catalogued expenses before turning his attention to the agency's finances. Quarterly taxes and his insurance premium were due next week, and he was short—even with Miss Winterjoy's check. He'd projected operating at a deficit for the first year, but…He grinned ruefully. Man, was his projection correct. He'd have to dip into his rapidly dwindling savings to cover M's small salary. He ran his fingers through his hair, creating oddly angled spikes.

Kalico leaned back in his chair and studied the crack that ran diagonally across his ceiling. He'd already cut his own salary to the bone. He could let M's go. He sighed. Not an option: she was invaluable. Besides, the sad and stoic young woman he'd greeted on her first day was slowly transforming into the warmer, more confident person he now knew.

His folks had offered him his old room at home—"just until the business got on its feet." That would save him over a thousand a month, and, God knows, they'd feed him.

His phone buzzed. "Hi, Mom." *How did she know?*

"Hi, Ben. Sorry your Ghost hunt didn't turn out better."

"How do you know about the Ghost sighting already? Don't tell me: M's updated our site."

"She did. That girl has flair. Listen: I wonder what that dog is running from."

"He's just spooked—excuse the pun. His owner's furious. Apparently, Ghost has a contract for a national commercial, and if the dog isn't back in perfect condition by the end of next week, he stands to lose a lot of money."

"Maybe Ghost is running to somewhere."

"Maybe. This sighting was encouraging. All the pet rescue groups and volunteer searchers are on alert. We'll find him. He's got to be hungry: he's been gone for over a week." He pulled up the husky's picture: the dog's sky blue eyes stood out against his silvery-white face.

"Speaking of hungry—Ben, your dad and I were wondering if you'd like to come over for pizza Friday night? Your sisters are coming, and we thought it would be fun to have a family pizza and movie night."

"Sure. I miss our Friday movie nights. Besides, I haven't seen Karla, Karen, and the kids since Christmas. I'll bring the popcorn."

"Save your money. We have Kettle Corn. See you at six."

Kalico resumed his contemplation of his ceiling. Moving home wouldn't be that bad. His folks were suffering from empty nest syndrome since Katie moved into the dorm at UT. He'd really be helping them out. And it would be only temporary—humiliating—but temporary. But cutting expenses was a short-term solution. He needed income. He needed more clients. Revise that: he needed better paying clients. Pet retrievals would never generate enough income. And walk-ins like Miss Winterjoy were rare.

Next week he had meetings with a local insurance agency and a new law firm. It would only take two or three contracts to establish enough predictable income to break even. Soon he'd be able to bring on another detective or two. He envisioned a bustling agency with multiple detectives. He'd have teams that specialized in different areas: insurance fraud, missing persons, recovery of stolen items, and surveillance. He would personally take the most intriguing cases and let an office manager take care of the administrative details and marketing. If he could just hold on....

He checked the clock: it was time to interview the intended murder victim, Nancy MacLeod.

Chapter Five

Downing a Red Bull, Kalico brought his Civic to a stuttering stop across the street from Nancy MacLeod's tan brick house. The Honda coughed. Now, what? Kalico's stomach clenched as he envisioned car repair bills. Right now, the best thing about his car was that it was paid in full.

He sighed and focused his attention on the MacLeod house. A white Honda Accord was parked in the drive, and the front door stood open save for a screen door. Raised beds ablaze with wildflowers—bluebonnets, Indian paintbrush, coreopsis, and wine cups—gave the impression that nature had been let loose in the yard. Another raised bed filled with their first spring blooms graced the far corner of the yard. Kalico recognized the hand of a skilled gardener. He shifted his gaze to the white stone house trimmed in blue next door: the Winterjoy place. A curtain in the window moved. Like her neighbor's, the front yard was meticulously landscaped, but with clean, geometric flowerbeds that left no doubt that nature was under the control of a practiced hand. Kalico turned on his tablet and pulled up his notes on Nancy MacLeod. He'd use the missing Pippa again as a way into his interview…

A sharp rap on his passenger side window caused him to drop the tablet. Damn. He turned to see Miss Winterjoy motioning to him to unlock his door. He did so.

"You can't park here. I asked you to be discreet…Good afternoon, Gladys. Yes, it's going to be hot today." She smiled and waved at a large woman who was walking an elderly terrier, then turned back to Kalico with a frown. "See. You've already drawn the attention of the block's busybody, Gladys Tatewell."

Kalico narrowed his eyes. *It takes one to know one,* he thought.

"I am not a busy body, young man," replied Miss Winterjoy.

How does she do that?

"I am a concerned friend—and you should never play poker! Now, get out of your car and follow me."

Kalico grabbed the folder with Pippa flyers, and trotted after Miss Winterjoy who marched to her backyard gate where she planted her feet and motioned to a stack of All Natural Texas Cedar Mulch. She then opened the gate and waited. Kalico frowned, paused, sighed, and placed Pippa's folder between his teeth before he bent down to pick up a bag.

He joined Miss Winterjoy in front of a bed of daffodils, now past their prime, and budding lavender irises. She removed the folder from his mouth and glanced at the little dog's picture. "Poor little girl," she murmured. "Just place the mulch there by the bulb bed, Mr. Kalico." He did so. "Good. Now, what's your cover story? You must be discreet. Nancy cannot suspect that I hired a detective."

"I want to meet Mrs. MacLeod and get her view of the accidents, so I was going to indicate that I was canvassing the neighborhood for Pippa, that way…"

"That will never do."

Miss Winterjoy marched out the gate and stopped by the bags of mulch. Kalico bent down, grabbed two bags and followed his client who had stopped in front of a large bed filled with hybrid tea roses. He dropped the bags, ruefully noting a mud stain on his khakis—his last clean pair of pants.

"Now, Miss. Winterjoy, you need to let me…" he began, but she had already returned to the front yard. Panting slightly, he trotted after her.

"Miss Winterjoy," he began again. "You must let me do my…."

"Of course, you want to get Nancy's version of the 'accidents.' You finish carrying the bags to the back and setting out the mulch—be sure to spread it evenly and no more than four inches deep—and I will arrange for the interview." She looked pointedly at him and then at the Cedar mulch.

"I am not your gardener." Kalico straightened to his full height, and glared down at Miss Winterjoy. Her ice-blue eyes met his brown. He blinked, sighed, and lugged more bags into the backyard.

For the next thirty minutes, Kalico hauled mulch, ripped open bags, and spread it evenly through flowerbeds and around blooming redbud trees. At some point, two yapping corgis rushed up to greet him, accepted belly rubs, then raced around the yard before dropping a much chewed tennis ball at his feet. He tossed it absent-mindedly, then stretched his back and admired his work. The beds looked dark and rich. Sweat trickled down his back; his khakis were filthy. The corgis returned; he threw the ball again. Only three bags left.

"Ben! Ben, time for a tea break. Come here and let me introduce you to my neighbor."

Kalico turned to see Miss Winterjoy beckoning to him from her deck. Standing beside her was a tall, slender woman wearing jeans and a blue "Librarians Do It By the Book" t-shirt. A wide-brimmed straw hat shadowed her face. He walked over to the ladies, corgis dancing at his heels.

"Ben, this is my friend, Nancy MacLeod. Nancy, Benjamin Kalico. He is being so kind as to help me in the garden this year." She smiled innocently, snapped her fingers at the dogs and pointed to a mat by her sliding glass door. The corgis begrudgingly left Kalico and lay down on the matt, heads between their stubby front legs, eyes and ears alert.

"Nice to meet you." Ben hesitated to offer his dirt caked hand, but Nancy grabbed it and shook it vigorously. He glimpsed a face that was all angles, highlighted by deep-set, golden brown eyes, and softened by straight bangs—a Katherine Hepburn face.

"It's my pleasure. I must confess, Mr. Kalico, that I am a fan. You do such important work—returning lost pets to their owners. Did you really have to sing to that cat? Sunny, wasn't it?" She laughed, a low musical sound. "Did Ghost literally vanish in front of your eyes?"

"Call me Ben." Kalico flushed, glad that he had not used the lost Pippa as an excuse to meet Nancy. "My assistant's blog exaggerates, but Ghost is elusive."

"I'd like to hear about your most fascinating cases," Nancy insisted.

"Do sit and have some tea," Miss Winterjoy interrupted. "These macadamia nut chocolate chip cookies are warm from the oven."

"Ma'am, do you mind if I use your bathroom to wash my hands?"

"Not at all. It's down the hall and to your left. Use the dark blue hand towel."

The two ladies watched Kalico leave.

"Such a polite young man...but since when do you need help in the garden?" Nancy asked.

"I'm not getting any younger and mulch is getting much heavier than it use to be." Miss Winterjoy sighed largely.

"I know what you mean, but still..." Nancy looked at her friend closely. "Emelia, you are up to something?"

"Nonsense. Sit and have some tea. How is your new flower bed coming?"

"Brilliantly. It's going to be all pink and white—pink dianthus and mounds of fragrant sweet alyssum." Nancy smiled. "Do not imagine that I don't know that you just changed the subject."

"Cookie?" Miss Winterjoy smiled.

"But how did the Kalico Cat Detective become your gardener? It's absurd."

"Ben, come and sit." Miss Winterjoy turned her attention to her bouncing corgis. "Boys! Down. I expect good manners. Now, sit and meet Ben properly."

Tails thumping wildly, the corgis sat. "Ben, this handsome gentleman on your left is Snowdon, and the incorrigible scamp on the right is Tregaren."

Ben knelt and the corgis shook hands politely. "No begging or it's back to your mat." The boys sighed and settled under the table.

Kalico sat down and drank deeply from a glass of the sweet, cold tea. He bit into a warm cookie and stifled a delighted moan. "Great cookie, Miss Winterjoy."

"Thank you. You may call me Emelia." She paused, a mischievous glint in her eyes. "Nancy was just asking me how you became my garden assistant."

Kalico took a big bite of a cookie, his mind racing. He could feel his neck flushing. *Rule number one when undercover: always have a back story.* His mind was blank.

"Yes. How did you two meet? And why is a detective doing yard work? I can't help being curious." Nancy smiled at them from under the brim of her hat.

"His mother," stated Mrs. Winterjoy.

"My mother?" He gulped. "Yes, my mother..."

"You've heard me mention Katherine, one of the docents at the Lady Bird Johnson Wildflower Center?

We were talking about garden projects last week, and I was complaining about mulching, when she suggested that I call her son to see if he would be willing to help an old lady out. I called, and Ben kindly agreed." She smiled innocently. "I had no idea that Katherine's last name was Kalico or that I was calling the famous cat detective."

An awful idea was forming in Kalico's mind. His mother? *His mother?* The best lies are based on truths, and he bet that Miss Winterjoy and his mother…

"It's very kind of you to volunteer to help," commented Nancy, still looking a bit skeptical.

"It's no problem. I always help my mom in the yard." He grabbed another cookie.

"Have you finished the Louise Penny for book club?" Miss Winterjoy changed the subject.

"Yes," replied Nancy. "I love Inspector Gamache, and I want to move to Three Pines."

"We belong to a book circle that meets every other week," Miss Winterjoy explained to Kalico. "We're reading *Still Life*, a fine detective story set in Canada." She looked pointedly at Kalico, then turned to her friend. "I can't believe it's been a month since your accident, Nancy."

"You were in an accident, Mrs. MacLeod? I mean, Nancy?"

"It was silly really—just a fender bender and a bump on the head."

"You could have been seriously hurt," interjected Miss Winterjoy.

"What happened?" Kalico leaned forward encouragingly and met Nancy's eyes.

"I was driving home from Margie's house—our book circle hostess for the night. She lives way out in Lakeway. It was late—about 9:00—and I don't like driving at night any more. The headlights are too bright.

Anyway, I turned left on Southwest Parkway, glad that oncoming traffic was sparse. I was coming up to the stoplight at Barton Creek when it changed. I stepped on my brakes—and nothing. I pumped them, but the car would not slow down." Nancy shuddered at the memory. She described the glaring red light, a dark SUV crawling through the intersection, her heart thudding as she pumped and pumped the unresponsive brakes. "I ran right through the red light, narrowly missing an SUV. I guess I panicked, turned the steering wheel too sharply, and ended up in a shallow ditch on the side of the highway."

"Did your airbag deploy?"

"No, thank heavens. I just wrenched my neck and dented my front bumper. Luckily, no one else was hurt." She sighed.

"But your brakes failed?"

"Yes."

"Had they given you any trouble before that evening?"

"No. It was stop and go getting to Margie's house, and the brakes were fine. Perhaps they were a bit—I don't know—mushy as I began the drive home." She shook her head. "Besides, Connor, my grandson, had just taken the car in for an oil change. And they checked the brake fluid, tire pressure—everything."

Miss Winterjoy looked pointedly at Kalico. "I'm grateful that you didn't reinjure your hip. I will never forgive myself. You see, Ben, normally we drive to book club together. But last month, I double booked my engagements. I went to dinner with my niece, so Nancy had to drive herself."

Kalico grabbed another cookie and stroked Snow's head. *Who*, he wondered, *would've known that Nancy was driving herself?* Aloud he asked, "Nancy, did you have an earlier car accident?" Miss Winterjoy imperceptibly nodded approval.

"No. I took a silly tumble in my kitchen that landed me in the emergency room."

"Sprained her wrist and bruised her hip. Lucky she didn't die," said Miss Winterjoy.

Kalico frowned, willing her to be quiet.

Nancy adjusted her hat and cleared her throat. "Too much fuss is being made of a little slip of the foot. I'm fine now."

Kalico leaned forward, again seeking Nancy's eyes. In a quiet, sympathetic voice, he asked, "But tell me, what happened?"

Excited barks drowned out his question as the corgis rushed to the sliding glass door.

"Aunt Emelia! Where are you? Trey! Snow! Boys? Where is everyone?" A young woman stepped out onto the deck. "Gentlemen, down!" They sat, vibrating with excitement, as she bent down to greet them. "Hi, Nancy."

"Lynn, dear. What a nice surprise. You're just in time for tea and cookies." Miss Winterjoy rose to hug her niece. "Let me introduce you to Benjamin Kalico."

Ben rose, scowling at the young woman who had interrupted his interview. "Hey," he growled.

"Hey." The niece glanced at him with clear blue eyes.

He looked at aunt and niece as they stood for the moment arm in arm. The girl was about 5'6"—two inches taller than her aunt—but their resemblance was uncanny—same upright posture, same heart-shaped faces, same blue eyes that missed nothing. Same annoying bossiness, he bet.

The niece's eyes narrowed, looking at him quizzically. "Aren't you the cat detective? Don't tell me Perdita has gotten out again, Aunt Em."

"Just detective," Kalico corrected.

"Perdita is fine. Ben is helping me in the yard." Miss Winterjoy smiled innocently.

"Since when do you need help in the yard?" Lynn hugged Nancy, sat down, bit into a cookie, and looked first at Ben and then at her aunt.

Kalico cleared his throat. "Nancy, was just going to tell me about the accident she had in her home."

"It was nothing, really. My foot slipped out from under me…"

"Oh, don't make her relive that awful night," Lynn interrupted, as Kalico scowled. "It's too dreadful. We're all just glad that she's recovered so well."

"Retelling an accident is part of the, uh, healing process," Kalico offered. "And I'd really like to hear…"

"Nonsense." Lynn pushed the plate of cookies over to him. "So you detect more than lost pets?"

Kalico looked pleadingly at Miss Winterjoy who smiled mildly at him. He picked up a tennis ball and threw it for the corgis who flew across the yard in ecstatic pursuit. He swallowed. "I operate my own private detection firm. We do surveillance, insurance fraud cases, cold cases. I'm even looking into a possible murder." The dogs had returned, so he threw the now wet and muddy ball again.

"Impressive. I'm amazed, then, that you have time to retrieve pets or help my aunt with yard work."

"I don't. I don't have time. In fact, I have to go." This interview was a bust. Kalico pushed back his chair. "Important client meeting." He turned to Nancy MacLeod. "It was a pleasure to meet you. Miss Winterjoy—Emelia—I will come by tomorrow to finish putting out that mulch."

"Ben, be sure to wear clothes more suitable for gardening," she offered.

He bit back a retort, and grabbed one more cookie. "Thanks for the tea. Great cookies." He knelt to give Trey and Snow farewell pats, nodded at Lynn, and made a hasty retreat through the backyard gate.

Lynn followed. "I'll show him out," she offered over her shoulder to her aunt.

Grinning, Nancy gazed at her old friend. "Now, I see what you're up to!"

Miss Winterjoy stayed silent.

Kalico was half way across the front yard, when Lynn's voice stopped him.

"Ben!"

Kalico sighed, turned, and looked down at the girl whose dark hair glowed red in the late afternoon sun. He waited.

"Okay. Give. What are you and my aunt up to?"

"I came over to help her move mulch."

"Really?" Lynn let out a sound that resembled a snort.

"Yes, really. I'm doing a favor for my mother. After all, Emelia is not getting any younger, and I had an open afternoon." He could feel his neck getting warm under her close scrutiny,

"You should never play poker!" She whirled around and disappeared through the gate.

"So I've been told," he commented to no one in particular.

Ten minutes later, stuck on MoPac in late Thursday afternoon traffic, Kalico fumed. "Damn. Damn, Miss Winterjoy, and damn her niece," he shouted at the mass of red tail lights in front of him. His elderly client had manipulated him into working in her yard, he'd ruined his best khakis, the interview had ended precipitously, and that niece of hers had snickered at him. *That cat detective.*

His anger evaporated. Who was he kidding? He was a joke. The niece knew it. Victor knew it. His parents knew it. His dad had warned him that he was undercapitalized. He should never have taken a missing pet case. He needed to go back to his business plan—such as it was—and find regular, well paying, two-legged clients. M's blog would have to go. No more pets—after Ghost and the five or six strays he'd already agreed to find. There was always the police academy. Or he could work for one of the bigger detective agencies—that is, if they'd hire a joke.

He pulled into the downtown Central Market and bought a six pack and a bag of Vinegar and Sea Salt Kettle Chips for dinner. He had reports to write and a business to save. Then his phone buzzed.

***

Kalico was running, running hard, Nikes pounding the uneven sidewalk, eyes fixed on the quickly retreating rump of a Boston Terrier-mix named Zoe who had developed sudden wanderlust at the advanced dog age of nine. He cursed under his breath as the dog cut across the main road and turned down an unlit side street. A scant ten seconds behind her, Kalico slowed to a jog, willing his eyes to adjust to the sudden gloom. He scanned left and right for the small black and white and brindle girl. There. Beside the fire hydrant. No. Just a shadow. There—movement by a shrub in the front yard of a duplex. Yes. Zoe was sniffing a shrub. She squatted to mark her territory.

Kalico unwound the purple leash he carried in his right hand and whistled softly. Zoe's large triangular ears rotated toward the sound. "Hey, Zoe-girl," he crooned. "How's the good girl?" He stopped four feet behind her, trying to slow his breathing and appear calm. Zoe turned, her white-tipped tail wagging, her body tense. "Don't run. I know you're a tired girl and want to go to your nice warm doggie bed." Kalico kept up a steady patter, willing Zoe not to run. Then he firmly ordered, "Sit!" She sat. Relieved, Kalico knelt and fastened the collar around her neck. She licked his hand, then heeled, walking calmly beside him as they made their way back to her home.

Gina Buonanotte sighed, laughed, and cried when she spotted the little terrier walking meekly beside the tall, thin, red-headed detective. "Zoe!" The dog yapped and began to pull on the lead. Hugs, dog-kisses, excited dancing, and more hugs followed, marking a joyful reunion. Kalico watched, grinning.

"Benjamin, I don't know how to thank you. If I had lost her—again—I know that Joe would make me give her up." She smiled at Kalico through happy and relieved tears.

"You're welcome, Gina."

"Come in. I have a check ready for you." She held open the door to her small suburban home. "I can't believe Zoe got out again." She cuddled the little dog. "We've blocked the gaps in the fence, the window screens are secured, and I'm so careful when I open the front door. But she just bolted when I went out to get the mail." She frowned at Zoe who had the grace to look ashamed. "If you had not come to help, I don't know what I would have done."

Kalico followed Gina and Zoe into a small living room littered with dog toys. A fluffy Kong rabbit squeaked under his foot; Zoe's ears turned toward the sound, but she didn't move in her owner's arms. This visit was Kalico's fourth—no fifth—to the Buonanotte residence. In fact, Zoe had been his first pet retrieval after he'd found the Diva. She had started him down the path of becoming a pet detective. *And she's going to be one of my last*, Kalico thought.

Gina gave him a check for $50.00. "I made lasagna for dinner—my nonna's recipe, straight from Napoli. Won't you join me? Joe's working late, and I'm too hungry to wait for him." Gina set Zoe down, and smiled. "It's the least I can do, since we ruined your dinner time."

Kalico breathed in the aroma of onions, garlic, and oregano. His stomach growled. Cookies, beer, and granola bars were distant memories. He should get home, but a man cannot live on cookie and chips alone....*Pet detective: will work for food.* He followed Gina and Zoe into the kitchen.

For the next hour Kalico devoured lasagna and garlic bread, drank red wine, and listened to Gina worry about her son, Joe Jr., who was struggling through his freshman year at the University of Oklahoma, about her husband, Joe, who was picking up extra hours at Sears to cover the cost of tuition, about her oldest daughter Paulina, a marketing rep for Whole Foods, who was dating the wrong guy.

Uncomfortably full, Kalico finally pushed away from the table, patted Zoe on the head, advising her sternly to stay home, said his good-byes, and surreptitiously placed Gina's check under a saucer on the table: *Pet detective will work for food.*

Chapter Six

Friday, 6 a.m. Kalico was once again parked near Carson Bolter's house. Keeping one eye on the darkened windows, he swallowed a scalding gulp of coffee and checked his emails. No sign of Ghost. No new missing pets. No queries from possible clients. Just a note from Miss Winterjoy: *"Be here at 9. Your report was better, but try to limit prepositional phrases."*

He groaned. If anything, his client's imperious tone strengthened his resolve of the previous night. He would give up fanciful cases like Miss Winterjoy's, he would stop retrieving pets, and he would establish himself as a serious detective worthy of serious cases. He frowned at the Bolton residence, willing Mr. Bolton to appear at the front door, leap outside, and break dance down the walkway. Kalico placed his hand on his camera. He would capture him in the act and save the insurance company thousands of dollars. He tensed as the Bolton's lights came on. The front door opened. He held his breath and raised the camera. Mrs. Bolton appeared, said something over her shoulder, and walked outside in a blue robe and fuzzy slippers to get the paper.

Two hours later, Kalico returned to his office, completed the Bolton report, and filled out an invoice for Lone Star.

"M's." he called. "Would you come in here for a moment?"

M's appeared in the doorway. A loose-fitting, dark blue and white shift over a black t-shirt and black leggings adorned her thin body. Emerald green socks peaked over the tops of well-worn Converse high top sneakers. She tucked a strand of silky, green hair behind her ear. "Okay, I know I went over the top, but you should see the positive buzz…"

"Over the top on what"

"Oh. You haven't read…? Never mind. What did you need, boss?"

M's never called him boss. "Over the top on what?" he repeated.

M's sighed, leaned over his desk, and hit a couple of keys on his computer, to pull up her blog. A bold headline screamed:

"Kalico Kaptures Kapricious Eskape Artist"

Beneath it there were two pictures. On the left, a tearful Mrs. Buonanotte hugged a soulful, doe-eyed Zoe. On the right, a foolishly grinning Kalico, red hair standing on end, accepted a lavish kiss from the terrier-mix. Kalico scanned the text:

Last night our intrepid detective traced the whereabouts of the five-time repeat offender and master escape artist, Zoe Buonanotte. After spotting the canny canine several blocks from her home, Kalico gave chase, risking life and limb—well, at least limb—as he raced after her through the mean streets of a dark, South Austin neighborhood….

Dazed, Kalico frowned, grimaced, then, to M's relief, chuckled. "Where did you get these pictures? And when did your writing become so, so…"

"Mrs. Buonanotte sent me the pictures last night. She said that you forgot and that she wanted the world to see what a remarkable job you do."

"I didn't forget," Kalico grumbled. "I decided that we need to downplay the pet retrieval part of the business. We need serious clients—ones with money."

"Of course," M's nodded. "And Miss Winterjoy suggested..."

"Miss Winterjoy?"

"Yes. She praised my blog and suggested that I add a more literary flair to my writing. The responses have been great." She smiled.

Kalico yanked at his hair. *Miss Winterjoy. He had four more days of putting up with her interference and bossiness—it felt like a lifetime.* But he liked seeing M's smile—he could almost see the girl who used to play with his sisters in their family room. To M's he said, "Please tone it down a bit, but good work on the blog. I have to report to Miss Winterjoy's house." He sighed. "Here's a *To Do* list. I want you to compile a list of law firms in our area. Focus on smaller ones—they're more likely not to have in-house detectives. Then, draft a letter of introduction for me. And, please, make sure this invoice is mailed today. I'll be back by early afternoon."

"Will do."

"Ghost seems to have gone to ground. Did the neighbors in Travis Country Circle have news of our boy?"

M's shook her head. "One man reported that a half of a chicken was stolen right off his grill. He thinks that he saw a flash of white disappearing into the brush. And several cats are missing: they suspect coyotes."

"I wonder if Ghost has learned to hunt."

"The manager of the Blue Valley Recreational Area said he'd post Ghost's picture and keep an eye out when he walks the trails." She paused to tuck a loose strand of hair behind her ear and cleared her throat. "I thought, maybe, that I would hike there later today." At

Kalico's thoughtful silence, she rushed on, "I'd like to do more field work. I know we could use the bonus money."

"M's, I'd appreciate the help—as long as it does not interfere with your school work. But not by yourself right now and not with Ghost. If the husky has discovered his inner wolf, he could be dangerous."

M's shrugged, disappointed.

"I've got to meet Miss Winterjoy." He turned at the door. "How'd the exam go?"

M's grimaced. "I won't know until next week."

"Why not come over to my folks' house this evening? It's pizza and movie night. All of my sisters will be home, and Katie says she needs another vote against the latest Nicholas Sparks' movie."

M's hesitated. Kalico watched conflicting emotions play across her face before it hardened into impassivity. "Can't tonight," was all that she said.

Kalico shrugged and left, the question he'd been wanting to ask unspoken: *What happened to you, Melissa?*

***

Miss Winterjoy opened her front door before Kalico had a chance to knock and ushered him into her dining room. The corgis, Snow and Trey, danced around his feet, barking excitedly, refusing to quiet down until he had knelt and properly welcomed each boy with head pats and butt scratches.

"Boys, settle!" commanded Miss Winterjoy. They settled. She motioned Kalico to a chair at a polished mahogany table. He settled too. Then she sat across from him, placed a pair of reading glasses on the tip of her nose, and opened a manila folder. She slid a copy of his latest report to him—marked in red—as she scanned the original.

He looked down at a spider web of red ink. Individual words and whole phrases were crossed out. He flashed back to senior high school English and shuddered. *Use active voice. Limit prepositional phrases. Add concrete detail here.* Comments filled the margins. At the bottom: *Strong organization of facts. Style shows improvement.* Kalico felt ridiculously pleased by the praise. He took a breath, ready to speak, but Miss Winterjoy, eyes still on the report, held up a hand. Kalico stayed silent.

A slight motion behind his client caught his attention. An elegant calico cat was perched on the china cabinet. She sat up straight with her tail wrapped around her front paws. Ears were alert and golden eyes stared into his.

"Perdita, come and meet Mr. Kalico," invited Miss Winterjoy.

The cat yawned.

"You have clearly organized and presented the facts of Nancy's automobile accident." She gazed at him over the tops of her glasses. "I am pleased that you note, and I quote, *the possibility of her brakes having been tampered with*. You also acknowledge that Connor had *the opportunity* to sabotage her car. Good."

"But, Miss Winterjoy…"

She held up a hand to silence him. "I recognize that you are not convinced that someone is trying to harm Mrs. MacLeod. But I can see that you are keeping an open mind—and that is all I ask."

"I will follow up on the car accident, and I intend to interview Mrs. MacLeod about the first incident. But," Kalico shrugged. "Accidents happen. Opportunity does not equal motive. Besides, other people—including the garage mechanics—had access to her car."

"True. But Connor knew that I would not be driving us to our book group that night. He'd know that his grandmother does not like driving at night anymore."

"Did anyone else know that Nancy would be driving herself?"

"No." Miss Winterjoy frowned. "But…"

"But what?" he encouraged.

"Nothing. Now, let's plan out your next move."

Ten minutes later, Kalico had his marching orders, and, as he expected, they included yard work. But this time he was prepared: he pulled work gloves and a cap from his back pocket as he exited the house.

Miss Winterjoy observed Kalico as he put on a baseball cap and work gloves, grabbed the loppers that she had placed on the front porch for him, and climbed a ladder, and began to prune the giant shrub from the corner of her roof. "Down, boys," she said absent-mindedly to the dogs who ignored her and continued to scratch at the front door. "What do you think of him, Perdita?" The cat rubbed her head against her owner's legs and purred. "I like him too." She sighed. She hoped again that she was imagining that Nancy was in danger, but the knots in her stomach belied that hope. She pulled back the front curtain. Kalico was walking over to the MacLeod's—right on time. *At least she is safe for now*, she thought.

Kalico knocked on Nancy MacLeod's green front door and waited. A dog began to bark, and he heard. *Moody, quiet! Moody, down. Down!* Nancy opened the door and smiled a greeting as she held a wiggling tan and white Jack Russell terrier by the collar. "Why, Benjamin. What a nice surprise! Moody, quiet!" Moody continued to bark.

"Good morning, Mrs. MacLeod. I just finished pruning Emelia's ligustrum and wondered if you'd like me to lower a couple of the shrubs from your roof?"

"How thoughtful." She smiled and pushed the screen door open. "Come in and greet Moody. I have breakfast on the stove."

He lowered his hand for the dog to sniff, accepted a lick on the hand, then followed Nancy to a sunny yellow and white kitchen where bacon and eggs were sizzling. His stomach growled. Today she was dressed in white pants, and a white tee-shirt, with a gauzy, long-sleeved white over-top. Soft brown curls, touched with gray framed her face.

"Emelia is afraid that I'll climb the ladder and do the pruning myself, isn't she?"

Kalico shrugged.

"I took a little tumble a few weeks ago, and my hip still hurts, so my balance is off," Nancy explained. "So, yes, I would appreciate you taming those monster shrubs. Did you know that ligustrum can grow to over forty feet?"

"I believe it. But I'm sorry you hurt your hip." Kalico followed the opening that Miss Winterjoy had predicted. "What happened?"

"Just a stupid accident." Nancy moved to the refrigerator, took out three eggs, and broke them into the frying pan. "You'll join us for breakfast, won't you? My grandson, Connor, will be down in a moment." She took out a plate, a juice glass, and silver and set a third place at her counter high breakfast table. "Please, sit."

Miss Winterjoy's instructions played in Kalico's head as he pulled up a chair. *Now Nancy will invite you for breakfast and that will give you a good chance to question her about her first accident and—if we're lucky—for you to meet Connor."* Aloud he said, "It smells good. Thanks."

"Coffee?"

"Please. Black." Nancy placed crisp bacon on paper towels to drain and turned the flame under the eggs on low. Then she poured two cups of coffee and joined Kalico at the table. "Connor! Breakfast is almost ready," she called in a clear, high voice.

There was no response.

"Now, where was I?"

"You were going to tell me about your accident," Kalico prompted.

"Oh, yes." She frowned. "Something woke me at about 2 a.m. I suppose it was Connor coming home from work. I decided to get up and come downstairs for a glass of juice—something I do most nights. I remember taking a glass from the cupboard and stepping toward the refrigerator when my foot slipped out from under me, the glass shattered on the tile, and I landed hard on my left hip."

"That had to hurt!"

"Yes, indeed." Nancy moved to the stove and removed the eggs from the burner. "Connor!" she called again, before spooning fluffy scrambled eggs onto Kalico's plate, accompanied by crisp bacon. "But mainly, it was frightening. I couldn't get up. I felt like that poor, old woman in the commercial: 'Help me! I can't get up!'" She frowned and sighed at the memory. "Poor Moody did not know what to do. She barked and whined, then she just curled up next to me."

"What did you do?" Kalico took a mouthful of eggs. "These are delicious, by the way." Moody gently placed a paw on his knee.

"Thank you. Moody, no begging." The dog kept her paw on his knee., and Kalico slipped a small piece of bacon to her. "I tried to pull myself up, but the pain was intense, so I began yelling for help, and then Connor came…"

As if on cue, Conner came into the kitchen and slumped into a chair.

"Good morning, dear." Nancy's face glowed with pride. "Benjamin, this is my grandson, Connor. He's a junior at UT. Connor, say hello to Benjamin Kalico."

"Hey." He did not look up from his smart phone.

"Hey." Kalico took the opportunity to observe Miss Winterjoy's prime suspect, who began to devour his breakfast, eyes still fixed on his phone. He was tall and angular like his grandmother, dressed in jeans and a purple *Keep Austin Weird* t-shirt, and he seemed to be only partially awake. "Your grandmother was telling me about her fall, and how you saved the day," he prompted.

Connor frowned at his grandmother. "Lucky I heard her with my bedroom door closed. Gran, you need to get one of those alert buttons. God knows how long you would've been on that floor…"

"I'm not some old woman who needs to wear an alert button around her neck," Nancy replied rather sharply. "And, please, put that phone away."

Connor stared more intently at his phone, thumbs moving furiously.

"Connor! No phones at the table. Put it away now." Nancy stared at his lowered head until he looked up. Their eyes locked; he looked away first and placed his phone in his pocket.

"Benjamin is here to trim the shrubs for me," she said pointedly, changing the subject.

"I told you that I'd do the darn shrubs." Connor continued to shovel eggs into his mouth.

"That was two weeks ago."

An uncomfortable silence settled over the table. Kalico watched the dynamics thoughtfully.

Moody barked, breaking the silence and jumped to her feet, then the doorbell rang, signaling visitors. Nancy rose to answer the door.

"So you live with your grandmother." Kalico observed and smiled.

"Yea."

"I'm considering moving back in with my folks until business picks up," Kalico confided ruefully.

Connor looked up. "Think hard before you do it, man. I mean, it'll save you money but there's a price."

Women's voices mingled, laughing and chatting in the front hallway.

"What price?"

Connor was about to respond when his phone buzzed, and Kalico lost him again to the screen. Done texting, the young man rose, and grabbed another piece of bacon. "I have to get to class."

Nancy bustled back into the kitchen. "That was the girls delivering books for our charity flea market." She turned to Connor. "Oh, do you have leave already? What time will you be home? Shall I keep dinner warm?"

Conner put a backpack over his shoulder. "I gotta run. Big stats test." He strode quickly to the front door.

"But dinner?"

"I have the late shift at the restaurant."

Nancy sighed and turned to Kalico who was placing his dishes in the sink. "Don't bother with the dishes. I'm just going to put them in the dishwasher." She absentmindedly placed her plate on the floor for Moody to clean. "Poor boy," she said looking toward the front door. "He has such a busy schedule with school and work."

"Sounds like it." Kalico waited, sensing that Nancy wanted to share something with him. She continued to stare at the front door.

"I don't know what I expected when I told my son that I would let Connor move in. You see, he got into a spot of trouble...." She sighed and shook her head.

Kalico waited, but Nancy just smiled at him. "Now you go ahead and trim those shrubs before it gets too hot."

"I will. And thanks so much for the breakfast."

"You are very welcome."

Five minutes later, Kalico was atop a ladder wrestling a ligustrom. Each time he pruned a branch, another one seemed to spring up in its place. He leaned against the rooftop and went over what he had learned from his interactions with Nancy and Connor and could find little to suggest that Nancy's fall was not an accident. Mrs. MacLeod moved gracefully and confidently around her home, but even the most coordinated people stumble. Connor appeared to be an ordinary twenty-something—a little monosyllabic and self-involved. Kalico wondered what 'spot of trouble' the young man had gotten into. And, he noted, Connor never made eye contact or thanked Nancy for breakfast. Poor manners would place him as Miss Winterjoy's top suspect. His relationship with his grandmother was not without tension.

"It looks so much better!"

Kalico looked down to see Nancy, now wearing a wide brimmed straw hat. She carried a pair of shears, gloves, and a bright purple floral bag. Moody sat beside her, gazing up at Kalico.

"Thanks." He watched as the woman and dog made their way to the front garden bed where Nancy began to efficiently deadhead her deep red Celebrity rose bushes. The day was beautiful. The sun felt good on his skin, doves were calling, he was being paid an exorbitant amount for yard work, and Nancy was safe. Kalico began to whistle under his breath as he renewed his attack on the ligustrum.

Staccato barks brought Kalico out of his reverie. Moody was frantically dancing at the base of the ladder. As he looked down, the little terrier sped across the lawn and stopped at a white mound. It looked as if snow had fallen among the red roses. Then it registered: that white mound was Nancy.

Kalico flew down the ladder, hit the ground running, pulled his phone from his back pocket, and punched in 911. He knelt by Nancy. "Moody, quiet! Down!"

"What's your emergency?"

"Medical emergency at 3000 Hummingbird Way. Please send help."

"An ambulance is on its way. What is the patient's condition?"

Kalico felt Nancy pulse—it was rapid and very weak. Her skin was pale, and she was gasping for air. A rash was forming on her left arm.

Miss Winterjoy appeared at his side. "It's anaphylactic shock," she announced. She grabbed Nancy's purple bag and dumped its contents onto the lawn. She dropped to her knees, quickly sorted through mosquito spray, sunscreen, lip balm, and tissues. "Where's the EpiPen? Where's the pen?" Momentary panic welled up in her chest, then she took a deep breath. "Benjamin, go. There should be an EpiPen in the downstairs bathroom. Run!"

Kalico was running to the house before Miss Winterjoy finished her order. He flew into the downstairs bathroom, threw open the medicine cabinet, and scanned its contents. No epinephrine. He next took the stairs two at a time, found the master bedroom and bath. Again: no EpiPen in the medicine cabinet. As a last possibility, he opened the draw of a bedside table. There. He grabbed the medicine and ran. In the distance he could hear the faint sound of sirens.

Miss Winterjoy was cradling Nancy's head in her lap.

"Got it." Kalico announced.

"Hurry. Hurry."

He ripped open the packet, swung his arm, aimed the orange tip of the auto injector against Nancy's outer thigh, and pressed until he heard a click.

"Got it." Kalico announced.

Chapter Seven

Moody's whines escalating into the screech of sirens. Kalico running to meet the EMTs, shouting information. Strong hands guiding her away from Nancy. Red lights flashing. EMT's efficient and brusque: "Sixty-nine year-old female. Anaphylactic shock. One dose, 3 milligrams, of epinephrine administered. Pulse rapid. Patient unconscious." Red rose petals like splattered blood caught in the gauze of Nancy's shirt. Kalico's arm bracing her as the ambulance swallowed the stretcher carrying her dear friend.

Miss Winterjoy took a shuddering breath as she replayed the events of the last five—or was it fifteen—minutes. Things happened so fast, yet they had seemed to play in slow motion. Now she was positioned in the passenger seat of Kalico's Civic, barreling down Highway 71 toward South Austin Medical Center. Her mind repeated a single prayer: "Please, God, let her be okay. Please."

Kalico glanced over at his client. Her hands, white knuckled, gripped the brown bag in her lap, and her lips moved silently. "Nancy is going to be okay. We got the epinephrine to her, and she's in good hands. Breathe, Miss Winterjoy."

Uncharacteristically following directions, she indeed took a deep breath. She straightened her spine and focused on the road ahead. "How soon...?"

"Next exit."

"Moody?"

"She's in the house."

"We have to turn back. We need Nancy's purse."

"You're holding it."

"Yes. Oh, yes. It's got her insurance information. Did you lock the house?"

"Yes, ma'am. The keys were in her purse."

"Connor!"

"We'll call him when we get to the hospital."

Kalico took the hospital exit and screeched to a halt at the Emergency Room entrance. Miss Winterjoy leaped out of the car and disappeared through the wide, glass doors. After parking the car, Kalico joined her in the crowded waiting room.

"Any news?" he asked.

"No. They took her back to a treatment room. The nurse said that a doctor would come out soon."

They waited in silence. Coughs echoed throughout the Emergency waiting room. A baby wailed, a pale, young woman shivered in the arms of a young man, and a middle aged woman pressed a white cloth, now pink with blood, against a gash in her hand. Eyes stared glumly at the green doors that led to the treatment rooms. Some people read magazines; others focused on their phones. A couple of people slept.

Miss Winterjoy, sitting ramrod straight, her hand clutching Kalico's arm, kept her gaze fixed on the nurses' station.

Lynn rushed in. "Aunt Emelia. How is she?" Lynn stooped to hug her aunt, who looked like a tiny, yellow canary—out of place in the gloomy room. She raised an eyebrow at Kalico.

"They took her back about an hour and a half ago," Kalico answered. "She suffered a severe allergic reaction to a bee sting, we think, and the EMTs administered a second dose of epinephrine in the ambulance. Once she's stable, your aunt can go back and sit with her until they ready a hospital room for her."

Lynn looked at Kalico quizzically over her aunt's head and nodded.

"How about you, Aunt Em? Are you all right?"

"Yes. Just frazzled. Benjamin has taken good care of me." Miss Winterjoy smiled at her niece. "Lynn, I'm so glad that you came. But what about your classes?"

"Not to worry. I found a great substitute." She settled herself into a hard metal chair. "Now, tell me what happened."

Lynn listened closely as her aunt related the morning's events.

"We were so lucky that Benjamin was there," she concluded.

"And exactly why were you at the house?" She turned to Kalico, her clear, blue eyes, disconcertingly like her aunt's eyes, narrowing on him.

"Just finishing some yard work. You know, trimming shrubs and what not. Have to get those branches off the roof or they could damage it, so….." God, he was babbling. He stopped.

"Indeed?"

Kalico met her gaze, but could feel a flush begin to creep up his neck. "Yes. You know those ligustrum." He laughed. "They could take over the world." *Shut up, you idiot.* He looked helplessly at Miss Winterjoy who smiled benignly and shook her head.

Lynn continued to gaze at him, then she shrugged. "Thank you so much for helping Nancy and my aunt. Sounds like you were quite the hero."

Not sensing any irony in her statement, Kalico blushed to the roots of his hair.

Lynn turned her attention back to her aunt and opened a large tote bag. She pulled out a thermos and two cups and poured hot, black coffee. "Drink this," she directed. "You've had a shock." They complied. "Now. I stopped by the house and brought Nancy's nightgown, robe, and slippers—just in case she has to spend the night here. Aunt Em, I also brought you a change of clothes, a sweater, and your Louise Penny novel."

"Thank you, dear. This coffee is just what I needed. Let me have that clean blouse, and I'll change." She sighed and looked down at the brown stain on her top. "Nancy, threw up on me after Mr. Kalico—Benjamin—administered the EpiPen."

"You go ahead. We'll hold down the fort here," Lynn reassured her.

"Come get me immediately if you hear...." Her eyes filled with tears.

"We will. Nancy's going to be fine—God willing." Kalico and Lynn watched the small figure walk slowly toward the lady's room. The usual spring in her step was missing, and she appeared suddenly small and old and fragile. Lynn sighed.

"She's tough. She's shaken but not broken," Kalico reassured her.

"Yes. Thanks. She's such a dear, really. She puts on a façade of being in charge and totally self-sufficient, but...." Lynn stopped. She turned to face him. "Now, Mr. Cat Detective: why were you really at Aunt Emelia's house? Give."

Kalico lowered his eyes.

"I knew it. Em always does her own yard work. But why does she need a detective?"

Kalico squirmed. He could not—would not—breach client confidentiality. He closed his mouth firmly, met her eyes squarely, and willed his blush to fade.

"Why would Aunt Em need a pet detective? Trey and Snow are fine, Perdita is an indoor cat, and Moody never leaves Nancy's side."

Goaded, Kalico frowned. "I am not a pet detective. I'll have you know that I'm a licensed private investigator for the state of Texas. I'm working on a big insurance fraud case right now and...."

"And?" Lynn smiled triumphantly. "So why are you working for Aunt Em?"

He was rescued from answering her when a white-coated doctor and Miss Winterjoy arrived simultaneously. "Doctor, how is she?"

Doctor Viola Millar looked at the chart in her hands. "Mrs. MacLeod is in stable condition. Her heart rate is still irregular, but the swelling in her throat has subsided. We're going to admit her to the hospital for forty-eight hours. In fact, we're taking her up to her room now."

"Oh, thank God."

"She was lucky that you administered the epinephrine when you did—a few minutes delay could have proved fatal. We advise all patients with severe allergies to carry an EpiPen with them at all times."

'Nancy always has her medicine within reach. Always," asserted Miss Winterjoy. "For some reason, it just wasn't in her bag...." She stopped and exchanged a look with Kalico. He nodded.

The doctor continued. "She's going to need bed rest and quiet. She's complaining about pain in her left hip, so we'll send her to x-ray later this afternoon. She's asking for an 'M' and Moody and Connor?"

"I'm Em, and Moody is her dog. Please tell her that her little dog is fine and a hero because she alerted us that Nancy was in trouble. We've left messages for Connor, her grandson." Again, she looked pointedly at Kalico who tipped his head slightly in acknowledgment. The exchange did not go unnoticed by Lynn.

"I will. Now, you folks might as well get some lunch. You should be able to visit her at one o'clock or so." The doctor hurried back through the green doors.

After a few minutes discussion, the trio settled on a plan. Miss Winterjoy would stay at the hospital with Nancy. Kalico would drive Lynn to her aunt's house to pick up her car and drive it back to the hospital.

"Here's a list of what Nancy will need." Miss Winterjoy was in charge again.

Lynn read her aunt's precise handwriting aloud: "Shampoo and conditioner, make-up case, tooth brush, green pants suit, and blood pressure medicine."

"Bring Moody over to the house—the boys will keep her company. And, please, call Connor again. Nancy will want him here." She turned her attention to Kalico. "Benjamin, I know that you have work to do," she said pointedly. "Thank you. You showed great presence of mind during our crisis. If you hadn't acted so quickly…" Miss Winterjoy paused, her eyes glistening.

"It was a team effort." Kalico surprised Miss Winterjoy and himself by hugging her. "Call me if you need anything, and please let me know how Nancy is doing. I will be in touch."

"Yes. Yes, I will." As she watched the young people walk away and exit the hospital, a new idea began to tease her brain. She smiled to herself, then removed a murder mystery from her purse and began to read.

***

Kalico glanced at Lynn who was perched in the passenger seat of his Civic. As the young woman wrinkled her nose, he became aware that odors of wet dog, sweat, French fries, and something musty pervaded the small space. He rolled down a window. He nodded at the backseat that was piled with dirty clothes.

"Sorry about that. I haven't had a chance to do laundry." Kalico wasn't about to tell her that he was hauling his dirty clothes to his mother's house to wash.

They rode in silence. Kalico maneuvered his little car easily through Austin's Friday afternoon traffic, replaying the morning's events. He couldn't believe that it was only a little after one. Two hours in the emergency room's gloom had felt like days, and he would not have been surprised if it had been dark outside.

"The waiting room swallows one, doesn't it?" Lynn echoed his thoughts. "It's hard to believe it's still springtime." She rolled down her window.

Aware that she was studying his profile, he wondered what she saw. He hoped that she recognized that he was not a con man intent on duping her aunt out of her life's saving.

Kalico commented, "Your aunt is a champ in a crisis."

"She is, but I don't recall ever seeing her so shaken. I would hate to see someone take advantage of her."

Kalico choked. "You don't think that I would…"

"Then tell me what the two of you are up to—and don't give me that line about yard work."

"I can't. Really."

"You can. Aunt Emelia and I don't keep secrets."

"Sorry. You need to ask your aunt." He looked at her. Arms crossed, chin out, and eyes narrowed, she looked like a younger and angrier and equally stubborn version of Miss Winterjoy. "It's no use jutting your chin at me. I have three sisters, and I can withstand all forms of coercion."

Lynn sighed. "Can you at least reassure me that she is not in any danger?" Her blue eyes implored him.

Kalico sighed. "Miss Winterjoy, to the best of my knowledge, is not in any danger."

"Ah ha!" Lynn trained her eyes on his face. "Then she must have hired you for someone else. Who could it be?"

Lynn fell silent, and Kalico gratefully turned onto Hummingbird Lane. As he pulled into Miss Winterjoy's driveway, Lynn asked quietly, "Is it Nancy?"

Kalico swore silently under his breath.

"I'm right, aren't I? Aunt Emelia has hired you because she's worried about Nancy." She sat back triumphantly. "But that's ridiculous. Who would want to harm Nancy? She's the dearest person—a children's librarian, for heaven's sake."

Kalico pressed his lips together, turned off his engine, got out of the car, and crossed the lawn over to the MacLeod house, stopping by the rose bed. A right work glove lay discarded under a shrub beside Nancy's pruning shears. Her flowered purple bag, its contents sprawled out on the lawn, rested beside a straw hat about three yards from the glove. Lynn bent down to pick up the bag.

"Stop!"

"It's her Vera Bradley bag..." Lynn began.

"Just give me a moment."

Lynn complied. She watched as Kalico took out his phone and began to systematically take pictures. He circled the rose bed, then walked into the center. He knelt down by the discarded glove and shears, rose, carefully plucking something from a shrub. Next he walked to where Lynn stood by the purple bag, noted the spread out contents and took several more photographs.

"Detective at work?" Lynn asked mildly.

Kalico nodded, eyes still fixed on the scene. "I didn't see what happened, so I wanted to get a clear picture of events." He stopped. He could hear Moody barking from inside the house.

"Tell me." Lynn's gaze was direct and encouraging.

"Okay." He pointed toward the front of the rose bed. "Nancy began deadheading the roses here at the front of the bed, placing her bag most likely on the lawn, next to the sidewalk. She moved systematically and efficiently. You can see where she groomed these four bushes."

Lynn nodded.

He moved back into the flowerbed. "She began working on this center one, but stopped. You can see where there are still old blooms on the right side that need to be cut."

"Yes. This must be where the bee stung her."

Kalico nodded. "She dropped her shears and tore off her right glove. Then she ran out. See here and here"—he pointed to white pieces of fabric that clung to several shrubs—"where she snagged her blouse? I think she ran to her bag to get her EpiPen, but when it wasn't there…"

"What? Nancy always carried an EpiPen with her when she gardens."

"Not this time." Kalico shook his head, imagining the older woman's panic. "She started toward the house, but was already having trouble breathing. She collapsed here." He indicated a spot by the bag where the St. Augustine grass had been flattened and trampled by the EMT's.

"Go on," Lynn encouraged.

Kalico's shoulders slumped, and he suddenly felt tired. "Well, I heard Moody barking, but didn't pay attention until she stood right below the ladder, barking and circling. That's when I saw Nancy. I called 911. Seconds after I reached her, your aunt appeared. She yelled at me to get an EpiPen from the house, and I just ran, found one, gave Nancy an injection, and the EMT's appeared." Kalico took a deep breath, remembering his own panic when he could not find the medicine.

The young people looked at one another, the silence broken only by Moody's barks that were now punctuated with a kind of whine-yodel.

"You don't think that Nancy was a victim of foul play, do you Ben?"

He raised an eyebrow. "*Foul play*? Been reading Sherlock Holmes lately?"

"No, Agatha Christie, if you must know. But seriously, do you think that someone tried to hurt Nancy?"

Kalico ran his hands through his hair making it stick up at odd angles. He did not want to involve Lynn without Miss Winterjoy's permission. "No," he asserted. "She was the victim of a bee sting. Pure and simple."

"Yes, of course. A horrible accident. I'm going to get Moody before she barks herself hoarse."

"Good. I'll clean up out here."

Kalico watched the girl as she marched into Nancy's house, and listened as she greeted Moody before she closed the front door. He knelt by the purple bag, and checked its inside pockets—just in case they had missed the EpiPen. He carefully placed sunscreen, mosquito spray, a water bottle, and a packet of Kleenex into the bag. He then picked up the shears and glove, paused, took out a plastic bag from his pocket, and sealed the glove inside of it. After placing the bag in his car, he gathered fallen ligustrum branches and set them on the curb for pick up. Lastly, he returned the ladder to Miss Winterjoy's garage.

Lynn appeared at his side, a subdued Moody perched on her hip. The little dog's feathery tail wagged when she saw Kalico who scratched her behind the ears. Lynn inhaled as the detective's hand grazed hers and their eyes met.

"Strawberries."

"What?"

"Just strawberries," Kalico murmured foolishly. "You smell like strawberries."

Lynn stepped back and placed Moody on the ground. "Thank you so much for your help today. Aunt Emelia is right: we are lucky that you were here."

"A pleasure to be of service, ma'am." Kalico grinned and bowed formally, flourishing his hands before him. "We cat detectives have our moments."

Lynn laughed. "Really: thank you."

"Welcome." Kalico walked back to his car. "Lynn, who would know about Nancy's allergies?"

"Anyone who knows Nancy. She's allergic to bees—obviously—but also to honey, and nuts, and some citrus, and most perfumes. She has to be so careful."

"And is she in the habit of carrying her EpiPen with her?"

"Yes. Always." Lynn faltered. "Ben, you don't think someone...."

"No," he responded with more certainty than he felt. "Tell Emelia that I will be in touch."

As he drove away, Kalico viewed Lynn in his rearview mirror and saw her raise a hand in farewell, before she straightened her shoulders and moved purposefully to the house. He doubted that he had allayed her suspicions and wished he could be honest with her. It was time for Aunt Emelia to come clean with her niece.

Chapter Eight

"M's, where's the white board?" Kalico burst into his office and didn't break stride as he rushed to his desk.

"In the storage room. What's up?"

"Will you set the board up and find the dry erase markers?" He turned on his computer, attached his phone, and began pulling up and printing pictures as M's wheeled out the pristine board and opened a new carton of markers.

"Ben, what's up?" M's planted herself squarely in front of his desk.

Kalico quickly brought her up to date on the day's events. He concluded, "I think we've got a real case."

"Mrs. MacLeod's not…"

"No. She's in the hospital and is going to be fine. But I believe we have an attempted homicide." He waited for M's response.

Her eyes widened with amazement. "So Miss Winterjoy was right."

"Looks like it." Kalico gathered the photographs from the printer's tray. "Where's the scotch tape?"

M's moved behind his desk, opened his top drawer and handed him the tape. "Before you get started, I have a few messages for you. First: your mother called and wants you to pick up popcorn for tonight after all. Apparently, your dad got into the Kettle Corn. And she asked that you be on time."

Kalico placed Nancy MacLeod's picture at the center of the white board. "Ben, did you hear me?"

"Yes. Popcorn. Dad's in the doghouse. Don't be late."

"Also Mr. Skifford called. He's increased the reward for Ghost to $2500.00. Some bad news though—he's not going to extend your retainer into next week." Ben dragged his attention away from the white board and looked at M's. "He said that he's going to trust the greedy public to find his dog."

Kalico shrugged. "Go ahead and post the new reward on all of our sites anyway, and send a special tweet to our volunteers."

"I already did," M's confirmed. Before Kalico could disappear into the white board again, she continued. "Two more things. I confirmed your Monday meetings with both the Santigo Insurance Company and the Lawrence, Gunderson, and Reed law firm. I also compiled a list of local law firms and drafted the letter of introduction that you asked for. You just need to proof read it and sign."

"Right. You're the best. Will you please call South Austin Hospital and find out Mrs. MacLeod's room number? Then have a small bouquet of flowers—no, have a small live plant, perhaps a geranium—sent to her room. Better use my personal credit card. The company card is...well, you know."

"Will do. I'll update the pet rescue websites and call the shelters too. We have three cats, six dogs, not including Ghost, and Merry, the hedgehog, on our retrieval list. Pippa's owner called again in tears.

"Okay. Let's not take on any more missing pets for now." Kalico taped a picture of a grinning Connor holding a beer and flashing the *hook 'em horns* sign on the board below Nancy.

He didn't notice when M's left.

Two hours later, she poked her head into his office. Kalico sat on his heels in front of the white board, now covered with pictures, notes, arrows, squiggles, and question marks.

"Ben, it's 4:00. I have to get to class."

He grunted.

"Mrs. MacLeod is in room 323." She walked over to his computer and placed a post-it note on his screen. "Do you need anything else?"

He grunted again.

"You'll need to leave for your parents' house in 90 minutes. Don't forget the popcorn."

Kalico waved a hand in acknowledgement.

"Okay. I set an alarm reminder on your phone."

Kalico's eyes didn't move from the board. He began writing something in black, erased it, and began writing again in red. He sat back on his heels.

***

The reception area phone buzzed, penetrating Kalico's trance. "M's? M's, can you get that?" he called, loathe to leave the white board. But M's had left for class, so he reluctantly picked up the call.

A young, breathless voice shouted into his ear. "Commander Kalico? This is Cadet Freddie. I can verify a Ghost sighting at Dick Nichols Park at 1700 hours. You need to get out here asap."

"Will do, Cadet. And good work. My ETA is 20 minutes. Do not approach the husky. I repeat: do not approach the dog."

"Time for a ghost hunt," he murmured as he rushed to his car. Last month when he was canvassing a neighborhood for a missing Rottweiler puppy, he had founded Kalico's Crusaders, a youth volunteer group. The children had becomes his eyes and ears for lost pets all over the greater Austin area.

Fifteen minutes later, he pulled into the Dick Nichols' State Park parking lot and jumped out of his Civic, scanning the area for Freddie. A noisy family was enjoying a picnic supper, runners pounded the cement trail, and several people were walking their dogs, but there were no boys around. *I'm at the parking lot. Where r u?* he texted. The response was immediate: *Southwest quadrant.* Squinting into the sun, he scanned the lot again. An elderly man was gently lifting an equally elderly, black miniature poodle from his ancient Toyota. A woman with two vocalizing Chihuahuas in her lap pulled into a space in front of him blocking his view. The two little dogs—a handsome tan boy and a petite, black and tan teacup girl—jumped gleefully from the car, noses to the ground. "Max! Kate! Wait!" The woman pursued them with leashes in hand. In the far corner of the lot, he spotted a little girl in camouflage, gazing at her phone.

"Freddie?"

The girl looked up. She was about ten years old, petite, with brown hair pulled back in a high ponytail. Recognizing Kalico, she came to attention. "Cadet Freddie reporting for duty, Commander."

"At ease, Cadet." Kalico smothered a grin. "Report."

The little girl stood with feet apart and hands behind her back. "Yes, sir." She pulled out a small notebook and began to read rapidly. "At 1630 Cadet Travis Brown and I began patrol. Our objective was to find Ruffles, a missing Yellow Lab. After making one round of the park, we began to question civilians. The Evans family reported that a huge, white dog stole a package of hotdogs and ran off in that direction." She pointed toward a wooded area in the center of the park. "We scouted the area. Cadet Travis found the empty hotdog package. We continued up the trail for approximately ten meters, when we saw Ghost." Freddie's voice rose in excitement, and she lost her military composure. "Man, he was big and gorgeous. Blue eyes—just like in his pictures, and the whitest coat ever. He just stared at me, then he vanished. I swear." She held up her right hand. "One minute he was in front of us, and the next—just gone. I wish he were my dog. Mom won't let me have a dog. She says that they're too much trouble, but I'd take care of it."

"Excellent report." The girl snapped back to attention. "Where is Cadet Travis now?"

"His mother called him home for dinner," Freddie sniffed in disgust, as though she was reporting a deserter.

"Do you have your parents' permission to, uh, patrol here? It's almost sunset."

"I do not have to report home until 1800 hours."

Kalico's phone alarm began to chime: 5:30. He was supposed to be at his folks' house. He sent a quick message to tell them he would be late. "Okay, show me where you saw Ghost." He was alarmed at the girl's willingness to go off alone with a stranger. He made a mental note to remind Freddie about stranger danger—after she led him to the missing husky.

Freddie took off down the paved trail with Kalico jogging behind her. She veered to the left onto a narrow dirt path, slowing her pace. They moved quietly through a grove of cedars and live oaks that suddenly opened up onto a grassy meadow, filled with wildflowers. The angled sunlight made the Texas primroses, Mexican Hats, and Indian Paintbrush glow.

"He ate the hotdogs here." Freddie pointed to a spot just off the trail where they could see bits of yellow and red plastic.

"Quiet." Kalico held up a hand took the lead. "We don't want to spook him."

They progressed down the trail in silence. Freddie tugged at his sleeve to signal stop. She pointed. "He was just there by that little tree," she whispered.

They continued up the trail until it intersected with the pavement. The light was growing dim and the air, chilly. "We'd better get back," Kalico said, but did not move. Freddie was still and as silent as a statue beside him. Suddenly, the hair on Kalico's arms stood on end. Was it the cold or something else? He held his breath and listened. A soft rustle of branches. The wind or...?

"Ghost," he called softly. "Come here, boy. Ghost..."

Eyes glinted in the brush across from him then vanished.

He released his breath. "Let's go," he said in a normal tone.

Freddie marched dejectedly beside him. "Sorry," she said. "I thought we'd get him."

"You did a great job." The little girl looked doubtful. "No, really. You came closer to Ghost than anyone else so far. Exemplary work, Cadet."

Freddie beamed. "Really? Thanks."

"Thank you. And I bet he stays in this area—there's food, water, and shelter."

"I'll patrol this weekend and after school," the girl pledged.

"But not by yourself. Cadets always go on reconnaissance in teams. It's a matter of safety and accuracy. Agreed?"

"Agreed." She began to skip.

"And do not go off with strangers," he added.

"I know better than to do that," she scoffed, insulted that the commander would consider her such an ignorant baby. "Besides, I know you."

"You do?"

"Sure. I check your website hourly. We just gotta get lost pets to their people."

"We do," Kalico affirmed. "So your dad's in the military?"

"Yes. Mom too. How did you know?" Freddie looked at him with admiration.

"High powered detective skills," he laughed.

"Grandpa Jim is a Vietnam War hero. He took apart bombs. I'm gonna do that when I get older."

The parking lot came into view. "Are you okay going home alone? It's almost dark."

"Sure. I just live across the street."

"Okay, then. And, Freddie, again good job."

The girl grinned and saluted. "I'll be on duty here all day tomorrow," she promised. "We'll find the Ghost for his person."

He watched as the girl safely crossed Escarpment. The western sky glimmered pink and peach and gold as Kalico drove to a convenience store to buy popcorn and made his way to his parents' house. The Kalico clan had saved pizza for him and were eager to hear about his ghostly adventure. If he retrieved the husky, he would share the reward with Freddie.

Chapter Nine

Emelia Winterjoy watched the sun set through the horizontal blinds of a third floor hospital room window. For a moment a few clouds were touched with brilliant colors, then they faded to gray and white, and night descended. *Isn't this a metaphor for life?* she thought. She tucked a strand of short white hair behind her ear —hair that a young man had likened to rich mahogany a thousand years ago.

"We have to stop meeting this way," a hoarse voice whispered behind her.

"I know! The food is mediocre and the accommodation not at all luxurious," she responded lightly, walking over to Nancy MacLeod's bed and picking up a tall plastic water glass. She placed the straw beneath her friend's lips and held the glass as the patient drank.

"Thanks, Em. Now isn't this just a fine kettle of fish?" Nancy frowned at her swollen right hand and forearm that nestled in a foam contraption. Her face and eyes were still red and swollen.

"Three hospital visits in as many months are a bit excessive, Nancy."

"Agreed! I should be accident-free now for a good long time." She smiled optimistically. "You know what they say: third time's the charm."

"From your lips to God's ears." *They'll be no more accidents if I can help it,* she vowed silently. Aloud she asked, "How are you feeling?"

"Ready to go home and sleep in my own bed." She attempted to sit up, then sank back into her pillow. "Oh, you brought my throw." She ran her left hand lovingly over the rich greens and blues of the hand knitted throw. "And my pictures!" In the first, her late husband, Gareth, posed with their son, Patrick, who was proudly holding baby Connor in his arms. In the second, Gareth was playing tug of war with Moody. In the last, four ladies in Sunday dress were toasting Nancy.

"Lynn brought them by earlier when you were napping. And see your flowers?"

"They're lovely. Will you read the cards to me?"

Emelia placed her reading glasses on her nose. "These white daisies are from Lynn. The card just says, 'Bee-have and you'll be home before you know it!' She spelled behave with two e's—very punny." Nancy laughed. "This garish bouquet is from the book club girls. The card just says, 'Love you!' Margie's handwriting, of course! And this pink geranium is from Benjamin Kalico."

"So thoughtful!" Nancy sighed.

"Connor was here too," Emelia reassured her friend. He had finally shown up late in the afternoon. To do him justice, he had seemed genuinely upset and explained, inarticulately as usual, that he'd turned his phone off during an exam and forgot to turn it on again. "Do you remember?"

"Yes, vaguely. Poor dear. He just hates hospitals—ever since his grandpa...." Nancy shook her head as if to remove a painful memory.

"Connor had to leave for work, but promised that he'd see you tomorrow during visiting hours."

"Good. He cannot risk losing his job. He's trying so hard to be responsible."

Emelia did not comment but looked skeptical.

"No, really, he is. Who has not acted rashly in their youth? He has turned a corner and is making up for his mistakes now."

"I don't recall that *we* ever acted foolishly."

"Then, Emelia, your memory is failing you," Nancy asserted. "Remember that time on 6th Street...."

The two old friends chatted comfortably. At 7:00 a nurse bustled into the room to check Nancy's temperature and blood pressure; an orderly delivered a bland chicken dinner with banana pudding—which Emelia ate. Kalico called for an update on Nancy's condition, and Lynn called to wish her a good night.

"Emelia, you should go home and get some sleep."

"I will, dear. I'll just keep you company until visiting hours are over." Her phone buzzed, and she glanced down to read a text from Kalico. It contained a single question.

"What was that?"

"Nothing. Just Lynn telling me that the dogs and Perdita are fed. Moody misses you," she prevaricated. Then thinking of Kalico's question she added, "Lynn mentioned that there was a big box of books in your foyer. Did you want it moved into the garage or taken to Half Price?"

"Heavens, no. The girls brought the books over this morning on their way to bingo. They're for our Reading is Fundamental program. Every child will receive a brand new book." She smiled. "Oh no. Did someone call the library?"

"Yes. They know you will not be in tomorrow."

"But who will take over the Saturday story corner? I hope it's not Marion; she just can't create character voices. I do wish...." Nancy plucked at her sheets nervously.

"Nancy, you need to stop worrying. Remember your blood pressure. I'm sure Story Corner will survive without you this once."

At 8:30 Miss Winterjoy wished her friend a good night and made her way out of the hospital. Stepping into the crisp March air, she felt the weight of the day lift momentarily. She texted Kalico: *Nancy secured for the night. Box delivered by book circle group. I expect your report first thing in the a.m.* Then she went home, cuddled her dogs, and, although she disapproved of drinking alone, poured herself a glass of red wine.

Chapter Ten

Kalico pounded toward the basket from half-court, feinted right, pushing Victor back with his hip, then turned left, jumped, and sank the shot. *Swish!*

"Nice shot." Victor bent over, hands on knees, trying to catch his breath. Although a cold front had come in over night dropping the temperature into the lower 60's, he was sweating profusely.

"Too many doughnuts?" Kalico dribbled the basketball lazily.

"Ha. Ha. Too much of Gabriella's cooking. I've gained the newlywed ten."

"More like twenty."

Victor rubbed his belly and laughed. "Just more of me to love. Speaking of food, let's go to Kerby Lane. I'm hungry for pumpkin pancakes."

"Can't. I've got a lot of work to do today."

"What? A wandering weimaraner? A lab on the loose?"

"Something like that," responded Kalico, determined to not let Vic get to him.

"Frankly, you're looking a little worse for wear."

Kalico nodded ruefully. "Been sitting in a meadow since 5 a.m., watching for a ghost."

Victor decided not to ask. "We're taking applications for the next Police Academy class. Think about it. We could partner up." He laughed.

Suddenly serious, Kalico replied, "I will." The idea of a regular paycheck with benefits, greater resources, and more help was appealing.

"Good. Gabi would like you to come to dinner next Sunday. She's making enchiladas."

"Great!"

"She's got this friend, Isabella that she'd like you to meet. A real beauty."

"Vic, please. No set ups." Kalico had decided long ago that he wouldn't date until his business was established. He didn't have the time or the money that women required. "See you next week?"

"Same time, same place. And don't forget about dinner."

Kalico pulled a tattered burnt orange sweatshirt over his head, jumped in his Civic, and drove to the Jiffy Lube on Brodie Lane, the garage where Connor had brought his grandmother's car to be serviced the day of her accident. He asked for an oil change and reviewed Nancy's service history as he waited. He had lifted it from her Accord's glove compartment just that morning. The car's oil had been changed, air filter replaced, and transmission fluid topped. According to the history, her brakes had not been inspected. As he paid, Kalico conversed casually with the on-site manager. He hadn't had any staff changes in the past six months

Next Kalico drove to Alvarez Automotive where Nancy MacLeod's car had been towed after her accident. He reread her accident report before he walked into the cramped office.

"How can I help you?" A stocky Hispanic man with thick, white hair greeted Kalico from behind a service desk.

"Mr. Alvarez?"

"Yes."

"My name is Benjamin Kalico. I'm a friend of Nancy MacLeod's. She asked me to follow up on the accident she had last February. The insurance company is giving her some grief over its settlement."

Mr. Alvarez nodded in sympathy. People pay their premiums but the companies never want to make good on their claims.

"She drives a 2005 Honda Accord LX that you repaired," Kalico paused to check the date, "the week of February 23."

"Yes. Mrs. MacLeod. My granddaughter goes to her Story Time at the public library every third Saturday. Don't let that insurance company shortchange her. Let me pull up her file."

As the man went to his computer, Kalico looked around the office. The shop had a long history in South Austin, was family owned and operated, and had received numerous, positive customer reviews.

"Here it is." His printer began to whir. "Mrs. MacLeod was lucky not to have been seriously injured. Her driver's side bumper was crumpled and left tire flattened. We did the bodywork, replaced the tire, and realigned the car."

"Mrs. MacLeod said that her brakes felt mushy."

"We also did a full brake inspection." He squinted at his mechanic's notes. "Her brake pads were wearing thin on the right, and her brake fluid was low."

"Did your mechanic notice any holes or cracks in the fluid lines?" Kalico asked.

"No. Just signs of aging. We recommended pad and line replacement which we completed."

Kalico jotted down a note on his phone. "May I have a copy of your service report for Mrs. MacLeod's records?" Mr. Alvarez handed him the pages still warm from the printer. "Except from general wear and tear on the brake fluid lines, is there any other reason why a car's brakes would lose pressure?"

"There could be small leaks in the fluid lines that a general inspection would not catch." Mr. Alvarez rubbed his palm against the stubbles on his chin. "Of course, someone could drain fluid from the system."

Kalico nodded, thanked him and left. He checked the time: 8:50. He went to his apartment, showered and changed, silently blessing his mother for the clean clothes. He needed to visit Nancy. But first he stopped at his office to add the names to his white board that Miss Winterjoy had texted to him. Then he carefully opened the baggie with the right gardening glove, inspected it, nodded to himself, and resealed it. He'd need to stop at Whole Foods for a small purchase before visiting hours.

***

Settled at the end of the small sage loveseat in Nancy MacLeod's hospital room, Emelia Winterjoy calmly knitted a red cape for her corgi, Snowdon, as her bright and ever-watchful eyes surveyed a lively scene. Margie, Susan, and Jane had bustled in shortly after 9 a.m. with books and flowers, dark chocolate and crossword puzzles. They buzzed around Nancy gossiping, laughing, and sympathizing—all talking at once.

"My granddaughter, Louise, has been accepted to Rice. Now, we're waiting to hear about scholarships..."

"I think Rosemary Martinelli had a little something done around her eyes. We ran into her at Nordstroms and..."

"Kale and soy salad with blueberries, salmon, and whole grains. Nance, you need to try this anti-inflammation diet..."

The patient was holding court, obviously enjoying the attention. She sat up in bed, a green scarf around her neck and her colorful throw over her lap. Emelia had brushed her hair and applied her make-up earlier. Still, tension showed around her eyes, and her hand was throbbing. Emelia determined to shoo the visitors away shortly.

For now, she let the activity float around her as she reviewed her long and, at times, difficult conversation with Lynn earlier that morning. Her niece had demanded to know what was going on. As Emelia shared her suspicions, Lynn had been alternatively skeptical, alarmed, thoughtful, and, finally, cooperative—with reservations, especially with her decision to employ a detective. But at least they had a plan: Nancy was not to be left alone. They would share guard duty—easy enough while Nancy was in the hospital, more problematic when she returned home.

She glanced up to see Kalico standing in the doorway, observing the scene. He nodded at her when she caught his eye.

"Benjamin, come in!" Nancy called brightly. "How good of you to visit! Come in and meet the girls."

Kalico stepped into the room as the three women turned simultaneously to see the new visitor.

"Let me introduce you." Nancy indicated a stocky woman with short gray hair and intelligent hazel eyes filled with curiosity. "This is Margie David." She next nodded to a woman with shoulder-length silver-blond hair. This is Susan Jankowsky. And last, but not least, let me introduce Jane Roundtree." A small and very round woman with short brown hair and brown eyes framed by dark oval glasses nodded at him. "Ladies, this is Benjamin Kalico." She paused for effect. "He saved my life."

Instantly, Kalico found himself surrounded as each woman thanked him, exclaiming, and firing off questions. Margie shook his hand firmly, Susan enveloped him in a perfumed hug, and Jane took his hand in both of hers and pumped it.

In her best English teacher's voice Emelia interrupted: "Ladies, quiet, please. Let the young man breathe." They obeyed.

Extricated, Kalico moved to Nancy's bedside and took her outstretched left hand. He'd hoped to speak to her alone, but he was grateful to meet the book circle in person. Now he could put faces to the names he had written on his white board last night.

Nancy squeezed his hand and said simply, "Thank you."

"Any time," he responded lightly.

"Let's just pray there's not a next time," offered Jane, blinking rapidly behind her big glasses.

They all concurred.

"But tell us about the accident from your point of view, Benjamin." Susan leaned forward, prepared for a good story. "Emelia says that you acted with alacrity and great presence of mind."

Kalico retold yesterday's events, warming to such an attentive audience. Emelia added a detail here and there, once reprimanding him for being too hyperbolic. "The events were dramatic enough; there is no need to embellish."

When he finished, Nancy's eyes glistened. "You and Emelia are my guardian angels."

Emelia sniffed. "No one has ever accused me of being an angel. And don't forget Moody."

"Of course, my Moody-girl."

"So Ben," began Susan, "you're a handyman? I have a large redwood deck that needs refinishing..."

"Don't be daft, Suse," interrupted Jane. "Benjamin Kalico—K-A-L-I-C-O—he's a detective."

"How exciting!" Margie, a devoted mystery buff looked at Ben with renewed interest.

"You found that famous Siamese cat a couple of months ago, didn't you?" Jane peered at him over the tops of her glasses.

"Yes. But she was a Persian."

"I remember that now. It was all over the news." Susan leaned forward. Her silver earrings glinted in the artificial light. "Being a detective must be so exciting."

"Sometimes," Ben surveyed the circle of interested faces. "But there's a lot of research, surveillance, and foot work. You know what they say: there's tedium punctuated by moments of high anxiety."

"Have you tracked down any nasty criminals?"

"He's not some bounty hunter, Margie," corrected Emelia.

"Not really. I specialize primarily on pet retrievals and leave the heavy lifting to the police."

"That's a nice service, I guess," said Margie, disappointed.

"It is." Emelia broke in, deciding to change the subject. "Have you all finished this month's novel?"

Everyone in the book circle nodded except for Susan. "I'm on the last part, so don't say anything! I can't wait to find out who done it."

"I guess our meeting will have to be delayed," said Jane.

"I don't see why it should," said Nancy. "They're going to release me tomorrow, unless I can talk the doctor into letting me go home today. I'll be fine for our meeting. Besides, it's at Emelia's, so I only have to walk next door."

"Good. I'll bring the spinach salad," said Margie.

"I'm good for dessert," said Jane.

"I'm making my famous potatoes au gratin," said Susan.

"And I'm roasting a pork loin," Emelia stated, then she added, "Ladies, I think it's time to leave so that

Nancy may rest. I'll walk you out." Amidst a flurry of farewells, she efficiently herded the group out the door.

Kalico stayed behind.   "That's quite a trio."

"Good friends. We've known each other for ages."

"How are you feeling?"

"Ready to go home," Nancy responded, but she rested her head on her pillow and her left hand worried the throw.

"That's a beautiful blanket," Kalico commented, as he tried to figure out how to move the conversation to the missing EpiPen.

Nancy smiled. "My mother-in-law made it for our first wedding anniversary." She indicated a framed photograph on a little side table. Kalico brought it over to her.

"That's my Gareth." She pointed to a laughing man in a gray suit who had his arm around a shaggy-haired boy of about ten. "And that's our son, Patrick. He's a lawyer. Practices in the Bay area."

"Connor looks just like him."

"The MacLeod men are handsome and charming."

Kalico would never have associated charm with Connor. He wondered where her beloved grandson was anyway.

"Connor will be in to visit me later," Nancy said, as though reading his mind. "Poor boy, he hates hospitals Ever since…" She paused and closed her eyes as if to block out a dark memory.

"Ever since what?" Kalico prompted quietly.

"Since the accident."

Kalico waited as Nancy gathered her thoughts.

"Connor adored his grandpa. When he came to visit during the summers, the two of them were inseparable. Gareth took him swimming at Barton Springs, hiking on the greenbelt, and biking around Town Lake. They went fishing and on campouts. I think Pat was too busy building his law practice to do things with his son, but Gareth relished being a grandpa."

"What happened?"

"One early July morning, the boys—Gareth was as much of a boy as Connor— went out for an early morning bicycle ride around the neighborhood. I remember wishing them a good ride and reminding them to be back in thirty minutes because I was making French toast—Connor's favorite. Forty-five minutes later, I was fuming. But neither Gareth nor Connor possessed a sense of time, so I just turned off the stove. Then the phone rang: it was the hospital. Gareth's bike had hit a stone in the road, and he'd been thrown over his handlebars. He'd broken his collarbone and his right arm and was going into surgery."

"And Connor?"

"He was shaken but fine. We sat in the waiting room together until Gareth came out of surgery. When he woke up, he was fine. In some pain and in a brace, but, otherwise, fine. We visited for a while, he asked me to smuggle in some of my French toast, and then I left the room to get him a cup of ice. I wasn't gone more than a minute." She shook her head at the memory. "I was walking back to the room, when I saw Connor standing outside in the hall. He was crying with his arms gripped around his body as though he were holding himself together. Commotion filled Gareth's room—doctors and nurses were shouting orders ...."

"It must have been terrifying."

"Yes. It was. Gareth died. An embolism, they said." Nancy looked lovingly at her husband's picture. "I never got to say good-bye."

"I'm sorry."

"We had twenty-three good years together, but that was not enough. I guess, no one ever has enough time."

She sighed. "Connor was in the room when his grandpa died."

"Poor kid. Man, I can understand why he'd avoid hospitals!"

"Yes. He hides it, but he's very sensitive."

"He's lucky to have you," Kalico said sincerely. "Nancy, a quick question: do you normally keep an EpiPen in your gardening bag?"

"I do. Always have." She lowered her head. "I must have forgotten to put one into the new bag I got for Christmas. Forgetting things is the curse of growing old."

"I can never recall where I put my car keys. I don't think losing things has much to do with age." Kalico placed a comforting hand on her shoulder. "I had better go before Miss Winterjoy rousts me out of here."

"Thank you again, Benjamin. And thank you for the beautiful geranium."

"You're welcome. Feel better soon." He moved toward the door, paused, and turned as though just remembering something. He pulled the small bottle he had purchased at Whole Foods out of his pocket. "I almost forgot. My mother sent this bottle of lavender for you. She's into aroma therapy and says it will bring relaxation and sweet dreams."

"That's so thoughtful." Nancy looked at the lavender for a moment, then held it out to Kalico again. "I'm afraid that I'm allergic to most scents. They make my skin break out into little red bumps. But do thank your mother for me."

Kalico pocketed the lavender, repeated his good-bye and left. He wanted to get back to his office. His suspicion had been confirmed, and he needed to mull over what he'd learned today. Moreover, as a text from Miss Winterjoy had reminded him, he had a report to write. *There are no good excuses for turning in work late. Late work suggests poor time management and impedes productivity.* He could just see her putting a zero next to his name in her grade book.

Chapter Eleven

A light drizzle began to fall as Kalico circumnavigated the mile loop at Dick Nichols Park. He zipped up his jacket as he turned onto the dirt trail that led to the meadow. As he expected, the area was empty, save for a few early Sunday morning dog walkers. He wound the dog leash around his left hand. The tip of an animal control pole peaked out from the top of his backpack that also contained gourmet dog treats and food.

He squinted through the drizzle toward the last area Ghost had been spotted. A huddled figure dressed in black perched on a small boulder several yards away from the dense brush.

"M's?"

The girl turned haunted eyes toward him. "I had him, Ben. I had Ghost." She turned her head away. "I had him."

Kalico sat down on his heels. "Tell me," he said softly.

"I got here at 6:30, set out food, and waited." She pursed her lips together. "You're right by the way: a stake out is an uncomfortable bore. I was just about to give up, thinking that maybe Ghost does not want to be found. After all, he made his escape; he's free unlike...." She lowered her head. "Then I heard a faint rustle in the grass and saw a white shadow float through the cedars. He stepped out, right over there." She pointed to a small break in the brush. "He's magnificent. He stood on alert: head up, ears forward, aware of my presence. I could tell that he wanted to eat. He took two steps toward the dish when a woman being pulled by an unruly brindled mutt appeared from nowhere." She clicked her tongue in irritation. "She let her dog eat Ghost's food."

"How long ago was that?"

"Fifteen minutes."

"It's starting to rain harder, and you're shivering. Let's go." He held out a hand and pulled the girl to her feet. He removed his jacket and draped it over her shoulders.

A slight grin lightened her features for a moment. "Very Sir Walter Raleigh of you," she quipped.

"Forget it. I'm not putting my jacket across any mud puddles."

They walked slowly along the dirt path.

"Ben, I'm sorry. I know that I should not have come out here on my own. I'm so stupid. I wanted to surprise you: rescue Ghost and get the reward money for the agency. Help pay for my keep."

"You more than earn your wages. Sounds like you got close to Ghost. But it's best to be safe." He rubbed his thumb across a jagged scar. "A frightened animal can be dangerous."

"I don't know what I was expecting. I thought he'd start to eat, and let me slip on his collar. Stupid."

Kalico punched her lightly on the arm. "Stop being so hard on yourself, kid."

They trudged in silence.

Aware that he was entering forbidden territory, Kalico asked, "M's, you mentioned wanting to escape. Are things that bad at home? Your parents aren't...." He sought for the right word.

Through lips thinned into a straight line, M's replied. "No. Nothing like that. Dad just wants me to be his "sunshine girl," and Mom actually bought me a pink dress," she paused in outrage, "with ruffles."

Having grown up with three sisters, Kalico knew when it was best to remain silent. He waited, hoping that she would open up.

As they stepped onto the paved trail, two small figures raced toward them.

"Commander! Commander!" Freddie, still in camouflage, raced towards them, followed by a blond boy wearing khaki shorts and a bright red sweatshirt. "Commander Kalico! We're here. Have you seen Ghost? Sorry we're late, but Travis's mom made him eat breakfast." She glanced disparagingly at her companion. "I've been ready for hours and hours."

"Hi, Freddie. Nice to meet you, Travis." Kalico solemnly saluted them.

"Travis is excited to meet you," Freddie said. "We're ready for our orders." She came to attention and glared at Travis until he too assumed the correct posture. She looked curiously at M's.

"Cadets, let me present my lieutenant, M. Moon. At ease!"

The kids saluted. Smothering a grin, M's returns their salutation. "Cadets Freddie and Travis, I understand that you are both experts at reconnaissance. We greatly appreciate your help." M's improvised. "Ghost was spotted at approximately 6:45 a.m.—I mean, at 06:45—in the meadow. We do not expect him to come out again while the park is crowded."

"We could track him through the woods," Freddie suggested.

"We could, but we don't want to drive him away. Besides, it's beginning to rain. We'd better go in for the day."

Freddie was crestfallen. "But poor Ghost. He's going to get all wet, and he's hungry, and cold and…"

Kalico smiled reassuringly at the little girl. "He's got a big, thick coat. Remember, huskies survive in snowy climates. Also, he's smart. He'll find some kind of shelter during the storm." He crossed his fingers, hoping that he was telling the truth.

"I guess," Freddie said doubtfully.

"Come on, Cadets. Let's double time it!" M's jogged rapidly toward the parking lot, followed by Kalico. The two cadets soon passed her, racing and shouting down the wet pavement, stopping finally beside the bright yellow Beetle.

"We'll patrol again tomorrow after school," Freddie promised.

Travis leaned over and whispered something to Freddie. The girl frowned and shook her head. He whispered again.

Freddie grunted. "Travis can't patrol tomorrow 'cause he has to be tutored in math."

"Right. Thank you for your diligence. Remember, contact me if you see Ghost. Do not approach him on your own. That's an order."

The young cadets saluted and ran off.

M's removed the jacket and handed it to Kalico. "See you back at the office in a few, boss."

"It's Sunday. Go home. Put on some dry clothes. Read or watch TV. No need to work today."

M's chin jutted out stubbornly.

"Do the Montgomeries still prepare their famous Sunday brunches?" Kalico recalled fondly the times he'd feasted at the family's table on homemade blueberry muffins, cheese omelets, crisp bacon, and home fries. His stomach grumbled.

"Yes."

"Then go home and enjoy. I'll see you on Monday." He watched as she drove away and wondered if she would go home or find somewhere else to shelter for the day.

***

Kalico peeled off his wet socks, threw his soaked tee-shirt over a chair, and ran paper towels through his dripping hair. He found a ragged burnt orange sweatshirt in his desk drawer, pulled it on, then stood barefoot in front of his white board. The faces of Margie Davis, Susan Jankowsky, and Jane Roundtree smiled benignly at him, joining the photographs of Nancy and Connor, Miss Winterjoy and Lynn. He began to make notes under each name.

"That's quite a rogue's gallery you have there."

Kalico yelped, knocked over a chair, and dropped the folder he was holding, scattering papers across the floor. He turned to see Lynn Winterjoy, hands on hips, staring at him.

"Lynn! You startled me." He moved in front of the white board, attempting to block her view. "How did you get in here?"

"The door was open." She moved closer to him, her eyes still on the board.

Kalico gestured toward the door. "Let's go out to the reception area. Really, this information is privileged. I cannot allow…"

Lynn planted herself in front of the board. "Check your phone."

He did and saw a message from Miss Winterjoy: *Lynn and I conversed at length. Please treat her as my proxy. We have a plan. E. M.* Kalico shrugged, relieved that he would not have to hide things from Lynn, especially since she'd already guessed much of what was going on. He righted his chair and started gathering his scattered notes, letting Lynn absorb the patchwork of information. At one point she moved her face to within inches of the board, then stepped back again.

She tapped a finger beside a name, then followed an arrow to another name. Finally, she sat down in the chair in front of Kalico's desk, removed her aqua North Face jacket and loosened her rose-colored scarf. Kalico noticed how the soft light from the window created reddish blond highlights in her hair. Anger, worry, incredulity, and, perhaps, amusement played across her face.

Kalico met her gaze squarely and waited.

"I can't," she began. "You can't possibly…" She rose and paced around the room. "Ben, you don't actually believe that someone is out to kill Nancy, do you? All of this," she gestured toward the whiteboard, "is ridiculous. You seem to have followed Aunt Emelia down one of her rabbit holes!"

An image of the staid and proper Miss Winterjoy, dressed in a blue and white checked pinafore with a frilly white apron tumbling into Wonderland popped into his head. Kalico stifled a laugh. "Is your aunt given to falling down rabbit holes?"

"Not really." Lynn sank back into the chair. "But her whole life has been framed by stories—reading them, telling them, teaching them. I think that a seed of a good story planted itself in her imagination after Nancy's initial accident, and it's interfering with her common sense." She shook her head and shifted her gaze back to the white board. "And you!" Anger simmered in her blue gaze. "You're encouraging her delusion!"

"I'm gathering facts—as she hired me to do—to either dispel her delusion, as you call it, or to prove that there are grounds for concern."

"What possessed you to take her case anyway?"

"Lynn, listen. Your aunt is a force of nature. I'd accepted her retainer before I had a chance to think, but after…"

"You should have never taken that retainer!"

"Miss Winterjoy was determined that I should. I tried to return it after I did my initial investigation, but you know your aunt. She was adamant that I honor our agreement and finish out the week." Kalico smiled ruefully.

Lynn sighed. She knew her aunt's stubborn streak well. "Okay, so let me make sure that I have it all straight." She held up a finger. "First, Nancy has suffered three, potentially fatal accidents."

"Apparent accidents."

"*Apparent* accidents. Two," she held up another finger, "there are several anomalies that could point to someone tampering with her brakes to cause the car accident and stealing her EpiPen." She tapped her fingers on the red notes on Kalico's board.

"Yes. Red flags."

"And three, your suspects are comprised of four elderly women—including my aunt—, a college boy who happens to be Nancy's grandson, and apparently me!" Exasperated and amused, Lynn faced Kalico with her hands on her hips.

Kalico brushed a hand through his still damp hair, causing it to stand up at odd angles. "It's a matter of opportunity."

"To relieve your mind, then, I was not present at the book circle meeting the night of Nancy's fall, and I did not know that she was driving herself to Margie's house." She crossed her heart and raised her right hand as though swearing in court.

Kalico cleared his throat, stroked an imaginary white beard, and asked, "Can anyone verify that you were home the night of the first book circle meeting? A boyfriend perhaps?"

"I live alone, your honor. But my aunt will verify that I was not present."

"And your boyfriend?"

"There is no boyfriend at this time."

"Very good. And will your aunt also swear that she did not tell you about her decision to not drive to Margie's?"

"Yes. We did not speak that week because I was swamped grading AP essays."

Kalico relaxed and stopped playing judge. "I concede. You did not have the opportunity. And Miss Winterjoy is not a suspect either."

Lynn moved to the white board and reached up to remove her picture.

"Leave it, please." Kalico stopped her, then added with a grin as she looked quizzically at him, "I like it." After a moment's hesitation, she left it.

"Ben, honestly, do you think that someone is trying to harm," Lynn swallowed, "or even to kill Nancy?"

Kalico walked over to his small loveseat and picked up his wet socks, buying time as he formulated a response. He slipped his feet into his running shoes. "I don't know. Each incident is mostly likely an accident. In fact, there is nothing to suggest that her fall was anything but an accident. People fall in their homes all the time—especially older people." He fell silent and stared at the board.

"But?" Lynn prompted.

"But three accidents in less than three months could point to something more than bad luck. Someone could've tampered with her brakes. Someone could've have taken her EpiPen."

"By someone you mean Connor, don't you?" Lynn scowled.

"He did have both opportunity and means."

"And he is my aunt's chief suspect!" Lynn turned and walked quickly to the door, stopped, and gestured to Kalico. "C'mon. I'm starving and my brain hurts. Let's go out and have some lunch."

"You don't have to ask me twice for food." Kalico turned off his computer, grabbed his backpack, and escorted Lynn to his car. "I'll drive. Where do you want to eat?"

"The rain's stopped. Let's go sit on the deck at Hula Hut. Water always calms me down and helps me think."

"Great. Then you can tell me all about the plan Miss Winterjoy and you have concocted."

"Only if you buy me a margarita."

"Deal." And Kalico pointed his Civic south toward Lake Austin. They rolled down the windows to let in the cool, rain-fresh air, riding in comfortable silence. Kalico glanced at his companion, registering the sprinkle of light freckles across her nose and noting the lingering worry evident on her brow. Yes, margaritas were in order. He turned onto Lake Austin Blvd. Chicken Quesadillas, a frozen margarita, and a lovely companion: he suddenly felt light hearted. "Lynn, tell me about yourself."

Before she could answer, Kalico's phone began to bark. He nodded at her apologetically, and answered. "Hello. This is Kalico."

"Ben! It's Lois." Her voice was high-pitched and tense. "Stanley's missing. He's gone. I've looked everywhere." She choked back a sob. "Please, you've got to come."

Kalico looked at Lynn who nodded okay. "I'll be there in ten minutes. And, Lois, try to calm down. Stanley won't come out of hiding if he senses your stress." He made a quick U-turn. "We'll find him."

"Dog?"

"No, cat." Kalico waited for a wisecrack about being the cat detective, but Lynn stayed silent. "Stanley belongs to my parents' next door neighbor. I've known this cat since he showed up as a little ball of gray fluff outside of Lois's front door."

Eight minutes later, he pulled up in front a ranch style house with a deep front yard shaded by tall oak trees. Three teenage boys on bicycles grouped by the mailbox waved as Kalico parked. A tiny girl twirled on the lawn, chanting, "Kitty, kitty, kitty" to the sky. Five adults on the front porch turned in unison at the Civic's approach. Two women broke away and rushed toward the car as Kalico and Lynn emerged.

"Benji!" A plump, red-haired woman in her fifties hugged Kalico. "I'm so glad you're here."

"Call me Ben, Mom."

A petite woman in her early forties grabbed Kalico as his mother released him. "Oh, Ben. We can't find Stanley anyway."

"It's going to be okay, Lois. We'll find him." Kalico surveyed the crowd, trying to hide his dismay at the noise and activity. "I see you've gathered a search party?"

"Yes, yes. We've all been around the block at least a dozen times, but no Stanley."

Kalico's mother's attention shifted to the lovely young woman standing beside the car. "Hello. I'm Katherine Kalico." She smiled and extended a hand. "Please excuse my son's bad manners."

"Sorry. Mom, Lois, this is Lynn Winterjoy." Kalico made the introductions wishing his mother did not look quite so pleased or so curious.

"Nice to meet you both, but I'm sorry that it's under such circumstances," Lynn said.

"I'm afraid that we interrupted your—date?" His mother smiled delightedly at her son.

Kalico was at a loss for how to respond when Lynn chimed in. "We were just going to grab a late lunch at the Hula Hut. Finding Stanley is much more important."

"Yes! My Stanley. He's never been outside." Panic sparked around Lois, and she grabbed Kalico's arm. "What should we do?"

Kalico took charge. He directed Lois to email a picture of Stanley to him and to his mother. He asked his mother to create posters with the cat's picture and the Kalico agency's phone number. Then he called the gathered neighbors together.

"Hi, folks. Thank you so much for volunteering your time to find Stanley. We're getting pictures of Stanley copied for you to handout to people in the surrounding area." His mother nodded, smiled at Lynn, and hurried to the house next door. "I'd like us to search in concentric circles with Lois' house as the epicenter." He pulled up a neighborhood map on his iPhone. "Boys, since you're on bikes, why don't you scout these streets farthest from us? Remember to go slowly and quietly; look high and low. Do not go into any backyards without permission." He turned to a fit, young couple wearing matching Texas A & M t-shirts. "Jessica and Matt, would you take the next blocks in?" He showed them the streets on his phone. They nodded.

"We brought some cat treats—Seafood Medley," Matt offered. He then called and motioned to the child who was still dancing in circles around the yard. ""Leanne, come here now. We're going to search for the kitty."

"Stanley loves his kitty treats," sighed Lois.

"Terrific," concurred Kalico. He next approached an elderly man who leaning on a walker. "Hello, Mr. Douglas."

"What? Speak up."

"I said 'hello.'" Ben shouted.

"Hello! No need to shout. I came to see what all the commotion is about." He shook his head. "Stupid cat. Doesn't know when he has it good."

"I suspect he wants to get home about now," Kalico offered.

"True. True. So what can I do to help? Afraid I can't go traipsing around the block." Mr. Douglas looked ruefully down at the walker.

"Of course not. Would you be willing to be our lookout? Just sit quietly on the porch and watch in case Stanley comes home."

"Will do." He shuffled to the porch, slowly climbing the stairs step by step, and settled himself in a forest green Adirondack chair.

"Lynn and I will take the houses immediately around here." Kalico turned to the group of anxious faces. "Be sure to text me if you spot him. He's most likely to come to Lois, so don't approach him, and whatever you do, do not chase him. Any questions?"

Mrs. Kalico appeared at her son's elbow with a stack of flyers. Stanley's enigmatic golden eyes peered out from the pages. They handed out flyers, made sure everyone had Kalico's cell phone number, and the search party dispersed.

"But Ben, what do you want me to do? I can't just wait here." Lois paced nervously.

"Let's go inside, and you can tell me exactly what happened. Then I'll need to collect a few of Stanley's things to help us get him when we find him."

A few moments later, Kalico, Lynn, and Katherine were settled in Lois's living room. A cat's scratch tower dominated a corner of the room and a window mounted cat bed was set up in the front window. Various cat toys littered the otherwise pristine room and framed photographs of Stanley graced the mantle.

Lynn studied with interest the images of the rotund gray cat with four white mittens and a white tip on his tail. "He's a handsome, big boy," she commented. "Stanley's an unusual name, but it suits him."

"He's beautiful, isn't he?" Lois smiled mistily at her cat's picture. "He's named after my late husband. Every time I say his name, I remember my Stanley." She gestured toward a picture of a young man, grinning into the camera as he washed a vintage Mustang convertible.

"Lois, tell me about Stanley's disappearance. What happened today?" Kalico asked.

"I went to my dance class at the gym this morning, then did my grocery shopping. I guess I returned home at about noon or a little thereafter. Stanley greeted me at the door as usual and followed me into the kitchen, demanding his afternoon treat. I gave him his Catviar—he has such refined taste—then he went into the living room to nap in the window—or so I assumed." Her eyes scanned the room as though willing her cat to reappear.

"When did you notice he was missing?" Kalico prompted.

"I put my groceries away, then made a turkey sandwich for lunch, poured a glass of tea, came out here, and turned on the television. I began to eat and to watch a sweet Hallmark movie."

"I just love those!" Katherine interjected. Her son quelled her with a look. "Sorry," she said.

Lois continued. "After a few moments, I felt that something was wrong: Stanley was not perched above my shoulder, begging." She placed a fist in front of her mouth and her eyes filled with tears. "I panicked. I went from relaxed to full tilt crazy." Lois described that push of adrenalin as she realized her cat was gone. She'd raced around the house, calling his name. Then she'd seen it: the front door was ajar. Lois shuddered. She'd rushed out of the house barefoot, searched the yard, then ran into the street.

"That's when I found her, poor dear," said Katherine. "We searched the block, and then called you."

"I can't believe I left the door open, but Stanley has never even tried to go outside."

"Lois, you've given him a wonderful home. He's a pampered housecat, well fed, and well-loved. He was probably teased outside by a bird or a squirrel, then got scared, and is now hiding somewhere." Kalico patted her shoulder reassuringly. "I bet he's close and dying to get home!"

"I hope you're right. But what if...?" Her voice trailed off as fear and worry played across her face.

"No 'what if's'," Lynn and Katherine asserted in unison.

"Lois, I need a can of Stanley's favorite wet food, a toy, and his carrier. I'd like you to put food out for him in both the front and backyards, and keep the doors open—in case he finds his way home."

Lois gathered the materials Kalico needed quickly, pausing to stroke a fuzzy pink mouse.

"We'll text you when we find him. He's most likely to come if you call him, but you'll need to stay calm."

"I know. I know. But I don't know what I'll do if I've lost him. He's my," she choked on a sob. "He's my family."

"Ben will find him," Katherine said. "Now, let's set out that food. We'll search the house again and the backyard."

"Thanks, Mom." Kalico picked up the carrier with the Fancy Feast and the fuzzy mouse, and turned to Lynn. "Let's go."

Kalico paused on the front porch, where old Mr. Douglas was snoring softly. He pictured Stanley cautiously sticking out his nose, crouched low. He imagined the big gray cat, whiskers twitching, rushing at a grackle on the front lawn. Then Stanley would've watched the bird fly away. He looked back at the house, but a noise—a car, perhaps—startled him. Instinct told him to hide, so he....

"Which way?" Lynn stood beside him impatient to begin the search. Kalico moved to the trunk of his car, popped it, and removed a small backpack, two flashlights, a long-sleeved jeans shirt, and a pair of leather gloves. He handed a flashlight to Lynn. She raised an eyebrow questioningly.

"Stanley is a, shall we say, portly housecat. He is frightened out here in the big wide world and will seek shelter. He may be under a shrub, behind a garbage can, wedged between two fences, up a tree, or even down a curbside drain. We need to search slowly, high and low."

"What are the odds that someone will find him?"

"Fairly good. He's been missing for less than two hours." Kalico ran his hands through his hair—a gesture Lynn had seen before and no doubt meant he was less certain of finding Stanley than his words conveyed. She watched him don the backpack. Then he moved quietly up the street, and Lynn followed.

An hour and a half later, they sank onto a bench located in the center of a small park at the end of the street. No Stanley. Although the rain had stopped, gray clouds still loomed low overhead, and a cold, North wind, not unusual for the end of March, blew steadily. Lynn covered her nose and chin with her rose-colored scarf and nestled her hands in her pockets. Kalico sat hunched beside her, checking his messages.

"Anything?" she asked.

"No," Kalico sighed. "The rest of the volunteers have gone home." His eyes continued to scan the shrubbery.

"What now?"

"I've texted M's, my assistant, and she'll post Stanley's picture and notify all of our volunteers and the shelters to be on the lookout for him."

"Maybe he'll find his way home. He's got to be getting hungry. Besides he couldn't have gone very far."

"Maybe," Kalico sounded doubtful. "Even though Stanley is a senior citizen, if he was frightened or being chased, he could've travelled a couple of miles."

"Poor Lois," Lynn shivered.

"I guess we need to go back and tell her." Kalico did not move.

"I guess...." Lynn stayed seated, staring up at the branches of an Arizona ash, willing the lost cat to appear.

"I hate this!" Kalico's hands formed fists, and he scowled at the sky. "It's almost impossible to find a cat if he's missing more than a day. Where the hell could Stanley have gone?"

"Maybe a kind person took him in. He's obviously a house cat and, from what I understand, quite social?" Lynn offered.

Kalico's features lightened a bit. "Yes, that's always possible. It's just that he's so much more than a pet to Lois. Stanley appeared three weeks after her husband died. He immediately claimed Lois as his own, riding on her shoulder like a furry parrot, curling up on the pillow beside her, following her from room to room. I think she believes that her husband sent the kitten to comfort her." He shook his head. "Sometimes I think she believes that the cat is her Stanley reincarnated.

Losing him will be like losing her husband all over again."

Lynn placed a comforting hand on his arm. "Let's cross the street and go house to house again. In cases like this, action is always better than inaction." She nodded her head decisively, reminding Kalico of her aunt. She rose and held out a hand to Kalico. "C'mon. I want to see the cat detective in action!"

Kalico groaned, but allowed her to pull him to his feet. The wind had blown color into Lynn's cheeks and her blue eyes sparked with determination. Kalico felt momentarily light headed. "Say, after we find Stanley, let me take you out to dinner." He held his breath.

Lynn paused then grinned. "It's a date. I'm famished, so let's find that cat!"

They circled the little park one more time, then crossed the street to a two-story red brick home, beautifully landscaped and shaded by mature live oak trees that were just filling out with new green leaves. Lynn got down on her hands and knees to check the rain gutter while Kalico searched a border of Yaupon holly. He softly called in a falsetto, "Stanley! Here kitty, kitty. Stanley!" They moved quietly to the front beds rich and fragrant with dark mulch, and then progressed to the far flowerbeds, filled with purple iris and paperwhites. A rustle of leaves brought them to a halt. They held their breath, and Lynn pointed to the corner of the house. When she took a step forward, a squirrel burst into view, scrambled across the lawn and up an oak tree.

"Shoot," she sighed. "I thought we had him!"

"Shhhhh!" Kalico held out a hand. They listened to the hum of Mo-Pac traffic, the distant moan of a siren, the gentle whisper of wind in the tree branches. Then, faintly, a distinct and distant 'meow.' "Did you hear that?'

"Yes, but where did it come from?" Lynn whispered.

Again they listened intently. The squirrel broke the silence, chattering angrily above them. They looked up at the canopy of the tall Live Oak, and there, high above them perched on an upper limb they could just make out, the figure of a gray cat, his white tipped tail flicking nervously.

Lynn grabbed Kalico's arm, giggled, grinned, and exclaimed, "It's him. Oh, we found him. We found him!" She did a little happy dance.

Kalico smiled down at her and laughed with relief. "Thank heavens!" He returned his attention to the precariously perched cat. "Now, to get him down."

Lynn had her phone out. "Can't we just call the fire department?"

"No. They actually don't rescue treed cats." Kalico studied the stately old tree, noting its graceful symmetry, and scouting a climbing route to Stanley.

"Should I call Lois?"

"Hold off for a moment." Kalico imagined Lois's panic at the sight of her big boy literally out on a limb about thirty feet above the pavement. Her emotions would not help get Stanley down safely. He rummaged in his backpack and pulled out the can of Fancy Feast. Holding it over his head and within Stanley's view, he opened it with dramatic flair. "Here Stanley. Come and get your dinner. Come here, kitty," he called.

Stanley meowed more loudly in response, but did not move. The cat's back was toward the trunk, and he was settled about five feet out on a secondary branch that seemed to bow a bit under his weight and to sway slightly in the light wind.

"Let's give him a moment to think about his supper," Kalico directed, pulling Lynn away from the base of the live oak. They craned their necks and watched. Stanley remained frozen in place.

"I think he's stuck," offered Lynn. "Now what?"

"The way I see it, we have three options: 1. We could call a tree service company. They have the harnesses and skills to scale the tree, but are not necessarily experts with pets. 2. We could wait Stanley out, hoping that he will get hungry enough to turn around and come down without breaking his kitty neck. 3. I could go up and get him." Kalico studied the stately tree, tracing the way up in his mind. "Right now, I'm leaning toward getting him myself. The climb is fairly straightforward. I can go up the right side, cross over to the left at the midpoint, and climb to just below Stanley's branch. I think the branch just below him will hold my weight. If I can get below him, I can reach up and grab him by the scruff of his neck." Kalico was talking more to himself than to Lynn. "Yes, if I can position myself just below and a little bit behind Stanley, I can pick him up and bring him down."

"Ben, that sounds dangerous." Lynn lifted worried eyes to Kalico's face, which presented a heretofore unseen stubborn jut to his jaw. "I vote for the tree service and a call to Lois."

"I hear you, but that will take too long. We only have an hour or so before sunset, it's getting colder, and there's a chance of more rain tonight." He nodded emphatically once. "I'm going up." He handed her his phone and buttoned his jean shirt.

"Do you need the carrier? What about Lois? Ben!" But he was already six feet above her, shimmying up the rough trunk, preparing to hoist himself up to another branch. Lynn stood below, her eyes darting first from Kalico whose figure was being quickly being swallowed by dense leaves to Stanley, crouched and still above him. She held her breath.

Kalico worked his fingers into the ridges of the old oak's trunk; his right foot slipped, then rested on a convenient knob. He pushed up, got his left foot onto the next branch, and lifted himself up. He leaned against the trunk for a moment, breathing heavily and wishing that he'd spent more time on the climbing wall at the gym. He glanced down at Lynn, just making out her upturned face. *A lovely face*, he thought. He could hear Stanley's staccato meows. Chances were that he could turn himself around and come down the tree himself.

Kalico prepared to shift to the left side of the tree. If his calculations were correct, this move would place him just below Stanley. He hugged the tree, wedged his left foot into the juncture between the branch and trunk, and blindly swung his right leg around. For an instant—nothing. His heart pounded, and he began to slip. Then, contact. He shifted his weight, released the trunk, brought his left leg over, and rested precariously on a branch that groaned ominously under his weight. But the big gray cat was now within his reach.

"Hey, Stanley-boy. You certainly have gotten yourself out on a limb." Kalico spoke in a low, soothing voice. The cat's ears were flattened against his head and his tail flicked erratically. "Me too, come to think of it." Sure, he had reached the cat successfully, but how was he going to get the big boy down? A vision of Stanley and himself plummeting to the ground played itself out in his mind. *Stupid. What was he trying to do? Impress Lynn?* He should go back down; find a ladder; call for help. Stanley had been found. He was safe—for now. Just then, the cat inched forward away from Kalico. His branch shuddered and bowed.

Kalico held his breath as an idea formed. He slowly unbuttoned his jean shirt, keeping up a soft patter of talk. "Stan-the-man, Lois is worried about you. I know you want to come home, eat a good dinner, and curl up in your bed. You know me, boy. We go way back.

C'mon. Relax. Besides, you don't want to make me look bad in front of a beautiful woman." He moved a hand toward the cat, continuing to speak to him calmly. Slowly, slowly, he placed his hand on Stanley's back. He could feel the cat's muscles tense beneath his thick coat. "Don't do anything foolish, boy." He let his hand rest. Minutes passed. Then, Stanley's ears perked up, and Kalico could feel rather than hear a purr motor rumbling in the boy's chest. "Good, boy. Now, I am going to lift you off this branch. Easy. Easy."

He grasped Stanley by the scruff of the neck and lifted. The cat's claws dug into the bark for a moment, then released. Kalico pulled him into his chest, winced as the cat's claws pierced his skin, then quickly buttoned Stanley into his shirt. It was a tight fit, but it secured Stanley. He hugged him, then rapidly retraced his path down the oak, finally jumping three feet to the ground.

"Thank God!" Lynn rushed forward and hugged Kalico, instigating a startled hiss from his shirt. Stanley poked his head out from beneath the detective's chin, narrowing his golden eyes. Lynn laughed, stepped back, and snapped a picture.

An hour later, Stanley was safely home, having received a huge meal and countless scritches from neighbors. Kalico and Lynn were seated at his parents' kitchen table, eating grilled cheese sandwiches and rich tomato soup. Tired from the events of the past two days, Kalico let the conversation buzz around him, amused as his mother and sisters, who just happened to drop by, fired questions at Lynn. It was only after he had driven her back to her car and waved good-bye that he realized he had not asked Lynn about the plan she had concocted with her aunt.

Chapter Twelve

Emelia Winterjoy marched slowly forward, her eyes scouring the ground. She stooped periodically to peer under a shrub, run fingers through a dense patch of liriope, or examine the under canopy of a rose bush. Methodically, she crisscrossed Nancy MacLeod's front yard with extra special attention on the large rose bed where her friend had been stung. Forty minutes later, she had uncovered two tennis balls, a small, rubber porcupine with half of its quills missing, and a mud encrusted rawhide chew. But no EpiPen.

During the early morning's dog walk, she had found herself considering Kalico's latest report: *Although there is a possibility that Nancy's accidents were engineered, we cannot ignore the fact that they are most likely what they appear to be: accidents.* Perhaps, he was right. Perhaps, the simplest explanation is the best one. She sighed. Perhaps, she was becoming a fanciful old woman. Was she seeking excitement in an otherwise routine life? Perhaps. Had she read too many murder mysteries? Yet three potentially life-threatening accidents in less than three months…What were the odds?

The brisk walk had cleared her head. She would search for the missing EpiPen. Perhaps it had fallen out of Nancy's gardening bag and now rested unnoticed in the yard or in the house. Discovery of the pen dropped behind a chair would go a long way to indicate that the bee sting was, indeed, an unfortunate accident.

Emelia stretched to ease the tension in her lower back from bending over for so long. As she straightened, Connor emerged from the house and slouched towards her. *Stand up straight*, she thought. Aloud she said, "Good morning, Connor. Off to work?"

"Yea."

Stop mumbling. "Sunday brunch must be very busy, I suppose?"

"Yea." He moved to his car.

"I'm picking up your grandmother from the hospital early this afternoon," Emelia offered to his back.

"Uh, thanks." His eyes slid across her face, then he shrugged into the driver's seat.

Really! How could Nancy have such a monosyllabic hulk for a grandson? But she smiled and waved as he pulled away.

After he turned the corner at the far end of the block, she moved decisively to Nancy's front door, inserted her key, and stepped into the silent house. She paused in the entryway. The gardening bag usually hung from a peg on the wooden clothes tree. Emelia searched the floor beneath the stand, then patted down the coats and rain slickers, checking each pocket for the EpiPen. Nothing.

She surveyed the living room. A pair of men's Nike's were discarded in the center of the rug, a shirt was draped over the arm of the recliner, a mug—without a coaster—sat on the coffee table which was also cluttered with papers. *Really*, she thought, *Connor could clean up after himself.* She moved to the kitchen where dirty dishes were scattered on the counter. An empty pizza box and three beer cans filled the sink. Emelia shook her head and mentally rolled up her sleeves. It would be up to her to make the house fit for Nancy's return. *God knows, what I'll find upstairs.* At least, cleaning would insure a thorough search. She decided to begin upstairs and work her way down.

Grabbing the Nikes and shirt, Emelia climbed the stairs and pushed open the door to Connor's room. As she expected, the place was a disaster. A mountain of clothes crowned what was most likely an armchair, the unmade bed looked like it had been hit by a twister, the trash can overflowed, and a half-eaten slice of pepperoni pizza was stuck on the nightstand. She placed the shirt in the empty dirty clothes basket and set the shoes neatly in the boy's nearly empty closet. Her eyes scanned the floor: no flash of bright orange signaled the presence of the EpiPen. She moved next to the bed and glanced underneath it before turning her attention to the nightstand and gingerly opening the drawer—empty except for a pack of gum, three pens, and condoms.

A prickling sensation at the back of her neck made her heart flutter. She was being watched. Casually, she nudged the drawer shut, peeled the old pizza from the nightstand, and threw it in the overflowing trash basket. Then she turned and grabbed the sheets as though preparing to make the bed.

"Oh, Connor! You startled me," she commented, hoping that she did not sound flustered or, at worst, guilty.

The young man loomed in the doorway, silent and frowning.

"I'm just tidying up the house before I pick up your grandmother." She continued making the bed. "We don't want her to return to a messy place. She will need to rest for at least the next week. No exertion, the doctor said..." *Stop babbling, you old fool!* Emelia quieted herself.

"Grams leaves my room alone."

"Oh, of course." She dropped the covers.

Connor suddenly strode purposefully toward her. Emelia stepped back, banging her calf against the bedstead. She stifled a gasp and straightened to her full 5' 4", bracing herself for God-knows what. But the young man simply reached around her to grab a bowtie that was draped over his bedside lamp.

"Forgot my tie." He then waited as Emelia left his room, closing the door emphatically behind her. "Uh, thanks for taking care of Grams," he grunted. "Tell her that I'll be home by 4." He paused, brow creased, an unreadable look in his eyes.

"Connor?" she prompted, but he turned, ran down the stairs, and out of the house.

Emelia took a deep, calming breath. She waited until she heard Connor's car start and drive away, then she reopened his door and quickly searched his room. It pained her to leave the trash overflowing and the dirty clothes scattered, but she didn't dare clean. Had the look in his eyes been threatening? Worried? Sad? Guilty? Her mouth thinned into a determined line: she must protect Nancy. She returned to the hunt for the EpiPen, tidying as she went from room to room.

***

At eight o'clock Monday morning, Kalico found M's already at her desk, busily typing, and nibbling on a cinnamon bagel. Her hair was now a brilliant shade of chartreuse.

"Hey, M's. What's up?"

"Just updating our website. Nice save of Stanley."

"Yea. Don't know how the big boy made it up that oak, but I was never so glad to find a cat. Lois was frantic. And look...." He flourished a check for $200 before M's' eyes.

"Terrific. Endorse it, and I'll deposit it. Don't forget your law firm meeting's today." She looked pointedly at his jeans.

"Have my suit in the car." He grinned and looked over her shoulder at the screen. A picture of himself standing high up in the oak tree with Stanley perched on a branch above him filled half the page. A headline screamed: "Cat Detective Goes Out on a Limb to Save Beloved Feline." Two smaller photographs—one of Stanley's head poking out of Kalico's jacket and the other of a smiling and tearful Lois cuddling her boy— were inserted artfully at the bottom.

"Where'd you get those? Mom?"

"Lynn Winterjoy forwarded them to me with the pertinent details. She said to remind you that you owe her a dinner." M's raised an eyebrow and grinned.

"Sure. Thanks." Kalico tried to look nonchalant.

M's grin widened. "She seems interested, Ben."

"She a client's niece. Besides, I'm far too busy," he frowned. *And far too broke*, he added to himself.

"C'mon, Ben. You know you're a stud-muffin," she giggled, a sound Kalico had not heard in over a year. "Go for it!"

"Enough!" he tried to frown but a laugh escaped him. "You're reminding me of the time you and Katie torpedoed my date with…."

M's dramatically placed a hand on her brow and pretended to swoon. "The glorious Tiffany DeLong."

"Yes. If I recall—and how could I ever forget— Tiffany, a golden goddess of a girl, and I were standing on her porch after a movie date. A crescent moon was shining. I swear her hair looked like liquid silver. I was going in for a kiss when…."

"When Katie sneezed! We waited behind those bushes for hours. We just wanted to see your moves!"

"You just wanted to spy on me and embarrassed me." He laughed at the memory of the two little girls emerging from the shrubs. "I never did get that kiss—or a second date."

"If I remember it right, you managed to get plenty of kisses in high school!"

"What?"

"Katie didn't always sneeze!"

Kalico groaned. "You two were little devils!"

M's nodded in agreement. "But, seriously, Ben, Lynn seems nice."

"She is. Any news about Ghost?"

"No more sightings at the park. I must have spooked him. I bet he's on the move again." She sighed. "I'm so sorry." Then she added, "The next time you go after him, I'd like to come along. You know, get some on-the-job training." She laughed self-consciously."

"Sure. I appreciate the help."

"I'm going over to the animal shelter this morning to see if Pippa or any of the others have been rescued."

"Great. There's not much else going on today. Go home and relax."

M's faced froze into an expressionless mask. The giggling girl was gone again.

"Trouble at home?" he asked gently.

"Status quo."

"You know if you ever need to talk…." Kalico looked at his assistant's bent iridescent head. She did not look up, so after a moment, he went into his office. M's would open up in her own time.

He settled in behind his desk determined to review his finances one more time and to double check the materials for his meetings with the two law firms before determining the next steps in the Winterjoy case. But first things first: email. Of course, the first correspondence was from Miss Winterjoy, followed by one from Lynn. He opened Lynn's first.

Ben:

Thanks for an adventurous evening. I will never forget Lois' reunion with her Stanley. A true love story! Please tell your mother how much I enjoyed the comfort food and conversation. See you soon, Lynn

Kalico found himself grinning as he shot off a quick reply:
Lynn:
Thank you for your help last night. Mom enjoyed meeting you too.

Probably too much, he thought, given his mother's late night phone call and not so subtle suggestion that he invite Lynn to the next Kalico family movie night. He continued typing.
Lois is busy showering Stanley with cat treats and says that she has made him promise to never run away again. Don't forget that you agreed to let me take you out to dinner.

Kalico paused—a spontaneous invitation out was one thing, but now he was committing to a date. He was in no position to date. No time. No money. And he was most likely going to have to move back in with his parents. He typed quickly before he could talk himself out of it.
Are you free Saturday evening? There's an amazing Detroit-style pizzeria that just opened. I could pick you up at 7. Ben

He hit send. Then he turned his attention to Miss Winterjoy's latest missive.

Mr. Kalico:
Nancy is home, she is tired, but feeling better. Lynn and I are on guard, but I am at a loss about how to protect her from Connor

whose most recent behavior is suspicious. It is imperative that we meet.

Attached is the list of names you requested. However, your reasons for widening our circle of suspects elude me. Shall we say 3 p.m. at my home on Tuesday? Emelia Winterjoy

Kalico affirmed the meeting. The list of names was comprehensive; it included Nancy's co-workers and neighbors who had access to both her car and her home. After each name, Miss Winterjoy had included brief notes.

The final email was from Vic.

Hey, Bro.

Time to get your head out of the trees and your feet back on the ground. (A photograph of Kalico high in an oak tree appeared.) *I've attached the application to the Austin Police Academy. Seriously, consider it. Just imagine: you and me keeping the streets safe. Vic*

Kalico opened the attachment, paused, and then printed it out, placing it carefully on his desk—just something to consider.

For the next two hours Kalico reviewed his finances, made out checks for rent, insurance, M's wages, and other smaller business expenses. At least he had enough to cover the basics—minus any salary for himself. His rent was due in ten days, and he'd be short unless he took money out of his business reserve fund—again. He was astounded at how quickly his capital had dwindled in six months. At least today he would be marketing his agency to potential clients. He had to get his head in the game if he were to stay self-employed. No more chasing pets. No more indulging fanciful clients. It was time to get serious or lose his dream.

Resolved, Kalico locked his office. He would review his notes on the insurance agency and the law firm one more time, practice his pitch, and .... The phone rang: Zoe was gone again and Mrs. Buonanotte was frantic. Three hours later, Kalico dragged himself into his apartment and collapsed on the couch. Zoe was home, Gina Buonanotte was ecstatic, and he had a container of fresh-baked ziti as payment. But he had missed his two appointments.

Chapter Thirteen

At 11:30 Tuesday morning, Kalico paused just outside the door to his agency and frowned. Some jerk had inserted *C A T* written in orange permanent marker so that the nameplate read: The Kalico *CAT* Detective Agency. That would boost client confidence—if he had any clients. Santiago Insurance Company had agreed to reschedule. They did not subcontract, however, but indicated that he was welcome to apply for an in-house investigator position. He'd been tempted. Lawrence, Gunderson, and Reed had been less forgiving. They were just building their law practice and said that they would contact him if and when needed. Although he disliked marketing himself, Kalico determined that he needed to set up dozens of more such meetings to generate business.

Hearing animated voices, he paused in the doorway. M's and Lynn were bent over a book.

"You're right," Lynn acknowledged. "Mr. Rochester is manipulative. He does bring in Blanche Ingram to make Jane jealous. But why?"

"Because he enjoys locking women in rooms and playing mind games."

"That's certainly a possible explanation—if we see him as a villain. But, M's, why else would he manipulate Jane? Look at the text." Lynn, looked up and her eyes met Kalico's. She smiled hello.

M's frowned and scanned the book. "He says that he wanted to fix her attention and love."

"Good. Now, what obstacles stand in the way of Jane acknowledging her love for him?"

"Well, he is her boss and so much older."

"Yes, and?"

"So there's a difference in position and power?"

"Yes! It would be like you deciding to date Ben."

M's face registered horror, then she giggled, and Lynn joined her.

"Hey! Thanks a lot!" Kalico interrupted. "I'll have you know, I am quite a catch!"

"So your mother says!" M's retorted.

They all laughed. Kalico then ushered Lynn into his office after asking M's to see if she could remove the graffiti above their sign.

Lynn stood in front of the white board, frowning. "Mrs. Klein? Really? She's over 90!"

"Elderly, yes. But I just completed a criminal background check, and she makes Ma Parker look like Mother Teresa."

"You're kidding!" Lynn turned alarmed eyes to Kalico's, saw that he was trying to suppress a grin, and laughed reluctantly, but her frown deepened.

"Mrs. Klein dropped off a novel—a lurid romance, if your aunt's note is correct—at Nancy's for the book drive. Seems like everyone in the neighborhood as well as Nancy's co-workers had access to her house."

"This is all so, so…." She gestured at the board, then sank into a chair. Her hands nervously picked at her black skirt.

"Lynn, what can I do for you?" Kalico smiled encouragement.

"I can't stay. It's my grading period."

Kalico waited. "How is Nancy?" he prompted.

"Safely home and feeling a little better. Aunt Em is on guard. She's arranged for the ladies to rotate visits so that Nancy is rarely alone."

Kalico looked meaningfully at the white board. Nancy's protectors were all there as suspects. Never slow on the uptake, Lynn took a deep breath. "I know. I know, but Em is certain that Connor is…"

"The perp—if there is a perpetrator?"

"Yes. We had an awful row about it this morning."

"Tell me what happened."

Kalico listened attentively as Lynn related her fight with her aunt. After a sleepless night, she'd gone over to Emelia's before work determined to convince her to give up the notion that Nancy was in danger. "But Em is convinced that Connor is a potential murderer. She won't listen to reason. She's never liked Connor, and he knows it, so he always acts strangely around her. But I know that he loves his grandmother." She sighed.

Kalico, silent, murmured encouragement.

"Anyway, he has no motive." She rose and paced the room. "Em can be so stubborn. I told her that she was being fanciful, that she was prejudiced against Connor. And she…" Lynn's eyes darkened at the memory. "And she asked me if I thought she was 'in her dotage.' If I had ever known her to act without a good cause?" She stopped in front of Kalico. "God, Ben, she was so hurt and angry."

"It's a tense situation."

"Yes! I just want things to go back to normal. Accidents happen." Her phone beeped. "That's my alarm. I have to get back to school." She grabbed her purse. "And thanks for listening. I feel better."

"You're welcome. We can sort things out this afternoon. I assume you'll be at the meeting?"

"Yes." She moved rapidly to the door. "And Ben, dinner Saturday will be fine."

Before he could reply, she was gone, calling "Try hand sanitizer" over her shoulder. He smiled to himself: he had a date.

He came out to the reception area, where M's was busy scrubbing the door. "Hand sanitizer?"

"Apparently, it removes permanent marker." M's stood back and admired her work—the C A T had disappeared, except for the cap of the T.

"When you're done there, will you please call the next four businesses on our list and set up appointments?"

"Will do. But you cannot flake—not even for little Zoe."

"I won't. Any luck at the shelters yesterday?" Kalico changed the subject.

"No. But I spoke again with Pippa's owner, Alyssa. The dog is chipped, so we can't figure out why no one has turned her in—unless someone found her and just decided to keep her."

"Makes sense. A Bichon Frise puppy is cute—and valuable."

"I plan to canvass the neighborhood where she was lost again after class this afternoon. Alyssa authorized $20 an hour for up to ten hours. She's also posting a reward of $100 in addition to our finder's fee."

"I don't think you should canvas West Campus alone. That neighborhood's had some problems. I'll go with you."

M's nodded.

Kalico went back into his office to prepare for his meeting with Miss Winterjoy. It promised to be uncomfortable—at best.

***

At 3 p.m. Kalico was seated in a floral wing-backed chair with the calico cat, Perdita, curled in his lap and a cup of green tea balanced on his right knee. Miss Winterjoy, dressed severely in a charcoal gray pants suit, sat ramrod straight opposite from him. Her steel blue gaze was fixed on him, and she was silent and unsmiling. Even the antics of Trey and Snow, who obviously felt that they deserved one of the cookies set out on the coffee table, failed to elicit a response from their owner.

"I understand that Nancy is feeling better?" he offered.

Miss Winterjoy nodded slightly. Then she snapped her fingers sharply and pointed at the kitchen. The corgis paused mid-dance. "Sirs, enough!" She snapped again and the dogs, heads lowered, sulked to the kitchen and sank onto the tile with joint sighs. She returned her gaze to Kalico.

He wanted to loosen his tie and take off his jacket. He felt nervous sweat trickle down his back. "Miss Winterjoy," he began, "I want to go over my latest report on our case. As you can see…."

His client raised a hand to stop him. "I prefer that we wait for Lynn. I want her to join our discussion. I wouldn't want her to think that I had you chasing one of my fancies."

At that moment, excited barks announced Lynn's arrival. She rushed in, greeted the dogs, nodded at Kalico, and bent to kiss her aunt on the cheek. "Sorry to be late. A student needed help with a scholarship essay."

Miss Winterjoy allowed the peck on the cheek. *Must be like kissing an iceberg* Kalico thought. Lynn settled in the chair next to his. Silence descended. Only Perdita's strong purr was audible. Even the corgis seemed subdued, lying by Lynn's chair, their eyes focused on the cookies.

"Well," Kalico began. "I wanted to bring you up to date on…."

"Aunt Emelia," Lynn interrupted. "I want to apologize for this morning. I was out of line. Of course, I do not doubt that you have reason for your concerns for Nancy."

Miss Winterjoy studied her niece for a moment. "I, too, am sorry for my impatience. Now, Benjamin, enlighten us on your progress on this case."

Kalico cleared his throat, gingerly lifted Perdita from his lap and set aside the tea cup. He opened a folder and handed Miss Winterjoy a diagram that Lynn recognized as a simplified version of his white board. He proceeded to point out the people who had had access to both Nancy's car and to her gardening bag, assuming that all of them had knowledge of her allergies. He, then, eliminated neighbors, including old Mrs. Klein, assuming that they'd had little time to gain access either to Nancy's car or her medication.

"There are two main obstacles to our concluding that these incidents were not accidents. First, there's no physical evidence to indicate brake tampering. Mr. Alvarez, the mechanic who replaced brake pads and fluid lines after the car wreck, noted only usual wear and tear. Also, there's nothing to indicate that the missing EpiPen was stolen. Nancy cannot remember if it was in her bag. Second,…"

Miss Winterjoy raised a hand to stop him: "Connor was supposed to have his grandmother's brakes checked when he had the car's oil changed. Obviously, he failed to do so, and he lied about it!" She looked meaningfully at Lynn, who wisely remained silent.

"That's true. Nancy assumed that her brakes had been checked. We do not know if Connor directly stated that the work had been done, or why he didn't have the brake work done with the oil change."

Miss Winterjoy made a noise that sounded like an *harrumph*. "He certainly had the most direct access to the EpiPen. He was acting suspiciously—and even threateningly—when I last saw him."

"You were snooping in his room!" Lynn interjected.

"I was not snooping. I was searching for evidence."

"And did you find anything?" asked Kalico, as Perdita insinuated herself back onto his lap. He absent-mindedly began stroking her head.

"No. There is no evidence that the missing EpiPen fell out of Nancy's bag or was misplaced. It is simply gone. Therefore, someone took it."

"Or," Lynn added gently, "Nancy simply forgot to replace it."

"Because we old people are so forgetful?" her aunt challenged.

"Second," Kalico raised his voice, "I cannot find a motive for anyone wanting to harm Nancy. As far as I can discover, she is universally liked and has led a blameless life."

"No one, young man, beyond a certain age, has led a blameless life. Small thoughtless acts, little betrayals of trust, indiscretions, hurtful words, inattention—everyone is guilty, Nancy and myself included."

"Agreed. But people usually do not murder over petty grievances. Money, power, jealousy, revenge—these are the common motives."

"Connor would stand to inherit if Nancy were removed."

"But, Aunt Em, Nancy is not a wealthy woman. And wouldn't Patrick be her main beneficiary?"

"True. But I bet she left something to Connor. He is not trustworthy, he is a spendthrift, and I fear that he wants to get his grandmother out of the way." She folded her arms, a stubborn jut to her jaw.

Both ladies turned to Kalico who squirmed under the gaze of twin pairs of blue eyes. Annoyed that his hand had stopped the delightful pets, Perdita tapped him with a paw, claws partially extended. He resumed stroking her head. "I can see why you suspect Connor." He focused on his client. "He's in financial trouble, having run up..." He checked his notes, "a $7,000 credit card debt. He's living with his grandmother to cut expenses so that he can pay his father back. He's maintaining a strong B average at UT and working approximately 30 hours a week."

"Very laudable, I'm sure," conceded Miss Winterjoy. "But Connor is a boy who always tries to find the easy way out. In high school...."

"Aunt Em, that's ancient history. He learned from his attempt to plagiarize. Can't you accept that he's grown up?"

"Lynn, I do not understand why you insist on defending him."

"And I do not understand why you...."

"Ladies!" Kalico intervened. "Let me finish." He waited until they were again focused on him. "Miss Winterjoy, if someone wants to harm Nancy—and that is still a big if—I have concluded that it is not Connor."

"And how have you reached this conclusion?" she responded too quietly for Kalico's comfort.

He swallowed, fearing that he did not look very authoritative with a cat in his lap. He conscientiously avoided glancing at Lynn who could not disguise her delight. "Okay. Let's suppose there is a killer out who who is after Nancy. Let's suppose that each of her accidents was engineered. Now, if we profile the perpetrator, what could we determine about him or her?"

"Good question!" Lynn exclaimed. "I like this—it's a puzzle."

Miss Winterjoy looked thoughtful and her eyes sparked with interest. "I would say that our murderer is not impulsive."

"I agree." Lynn leaned forward. "And he does not want to get caught: he wants the crime to appear accidental."

"Good. So our perpetrator is careful, methodical, and non-confrontational." Kalico wrote these words on a blank sheet of paper. "What else?"

"I would say that he is patient. Wouldn't you, Aunt Em?"

"Yes. He sets something in motion by tampering imperceptibly with brakes or by taking an EpiPen, then he is content to wait for the outcome."

"Yes, he leaves the outcome to chance or to fate or to...."

"Or to divine retribution."

"Interesting thought. If fate or God play a part in Nancy's death, then the murderer could justify his actions."

"A twisted psychology certainly." Miss Winterjoy and Lynn exchanged smiles.

Kalico wrote: *Leaves outcome to fate.*

Lynn's brow creased in thought. "This person does not want to get his hands dirty. It's not a crime of passion."

"As the sayings goes, 'Revenge is a dish best served cold,'" offered Miss Winterjoy.

"Shakespeare?' asked Kalico.

"No. An old *Star Trek*," Lynn laughed.

"A centuries old proverb," corrected her aunt.

"Seriously, now," Kalico held the list of traits up to view. "Does this calculating, would-be killer sound like Connor?"

Miss Winterjoy leaned back in her chair; her shoulders slumped slightly. "No," she admitted. "No, it does not sound like Connor who, from my observation, is impulsive and careless, and messy." She recalled his bowtie strewn over the lampshade. "It's a wonder that he ever gets to school or to work on time and in one piece."

Lynn reached for a chocolate chip cookie. "I'm exhausted! But where are we now?" she asked Kalico.

"If we remove Connor from the list of suspects, we are left with people who are Nancy's closest friends and acquaintances." He conjured the faces of the elderly women. "Frankly, they're not the usual suspects. Therefore," Kalico ran a hand through his hair. "Miss Winterjoy, at this time, it is my professional recommendation that we disband the investigation." Kalico held his breath, unsure how his client would react.

"I am correct, am I not, Mr. Kalico, that I have you on retainer for one more day?" she asked quietly.

"Yes, ma'am."

"I surmise that if a crime had been committed, your next step would be to interrogate the suspects?"

"Yes, ma'am, but...."

"Then that is what I want you to do. Find out if any of our friends had the means, the knowledge, and the motive to want to harm Nancy." She nodded her head decisively. "After all, most homicides are committed by someone the victim knows."

Recognizing an immovable object when he saw one, Kalico was at a loss how to respond. He pictured himself ushering each of the book circle women into Interrogation Room 3. Shaking his head, he glanced at Lynn, looking for help.

She complied. "But, Aunt, won't the ladies find it odd if Ben comes knocking on their doors asking questions?"

"Yes. But we must be thorough—Nancy's life is at stake." She rose, indicating that their meeting was over. "I will expect a full report."

"Miss Winterjoy," Kalico began, "isn't there some way that I could meet with the suspects in a less obvious way?" He paused for dramatic effect. "I wouldn't want to tip off the killer that we were on to him, uh—her."

"He has a point!" Lynn nodded decisively. "Everyone, including two of Nancy's co-workers who made your list, will be here tomorrow night for dinner and a book talk. Why don't you join us? It will give you a great excuse to speak with all of the suspects."

"Good idea. I should have thought of it myself, Lynn." Miss Winterjoy nodded in approval.

"Wouldn't my presence raise suspicion?"

"Not necessarily. We could say that you are there to offer professional insight into the methods of Chief Inspector Gamache," Lynn offered.

"Good, Lynn! And that Benjamin is with us as your special guest." Miss Winterjoy smiled broadly at the young couple.

"But I haven't read the book!" Kalico protested.

"Then you'd better get started." She handed him a copy of *Still Life* by Louise Penny.

Kalico shifted his gaze from Miss Winterjoy to Lynn. Both ladies were looking pleased with this decision. He hefted the substantial novel. Perhaps there were Spark Notes.

"And there are no Spark Notes for this novel," stated Miss Winterjoy, reading his mind. "There is no short cut to a great book."

Lynn walked Kalico to his car, affirming that he would arrive for dinner and book circle meeting at 6 p.m. Wednesday evening. "The novel is wonderful and a fairly quick read. And, Ben, thank you for diverting my aunt's attention away from Connor."

Before he could respond, she stepped quickly forward, placed her arms around his neck, rising onto her tiptoes. Reflexively, he placed his arms around her, feeling the warmth of her body and inhaling the sweet scent of vanilla. His heart pounded, and instinctively he leaned in for a kiss. Instead, Lynn whispered into his ear. "Don't look, but Susan Jankowsky just came out of Nancy's house and is headed our way. I want her to see you as my, well, boyfriend, not as a detective."

"Hello, you two!" Susan floated up to them, a vision in a swirl of blues and greens with a hint of purple. Her silver hair framed a broadly smiling face. "'In the spring a young man's fancy lightly turns to thoughts of....'"

"Apple pie!" finished Lynn, trying to pull away from Kalico who kept an arm around her as he turned to greet Susan.

"Not quite Tennyson's intent, but, yes, I bring apple pie." Susan arched an eyebrow at Lynn who pretended to ignore it. She studied the pair surreptitiously. She no doubt noticed that Lynn's young man was not conventionally handsome—that unfortunate red hair—but he had a pleasant face, and Lynn looked happy. Aloud she said, "Costco had a buy one get one free, so I dropped a pie off with Nancy, poor dear, and am delivering one to Emelia for tomorrow's night's meeting."

"I thought Jane was bringing dessert?"

"Yes, well, Jane's confections are not always, shall we say, edible?" Susan laughed, not unkindly.

"True."

"How is Mrs. MacLeod?" Kalico asked, tightening his arm around Lynn as she subtly tried to disentangle herself.

"Exhausted. Em wanted me to keep her company until 5:30, but she was so sleepy. I covered her with an afghan and tiptoed out."

"I'm sure that was best." Lynn frowned slightly. She moved out of the circle of Kalico's arm. "Ben, I'll see you tomorrow night. I had a lovely time."

"Me too. Mrs. Jankowsky, nice to see you again."

The women watched as Kalico drove away. "Lynn, do tell!" Susan looked like an elegant and exotic bird awaiting a treat.

"Nothing to tell—yet. We've just started," Lynn swallowed.

"But you like him! I can tell. And he's so much nicer than that last guy—what was his name?"

"Ah—the man who shall remain nameless. And, yes, I do like Ben."

"I'm so glad. You deserve someone really nice." And with that they escorted the apple pie into Miss Winterjoy's home.

Chapter Fourteen

Kalico pulled up beside M's' yellow Beetle, surprised that they had both captured rare parking spaces across from the University of Texas campus. M's emerged from her car with a folder filled with pictures of the seven-month-old Bichon Frise puppy, Pippa, tucked under her arm. The photograph showed a little white fluff ball staring out at the world with serious black eyes. She had slipped out of her collar and disappeared when her owner had stopped across from the Harry Ransom Center to chat with friends. That had been over a week ago. Her owner, Alyssa, had papered the campus with Pippa's image.

It was a good guess that the little dog had been scooped up by someone who'd decided to keep her. Kalico and M's planned to canvas the west campus neighborhood. They crossed 21 St., pausing for a moment to look at the Littlefield fountain and the iconic UT tower that rose behind it at the far end of the South Mall. Students lounged on the limestone wall that framed the dancing water, some with heads bent intently over textbooks; others, stretched out, enjoying the spring sun. They proceeded to the HRC, where little Pippa had escaped, and crossed the Drag, also known as Guadalupe St., a busy thoroughfare always bustling with students and traffic, street musicians and vendors.

"How could the puppy have crossed this mess safely?" asked M's, trying to keep up with Kalico's long strides.

For the next hour, they knocked on the doors of apartments, duplexes, lovely little bungalows, and stately homes. M's conscientiously noted the addresses where no one answered—placing a star by the houses where she could hear a dog bark.

"I like canvassing, Ben. It's like a great treasure hunt. At the next door, we may find Pippa."

"Or not," Kalico grumbled. "My feet hurt, and we only have another hour or so of daylight."

"Come on, old man." She pulled him along toward a small gray and white house, tucked behind tall Pecan trees and blooming Carolina jasmine.

M's pressed the doorbell and waited. The high-pitched yip of a puppy could be heard. The door opened about two inches, and a woman's voice asked, "Yes?"

"Good evening," Kalico began. "We're searching for a lost puppy, and wondered if you could help us?"

The door opened to reveal a woman in her late twenties. She was wearing a thick, fuzzy pink bathrobe over black sweat pants. Her light brown hair was mussed, and the gray eyes behind think tortoise shell glasses blinked against the light.

"So sorry. We didn't mean to wake you."

"No problem." She looked over the rims of her glasses at Pippa's picture. "I haven't seen him."

"Her. Could you keep an eye out? Perhaps, when you walk your dog?"

The woman stiffened and began to close the door. "I don't have a dog."

M's thrust a picture into her hand. "Our number is on the poster. Just in case…" But the door had closed firmly; the dead bold clicked.

"Let's call it a day," suggested Ben.

"But that woman has a dog. Why would she lie?" She stared at the closed door, and shrugged, not wanting to leave. The sound of footsteps rushing toward them made them turn.

"Missy! Ben! Hey, M's! Hey!" A tall redhead in bright blue shorts and an over-sized gray sweatshirt engulfed her in a bear hug.

"Katie!" M's managed to gasp as her feet left the ground.

"Oh, Melissa! And Benj. What a great surprise. What are you doing on campus?"

"Hi, Sis. We're looking for Pippa."

"Hi, Katie. No time to talk," declared M's, disentangling herself from her one-time-best friend's embrace. "On the job, you know." She showed her Pippa's photo.

"Poor little lost girl. You and Ben will return her to her owner."

"Let's hope so. Nice to see you, but we have to run." M's started to turn away, not seeing the pleading look Katie cast at her brother.

"I could use a cup of coffee before we tackle this block," Ben said.

"Yes. Let's have a coffee. Missy, I haven't seen you in months. C'mon. Let's go have coffee and catch up. Please."

"Sure, M's and I will join you at Starbucks."

Ten minutes later, settled in comfortable chairs, the girls sipped frothy chai lattes as Kalico drank a black coffee and watched the girls interact. Katie, elbows on the table and cup cradled under her chin, leaned forward willing M's to engage. M's, her black jeans and tee accenting the pallor of her skin, looked down at the table. Her shock of short and spiked electric green hair, today tipped with blue, evoked whimsy.

"Love the hair."

"Liar," asserted M's, but her tone was light.

"No, really. I do. It's exciting. In fact, I've been thinking of cutting my hair and perhaps going blue or even black." Katie swept a strand of thick red hair behind her ear.

M's snorted. "Never! A redhead's hair is a part of her identity! Isn't that what your mom said that time we got into the food coloring and tried to become brunettes like Katie Perry?"

"Yes! I'd forgotten…."

"Besides, your hair is a 'dazzling autumn sunset.' Remember Bobby Brent's *Ode to Katie* in the 9th grade?"

The girls laughed and for a moment it seemed to Ben like old times when the girls had been inseparable besties. Katie leaned forward. "Okay, Missy—sorry, M's—give. What's the story behind Ben and the new woman in his life?" She grinned mischievously. "Mom is thrilled. I think she's started to write wedding invitations!"

"Hey, leave my love life out of your conversation."

"What love life?" shot back Katie.

"Touché."

M's glanced at Ben before jumping in. "Her name is Lynn, and she's the niece of one of our clients. Didn't you meet her last night? She helped rescue Stanley."

"No. I had to stay late on campus. Midterms start this week." Stress lines momentarily appeared on Katie's brow, then as quickly disappeared. "Mom said that sparks were flying between them."

"Lynn is great. She's an English teacher at Bowie, pretty, and sane—unlike the other women Ben's dated. Remember Daphne?"

"You mean, Princess Daphne?" Katie placed her hand dramatically against her forehead, her voice deepened into an English accent. "Benjamin, get my sweater. Benjamin, my double espresso extra foam latte is cold. Benjamin, the car door won't open itself. Benjamin, chew my food for me!"

"And *she* broke up with *him*!"

"Enough, girls, or I'll tell Mom about the time you two snuck out...."

Katie held up her hands. "Okay. But Ben, is it true that you're considering moving back home?"

"No!" M's was horrified. "You'll never find a girl if you do that!" She shook her head. "It's so ironic: you may be voluntarily moving back home while I've spent the last year trying to figure out how to move out."

"Are things still tough at home?"

M's shrugged and took a long sip of her chai. She grasped M's arm with a warm hand and shook it playfully.

"Tell me about your quest to find the little lost Pippa."

Ben filled Katie in on the Bichon Frise's escape and the frustrating hunt for her, detailing the afternoon's door-to-door efforts. "We figure that someone found her and just decided to keep her."

"Without taking her to a vet to see if she's chipped?"

"I know." M's sighed.

Katie removed the lid from her chai, scooped foam from the cup's sides with a plastic stir and then licked the froth from the stir. Her eyes held a faraway look that signaled a Katie plan of action. "We must go back to the last house—where you thought you heard a puppy bark. Why would the owner lie about having a dog, unless she didn't want you to see it? I bet she has Pippa. Let's go!"

Katie grabbed her backpack and rushed to the door. "C'mon!"

Kalico and M's followed. "Katie, stop!" called Ben, but his sister was already half a block ahead.

M's sighed. "I don't know what it is about Katie, but it seems like I'm always following her into one adventure or another. Remember the time that Katie led me on a disastrous quest for pirate treasure in Zilker Park?"

"No, but I recall Katie's 'End Hunger' canned food drive that never seemed to end. You two filled our garage from floor to ceiling." He raised his voice, "Hey, Katie! Do you even know where we're going?"

"Hurry! You said San Gabriel, right?

"No. Rio Grande."

Katie rushed back, grabbed M's hand, and pulled her into a jog. "Let's save Pippa! She's probably been dognapped and is going to be sold on the black market."

Fifteen minutes later, breathless and laughing, the girls stopped two doors down from the suspicious house.

"The black market, Kit Kat?" Ben panted. "What have you been reading?"

Katie became suddenly serious. "Animals are sold to laboratories, to fur traders, and to foreign countries for food. A pure bred pup like Pippa could be sold to a breeder for a tidy profit, I bet. Have you been checking Craig's List?"

The Kalico outrage over injustice of any kind was contagious. M's cheeks flushed like Katie's. "Remember, there may not even be a puppy in this house. I just thought I heard a little yip."

"That's good enough for me."

Recognizing that stopping his sister from checking out the little house was futile. Kalico took charge. He determined that Katie would keep the woman of the house occupied at the front door, while he and M's checked out what they could see through the side and back windows. *Nothing like a little trespassing to get the old adrenalin working,* he thought.

Katie smoothed her hair and tied it into a ponytail. She discarded her sweatshirt to reveal a light blue Polo shirt and grabbed a notebook from her backpack. "I'll keep her occupied for five minutes. Synchronize watches—I mean, phones!" Then with a wink at Ben and M's, she marched up the walk of the gray and white house, and rang the doorbell. The woman, still in her bathrobe, answered the door. In seconds she was nodding and smiling and chatting away with Katie.

Ben pointed M's toward the right side of the house while he sprinted to the left. He was pleased to see that his assistant did not crouch down or try to make herself smaller. Instead she strolled confidently up to the side window—looking far less suspicious if a neighbor spotted her.

Katie's trilling laugh rose above traffic sounds as Kalico casually walked up to the kitchen window and peered inside. He saw a tidy cream and yellow room. Copper pans hung from hooks above a shiny chrome stove. A bowl—possibly a dog's water bowl—sat on the floor by the far cabinet.

Kalico continued down the side of the house to a wooden gate, thankfully unlocked. He placed his hand on the warm metal latch and stopped. He needed an excuse to enter the backyard. He pulled Pippa's slender pink leash from his pocket. If challenged, he could claim that he thought he'd seen his dog run under the fence. Pushing open the gate, Kalico moved rapidly. He looked in a small bedroom window. No movement. No dog.

He looked up to see M's entering the backyard. Suddenly ferocious barks erupted from behind a neighbor's fence. The girl froze, muscles tensed, prepared to run back through the gate. The dog's barks intensified. Kalico signaled her to stay still and quiet.

"Jake! Shut it!" growled a man's voice. Immediately, Jake's barking ceased. M's moved forward toward the sliding glass door, where Kalico joined her.

Slowly, they pressed themselves flat against the wall on either side of the door. At Kalico's nod, they peered inside at a living room that opened up to a small entry way. The woman's figure was silhouetted against the open front door. Scanning the room, they found no evidence of a dog, or any other pet for that matter. M's turned toward the side gate.

One last window seemed to present itself. M's raised herself on tiptoes to look through gauzy white curtains into a small bedroom that obviously served as a study. A desktop computer rested on a large desk covered with typed sheets of paper and Post-it notes. She gestured at Ben to join her. A small, metal dog crate, rested beside a Queen Anne chair, and inside it, contentedly chewing on a red, rubber Kong, sat a fluffy, white Bichon Frise.

Kalico and M's exchanged a silent high five.

M's danced from foot to foot as she waited beside Kalico for Katie to finish her conversation and come back down the walkway.

"Oh, you found Pippa! I can tell by your faces."

"Yes. There's a puppy in a crate in the lady's study. She lied," declared M's.

"Glorious." Kate danced a little jig on the sidewalk. She pulled out her phone. "I'm calling the police."

"Hold on, Kit-Kat. We don't know for certain the puppy is Pippa."

"The woman's a dog-napper! I say we go in there and rescue the puppy." M's hands were balled into fists, and she glared at the small house. "Who are we dealing with here, Katie?"

"Her name is Serena Moore, age 29, and she's a doctoral candidate in American History. She's writing the last chapter of her dissertation. I thought she was nice—certainly not my idea of someone who steals dogs or trades them on the black market." Katie sighed. "But graduate students are inherently poor, and she lied. She may have dog-napped Pippa for a reward."

Wavering between alarm and amusement, Kalico said, "I admire your passion, ladies, but do I need to remind you that we have no legal authority here? We cannot go in and seize a dog. Moreover, the police would consider a call like this frivolous, and...."

But M's and Katie ignored his protest, pushed past him, and marched up to the front door. M's knocked assertively three times.

Serena Moore, looking annoyed, opened the door. "Really, I'm working and have no time for more surveys or...."

"Ms. Moore, I work for the Kalico Detective Agency and have reason to believe that you are illegally harboring a missing Bichon Frise puppy named Pippa." M's squared her shoulders, looking steadily into the young woman's eyes. Kalico and Katie had her back.

Serena Moore blinked; her gray eyes glistened with unshed tears. "Oh," she sighed, her voice husky. "I know I should have told you about Abigail—uh, Pippa—when you were here earlier. I'm so sorry." She disappeared into her house for a few minutes, then returned with Pippa, squirming in her arms. She had found the puppy six days earlier—cold, hungry, wet, and muddy. Serena had scooped her up, fed and bathed her with the intention of taking her into a vet to see if she were chipped. But the little dog was so sweet and such fun company that one day became two, and the more days that passed, the easier it became for Serena to think of the newly named Abby as her own.

An hour later, the trio placed an excited puppy into her rightful owner's arms. Tearfully ecstatic, Alyssa laughed and cried, hugged Kalico, and M's and Katie and Pippa and then hugged them all again.

As Katie walked her brother and M's back to their cars, she glanced at her friend. "That was intense."

"I know!" M's grinned at Kalico, waving the reward check. "Two hundred and sixty dollars—not a bad afternoon's work."

Katie met her brother's eyes who nodded imperceptibly. She cleared her throat, "I've missed you, M's. If I did anything…Please know that I'm so sorry. I…"

"You didn't do anything. It's just that I've changed…" M's sighed.

"I've changed too, but that doesn't mean I don't want you to be my friend."

M's raised a skeptical eyebrow.

"Really, I *have* changed. After all, I'm almost twenty."

"In ten months!"

"But I'm walking through my twentieth year on earth." Katie nodded triumphantly.

"Okay. Let's see: do you still want to be a small animal veterinarian?"

Katie nodded.

"Do you still drench Mint Chocolate ice cream in Hershey's chocolate?" Another nod. "Do you stream reruns of *Veronica Mars*? Do you crush on *Sting*? Is *While You Were Sleeping* still your favorite movie?"

"Stop! Okay, maybe I haven't changed. But that means that I still love you and consider you my best friend." Katie chewed on her lower lip, then said softly, "Missy, you know that you can talk to me about anything. No judgment." She sent a silent appeal to her brother.

"That goes for me too," he said.

M's remained silent, but she returned Katie's goodbye hug and nodded at her boss.

Chapter Fifteen

Kalico whistled as studied his notes on the varied guests for the evening's dinner and book talk. He had finished his reading homework at 3 a.m. and had to admit that he'd enjoyed *Still Life*. Although he preferred true crime stories, Louise Penny's mystery was engrossing, her inspector smart and complex, and the Three Pines' setting a place everyone would want to live. He felt confident that he would be able to hold his own in the book circle. And, best yet, Miss Winterjoy had ordered him to include the reading time on his bill. The agency's finances were looking up for the month. He was not going to break even—damn the insurance bill—but he would be close, if he ignored the fact that he was paying himself below minimum wage. Alyssa Moore's check had been an unexpected bonus.

He grinned when he recalled M's excitement as they recovered Pippa. He believed that she had taken a small step back toward Katie. He had wanted to warn her against trespass; after all, Texas is an open carry state, so intruders in back and front yards were shot yearly. But he hadn't had the heart to dampen her enthusiasm. Her animated chatter had reminded him of the old Melissa.

Kalico pushed a comb through his hair and felt the stubble on his chin. A shave was in order. Although he viewed the evening as a way to appease Miss Winterjoy, he admitted to himself that he looked forward to seeing Lynn and planned to take full advantage of his role as her "special guest." As a professional, he intended to ferret out as much information from the guests as possible, so he had directed his client and her niece to encourage the ladies to reminisce. Did anyone have special knowledge of automobiles? What past jealousies or grievances could have prompted one of them to harm Nancy? He doubted strongly that a would-be murderer would be sitting at the dinner table, yet Nancy's accidents were suspicious. If nothing else, the evening could bring closure to Miss Winterjoy's case.

Promptly at 6 p.m. Kalico entered the Winterjoy home. Trey and Snow greeted him with joyful barks, Perdita arched her back and rubbed her face against his shin, and Lynn, laughing, rescued his mother's broccoli, cheese, and rice casserole from his outstretched hands. As he followed her into the kitchen where she set the dish beside a myriad of salad bowls and casseroles and pie plates, he could hear voices and laughter emanating from the living room.

"Aunt Em is plying the guests with white wine spritzers to loosen their tongues," Lynn whispered. Aloud she said, "Okay, let's make our entrance, boyfriend," and she linked her arm through his.

Kalico looked down at her. Soft brown curls framed her face; amber earrings glinted in the light, complementing her sleeveless, golden top. "I'm with you, girlfriend." He let her draw him into the next room.

A lively scene presented itself. Nancy MacLeod lounged on the sofa propped up by over-sized pillows. She wore a shear, high collared coral blouse with ruffles at the neck and wrists. Dangling silver discs shimmered at her ears. Moody, posted at her feet, grinned broadly and thumped her tail when she saw Kalico, but did not move. Beside her, Susan Jankowsky, elegant in white slacks and a white lace top adorned with a long, silver necklace, looked up smiling. Across from her, Margie Davis, in practical dark blue jeans with a matching jean jacket, and Jane Roundtree, resembling a little brown hen in an ill-fitting pants suit, nodded their welcome and then returned to their conversation.

Miss Winterjoy, who was handing a thin, middle-aged man a wine glass, noted the young couple's linked arms and nodded approval. "Welcome, Ben. I think you've met everyone except Randal Johnston. Randal, this is Benjamin Kalico."

Randal crossed the room to shake hands, seeming relieved at another male presence. Kalico recognized him from an earlier background check as the adult fiction librarian who had worked with Nancy for the past ten years. He was 37 years old, married with an eight--old son, coached his son's soccer team, loved sailing and photography. He had no criminal record—not even a traffic violation.

"Nice to meet you." Randal's handshake was cool and firm. "Say, aren't you that pet detective?"

"Just detective," Kalico corrected.

"Glad you're here. My wife and son are visiting grandma in Florida, so I thought I'd come to the book circle." He lowered his voice slightly. "Food is always terrific. And Louise Penny is a master at crime fiction."

"Yes, I…"

"Ben, come and greet Moody before she shakes herself to pieces," Nancy called, extending her hand.

"Excuse me." Kalico moved to Nancy, taking her hand. Suddenly, he was tempted to kiss it, like a gentleman in an old movie, but he bent instead to stroke the insistent little dog's head. "How are you feeling?" Although her make-up was done expertly, he could see red streaks, which lingered on her cheeks. Her eyes were still slightly swollen.

"Fine. But tired of answering that question—all for a little bee sting." She shook her head and smiled in a self-deprecating way. "I have discovered that healing is more difficult the older one gets. But I see my doctor on Thursday and should be able to resume normal activities."

"Nancy, that's terrific." Ben settled into an empty chair and Lynn perched on its arm. Kalico casually put his arm around her waist—just to steady her.

"I'm glad to get out my house this evening!"

"Yes, and with such great friends. How long has your book circle been meeting?"

"Oh, my goodness. We started in college—I think during our sophomore year. It must have been 1964. Fifty years ago."

"And you've been friends all of this time!"

Nancy flicked the rim of her glass, signaling for silence. "Ladies! My young hero here wants to know the secret of our friendship."

"Patience."

"Tolerance."

"Good food."

"Humor."

"How did your circle form?" Lynn asked, seeing an opportunity for the group to reminisce. "I know Em and Nancy have been friends for eons, but...."

"Not quite eons, dear," her aunt interposed. "We were fierce rivals in the fifth grade."

"Yes! Miss Bryant's reading contest," Margie exclaimed. "I did not stand a chance against those two."

"Our teacher gave us a long list of novels, ranging from children's books like *The Secret Garden* to difficult novels like *David Copperfield* and *The Grapes of Wrath*," Emelia explained. "Each book was assigned a star value: one star for a short, easy read and ten stars for adult novels."

"I can see that reading chart now: the gold stars lining up after our names. One week, I'd be ahead. The next Em would seize the lead. We left the other kids in our dust." She glanced sympathetically at Margie. "You did do well, Mar. Ten stars, if I remember correctly."

"Twelve. But you and Emelia: accrued over forty stars each."

"But who won?" Kalico asked, genuinely curious.

"We were tied with one week left of the contest. I picked up *Gone with the Wind*—a ten star book. Emelia was bogged down somewhere in the middle of *Wuthering Heights.*"

"Yes, I was lost on the desolate Yorkshire moors." She shook her head. "At ten years old I could not make sense of Cathy and Heathcliff's grand passion. And all the repeated names! I still cannot like that book."

"I felt certain that I was going to win the fifth grade reading trophy. But at the last moment, Ems picked up *The Scarlet Letter.*"

"Yes! Day and night for three days, I spent every moment reading. Used a flashlight in order to read after bedtime. I passed Miss Bryant's reading check questions and earned my final ten stars."

"I did not quite finish *Gone with the Wind* on time. Rhett Butler fascinated me, so I read and reread passages that featured him. As a result our teacher granted me only seven stars." Nancy sighed.

"You always did love the bad boys!" Emelia sniffed.

"Gareth was never a bad boy!" Jane interjected, pushing her glasses up to the bridge of her nose.

"Agreed. I only liked bad boys in fiction. In real life, I chose a truly good man."

"So, Nancy, that's where the idea for our library's Summer Star Readers program originated," Randal interjected.

"I re-commissioned that idea."

Miss Winterjoy rose. "All right everyone: dinner is served." She directed her guests to serve themselves buffet-style. Randal nudged Kalico to signal his appreciation of the feast. Spinach salad with ricotta and cherry tomatoes, pineapple and mustard glazed pork loin, scalloped potatoes, and homemade applesauce graced the sideboard. Soon the guests were seated, chatting and eating and complimenting the cooks.

"Save room for the desserts," Randal said, indicating a small table with an apple pie, lemon tarts, and a berry cobbler. "I've been eating pizza since my wife Joan's been gone."

As he ate, Kalico observed the group trying to spot any tension or unease when he caught Jane's dark brown gaze on him. She raised an eyebrow, then averted her eyes. When the individual conversations quieted a little, Kalico spoke up. "You all haven't finished telling me how the book circle began. I assume that Emelia and Nancy initiated it?"

"And you'd be wrong!" Susan asserted. "Our science major and future surgical nurse, Margie, set up the first meeting. If I remember correctly, she liked a young man in her sophomore Writing About Literature class, but was too shy to speak to him. What was his name again?"

"Travis. Tall, blond, with green eyes that could stop a bus." Margie pretended to swoon.

"Anyway, she asked Em and Susan, who were in her class, and they invited Nancy and Jane."

"And each of us invited a guy we wanted to get to know!" Susan laughed.

"And did this match making scheme work?" Lynn queried.

"No," Margie sighed. "Travis did not turn up, and the other guys drifted away after one or two meetings."

"But we persevered, earned A's in English, and became lifelong friends," Jane finished.

"That's so cool," Lynn stated. "I haven't stayed in touch with anyone from high school or college—yet alone elementary school. I guess I should spend more time on Facebook. Jane, how did you become a part of this motley crew?"

"Susan and I were dorm mates."

"The original odd couple," Susan interjected.

"Beauty and the beast, someone called us." Jane scowled at the memory.

"Oh, surely not!" Nancy exclaimed.

"Yes, they did. But we became instant friends. We both adored Joan Baez and Pete Seeger, molten brownies eaten directly out of the pan, and John Wayne movies!"

"Hold up there, Pilgrim," said Randal trying to imitate the Duke as he got up for seconds.

"Anyway, our book circle formed, and we've met ever since," Nancy concluded.

"Yes, through careers, marriages, births, and deaths. But our circle was not complete until Jane returned last year." Susan reached over and squeezed her friend's hand.

"Jane moved away during our junior year and returned from Arizona when she retired last year," Emelia explained.

"And I'm so glad that I did! To be back with my sisters of choice…there are no words." She dabbed at her eyes with her napkin.

As dinner progressed, Lynn and Kalico casually directed the conversation toward memories. The old friends recalled all night cram sessions, flirtations, anxieties over grades and majors, and road trips.

"Our road trips always ended in disaster!" Nancy declared.

"Oh, they were fun. And we all survived," corrected Margie.

"Barely!" intoned the others.

"Remember the skunks that invaded our campsite in Big Bend?" Emelia's nose curled at the memory.

"Aunt Em, you camped?" Lynn was incredulous.

"Reluctantly. Why people choose to sleep on the hard ground, I will never understand. But Susan's boyfriend *du jour* had decided to camp in the Basin over spring break, and so we followed."

"That was Frank—had a physique like a Greek god."

"And the intellect of a Greek olive!" deadpanned Jane.

"Anyway, someone—Jane—had a jar of peanut butter in her tent—skunk ambrosia."

"I woke up in the middle of the night with two skunks nosing at my sleep bag," Jane shuddered. "Susan screamed, the skunks sprayed us, and the rest was smelly history."

"And we had to ride back with the two of them stinking to high heaven!" Nancy laughed.

"Wasn't that the trip when our van broke down?" Jane redirected the conversation.

"Yes. We had a flat tire in the middle of nowhere." The ladies groaned in chorus.

"You'd think that five intelligent women could change a tire, but we were hopeless." Nancy shook her head.

"We took home economics, not shop, in school," justified Margie.

"What happened?" Lynn and Kalico asked.

"A handsome cowboy in a white pick-up truck stopped and changed it for us." Susan said.

"So all was well that ended well—to misquote the Bard," said Lynn.

"Sort of. Margie's father made us all enroll in an automotive repair class that summer."

"Susan, my Dad didn't make you," Margie corrected. "He made me enroll, and as a sign of solidarity, you joined me."

"Now we can all fix a tire, replace a battery, and change our oil!" Jane added.

Emelia pushed her chair back, declaring that she was going to put the kettle on and asking if anyone would prefer coffee as Lynn gathered the dinner plates. "Dessert now or after our book talk?" she asked.

"Now." Randal moved toward the apple pie.

"Later," the ladies said in chorus.

"Randal, you may have some pie now and more dessert later, if you like," offered Nancy.

"Great."

The group returned to the living room. Copies of the evening's novel appeared and the book talk began, informally led by Nancy. Kalico let the discussion buzz around him as he watched the interactions. Everyone loved and mourned the elderly victim, Jane Neal. Margie and Susan disagreed on the inspector's character. Nancy declared that she'd love to live in Three Pines, while Jane said that such a place would be claustrophobic. She disparaged the author's idealized view of village life. After an hour, the circle ended. The only business left was to set the time and place for the next meeting.

"Jane, it's your turn to select the book for next time," Nancy stated.

"I choose *Atonement* by Ian McEwan. It's a marvelous book, raising the question: Can someone atone for an unforgivable act?"

"*Atonement* it is, then. Jane, our potluck will be at your house, then, on April 19th."

"They're renovating my duplex, so it would be better to hold it at someone else's house. Or we could just meet at a restaurant?"

Discussion ensued until it was decided to meet at Margie's. As the circle adjourned to the dessert table led by Randal, Lynn held Kalico back. "Can you stay behind after the group leaves? Aunt Em would like us to share impressions."

"Of course." Kalico tucked her arm in his. "Let's guide the talk to relationships." He wanted to get a sense of any long-harbored jealousies.

In a few moments, encouraged by Lynn's rapt attention, each lady recalled past loves. Susan recounted meeting her future husband, Jefferson, at the dry cleaners—the most unromantic place imaginable. They'd discussed the benefits of having shirts laundered and pressed. They married the next month.

"Forty-two years together, three children, seven grandchildren: all because I spilled cranberry juice on my silk blouse!"

"Frank died six years ago of pancreatic cancer. It was brutal," whispered Lynn to Ben.

"You never know where romance will blossom," Nancy smiled. "I met Gareth in the new Undergraduate Library. I worked there part time to help cover tuition. I recall that I was shelving books on the Tudors when I heard a deep and resonant voice say, "Here, let me get that for you." I think I fell in love in that instant. That voice. How I miss that voice!" She paused as if listening to a distant sound. "Anyway, Gareth took a particularly weighty volume from me and placed it on the top shelf. I thanked him, not having the heart to tell him that he'd put a 900's volume with the 800's."

"Good heavens, Nancy. I'm surprised that you married him," Randal joked, taking a gigantic bite of berry cobbler. "Erroneous shelving is a serious offense!"

"Too true. Gareth asked me out right there in the English history section. We saw each other every day after until we married at the end of our junior year."

"Of course, we were all bridesmaids, forced to wear Kelly green tulle embroidered with pink roses!" Susan flourished her hands across her bodice. "Except for poor Jane! You came down with a horrible flu."

"I hated to miss the wedding, but I didn't want to spread germs and ruin the honeymoon!" Jane lowered her eyes regretfully.

Margie, next, recalled how her high school sweetheart reentered her life the day after she graduated from nursing school. Martin Davis had called out of the blue to congratulate her. They met for coffee, began dating, and they married two years later. "No grand romance, I guess, but I feel so lucky. I have spent my life with my best friend."

"Jane, were you every married?" asked Lynn, hoping that she was not being too nosey.

"No. Emelia and I are the old maids of the group." Her laugh held a small edge of bitterness or disappointment. "We never found our matches."

"Wasn't there that one boy in college?" Susan bit her lip, trying to remember.

"No. There was no one in college."

"A boy in your astronomy class…?" Susan frowned, but the memory evidently would not take shape.

"No. No one."

"But Em did find her match," Nancy said quietly. All eyes turned to Miss Winterjoy.

"Yes, I did." Her eyes held a faraway look and for a moment Lynn and Kalico could see the lovely young woman she had been.

"Aunt Em, please tell us about him. What happened?"

"It's ancient history."

"Please!"

Emelia gazed at the faces all turned to her expectantly. "His name was Paul Laurence. We met in an Introduction to Acting class. He was destined to be a leading man: tall, dark, and handsome, with the deepest blue eyes that seemed to be always laughing at me. We were cast in *The Glass Menagerie*. I was Laura, and he was my gentleman caller." She paused, a scene playing before her eyes.

"'Blow out your candles, Laura,'" Randal quoted under his breath.

Emelia shook her head. "We fell in love. Paul was killed in a convenience store robbery." She sniffed. "We only knew each other a few weeks."

Lynn rose and hugged her aunt.

"Em, we never knew!" exclaimed Susan, Jane, and Margie.

Miss Winterjoy pushed back her chair signaling that the evening was over. Lynn and Kalico volunteered for kitchen duty, while Jane and Susan filled seal-tight containers with left-overs for each guest. Margie delivered empty dishes to be washed so that they could be returned to their proper owners. Finally, in a flurry of activity, everyone departed.

Susan could be heard telling Jane: "No. Don't give me cobbler to take home. I can't resist sweets. It will be gone before I go to bed!" Nancy called to Moody, then sang, "Good night, Ladies! And Randal." A chorus of good nights followed.

Dishes and glasses neatly stacked in the dishwasher, pans washed and dried, left-overs placed in the refrigerator, Lynn and Kalico sank into the living room couch, followed a moment later by Miss Winterjoy who perched with perfect posture in the arm chair. Trey and Snow settled by her feet, and Perdita curled up in her lap.

"I'm exhausted!" Lynn yawned and stretched. "Who knew listening could be so tiring?"

"I must admit that I, too, am fatigued. But I must congratulate you two." She beamed at her niece and her detective. "You certainly got the girls to talk." She focused her attention on Kalico, whose arm had insinuated itself around Lynn. "What is your assessment, Benjamin? Did a prime suspect emerge?"

Kalico's mind raced, and he pushed his hands through his hair making it stand up at odd angles. He measured his words carefully: "I enjoyed the company and the conversation. Although I need a little time to process what I heard and saw, it seems improbable that any of your old friends would want to harm Nancy."

"What about Margie? She's still simmering over losing that fifth grade reading contest," offered Lynn, trying to lighten her aunt's mood.

"If she were the perpetrator, she'd want to kill me. I won the contest!"

Suddenly the corgis raised their heads, ears alert. Nancy appeared in the entryway, hands on hips.

"What are you three up to? Who wants to kill whom?"

No one responded. Lynn let out a gasp that turned into a nervous giggle. Kalico stared at his shoes. Only Miss Winterjoy looked directly at her friend.

"Come on, Emelia. Give. I could tell that you three were conspiring to take us all down memory lane tonight." With sudden insight, she turned to Kalico. "Ben, were you here as a book lover, a boyfriend, or as a detective?"

Kalico looked helplessly at Miss Winterjoy, who nodded her acquiescence. "As a detective," he admitted. "But I enjoyed the book talk and the dinner. Never had such a good pork loin and that apple pie...." Lynn elbowed him in the ribs. He shut up.

"Mr. Kalico is here tonight at my request. I have been deeply concerned, Nancy, about the accidents that have befallen you, so I hired a detective to see if there were any basis for my worry."

Nancy's mouth gaped open for a second, then she laughed delightedly and joined the trio in the living room. "Em! You are such a dear to worry about me, but really? A murder plot? And who is your chief suspect? Sweet and practical Margie?"

"I do not find your well-being a topic for levity. Anyone of your so-called accidents could have proved fatal."

"How could you imagine that any of our friends—our lifelong friends—could wish me harm?" Nancy shook her head. "And you two! You must have encouraged her."

Lynn protested as Kalico stepped in. "Miss Winterjoy requested that I look for any evidence that your accidents had been engineered, and to investigate anyone who may have had the means to tamper with your car or even to take your EpiPen. I was going to say...."

"Emelia Rose Winterjoy!" Nancy's voice held a dangerous edge. "Did you hire Ben to investigate Connor?"

"Since your accidents began shortly after Connor moved in, I felt that there was—shall we say—a slim possibility...."

"Enough! He is *my grandson*. Your other suspects are our closest friends."

"But Nancy...."

"I said, 'Enough!' Hiring a detective, setting up a dinner so you all could interview them without their knowing it—Em, your actions....I have no words!"

Kalico held his breath as the two woman locked eyes for what seemed like forever. He barely felt Lynn squeezing his hand. Then he saw Miss Winterjoy lower her eyes. She appeared to deflate, her ramrod straight spine contracting in on itself. Lynn started to rise, but stopped, as her aunt reassumed her posture.

"Nancy, I owe you an apology. I should not have gone behind your back. I should have addressed my concern for your safety to you directly."

Silence, broken only by the dogs' panting, descended on the room. Kalico inhaled and prepared to speak, but Lynn nudged him. Nancy rose and paced the room. Emelia's worried eyes followed her.

Finally, she stopped. "I don't know whether to slap you or hug you, Em. You really got carried away this time! Hiring Ben! I hope he charges you a fortune."

As the two old friends prepared to rehash all that had transpired over the past three months, Lynn and Kalico quietly left the room. They heard Nancy declare, "If I am to forgive you, you must promise me to stop this nonsense!"

Chapter Sixteen

The next morning Emelia Winterjoy slept in late—a most unusual occurrence. Had it not been for the intermittent "ding" of a cell phone, she might have slept in past seven. Trey gently licked her elbow as Snow rolled over, ready for a belly rub. Their mistress acknowledged her boys and sat up, still groggy from a deep sleep. Perdita emitted an indignant *meow* in protest at being dislodged from the pillow. "Sorry, Purr-purr." The phone chimed again. She reached for her phone, but no message appeared. Again: "Ding!" As her mind cleared, Emelia realized that the sound was emanating from somewhere in the dining room. A moment's investigation revealed a cell phone tastefully bedazzled in a pink cover. She could read a text message on it: *"Mom, hope it's not too early in Austin for you, but I have great news! Call me. Lizzie."*

The mystery phone belonged to Susan. Lizzie was Susan's youngest daughter, a staff writer for *The New Yorker*. Seven o'clock was definitely too early for Susan, who since she had retired from her position as an editor for *The Austin American-Statesman*, often slept in until ten or even later. *A shameful waste of daylight.* Emelia made a mental note to return the phone later that morning before running some errands.

At a few minutes after 10 a.m., she pulled into the Jankowsky driveway. The tan brick, two-story house was located in the Circle C neighborhood. Susan's metallic blue Audi was parked in front of the white, three-car garage. Emelia marched to the front door and rang the bell. When Susan failed to answer, she rang the bell again and knocked three times for good measure.

Perhaps she's taken up jogging again. I could leave the phone in her mailbox with a note.

She peered through the beveled glass in the door, but could make out only fuzzy shapes. Nothing moved inside. She shivered and turned to leave. *Probably out jogging*, she reassured herself. But worry nagged at her. *I promised Nancy to not let my imagination go wild.* As she began to walk back to her car, she felt someone watching and from the corner of her eye, she caught the rustle of a lace curtain at the front window. *I've become a ridiculous old fool*, Emelia thought as she stepped off the walkway into the front flowerbed, squeezed between two prickly Burford holly shrubs, and squinted through the glass into pair of golden eyes. "Delilah! You gave me a fright!" she said to Susan's fifteen year old black cat. "Where's Susan?" The cat began vocalizing and pacing back and forth on the windowsill. Emelia leaned in closer. *Was that Susan sitting in Frank's over-stuffed club chair?* She tapped on the glass. Delilah jumped down, flicked her tail, and bounded into the living room.

Emelia sprang into action. She dialed 911 and reported a possible medical emergency, clearly and succinctly reporting the address and the circumstances. Next she dug into the inner pocket of her purse pulling out sets of labeled house keys: NM for Nancy; LW for Lynn; SJ—she found her keys to Susan's house. Hands shaking, she unlocked the door. A loud warning *beep-beep-beep* of the alarm system startled her, but she ignored it and ran to Susan.

Susan sat still and upright in Frank's old, comfy blue chair. Her silvery-grey hair spread out against the chair's back, and her reading glasses, off-kilter, balanced precariously on the bridge of her nose. A novel, a Nicholas Sparks' romance—one of her friend's guilty pleasures—lay sprawled on the carpet. A mug of tea rested next to a bowl that held the telltale purple stains of berry cobbler amid a puddle of melted vanilla ice cream. *Susan loves, loved, her desserts, although she rarely allowed sweets in her house.* She wore creamy white silk pajamas, and her feet were bare. Oddly, her cheeks were delicately flushed, a contrast to the porcelain white of her hands and feet. Her eyes, wide and unfathomable, stared out beyond anything Emelia could see.

In minutes the EMTs arrived, rushing in with a stretcher and defibrillator. A stocky young man shouted questions at her. DNR? She could not recall what a DNR was… Dr. Munjabi appeared and gestured and shouted back at the EMTs. He was Susan's neighbor and their mutual primary care physician. It was only when the burglar alarm stopped screaming that Emelia registered that it had gone off at all. Kalico appeared from nowhere at her side, gently leading her away from the commotion in the living room. She glanced back at Susan: Dr. Munjabi knelt beside her; the uniformed men stood still and silent.

Kalico lowered Miss Winterjoy into a chair at the kitchen table. He took a pink cashmere sweater from a peg on the door and placed it around her shoulder, then busied himself by making coffee. As the automatic coffee maker began to drip, the older woman looked at him; her blue eyes dazed and glistening with unshed tears.

"I prefer tea."

"This morning you'll have coffee—black and strong."

Her posture straightened for a moment in protest, then she sat back. "I don't remember calling you, Benjamin. I don't know why I called you, but thank you for coming."

"No problem." He set a mug of coffee in front of her. "Drink. You've had a shock."

She sipped the hot and bitter brew. "I think I called you because you saved Nancy."

Kalico poured a cup of coffee for himself and sat across from her. "I wish that I could help Susan. I'm so sorry for your loss, Miss Winterjoy. Susan was a wonderful woman...."

They sat in silence, aware of muffled voices and the still body in the next room. Shortly, Dr. Munjabi came in his face somber. "A sad business, Emelia. A sad business."

"What can you tell us, Aaryan?"

"Susan died eight to ten hours ago, given the state of her body. I believe that she suffered a sudden and devastating myocardial infarction."

Emelia shook her head in disbelief. *Heart attack? Susan? She exercised, watched her diet, meditated.*

"As her doctor, I pronounced death, so unless the family requests an autopsy, there's no reason to transport her to the hospital."

"The family! The boys and Lizzie—they don't know. I have to call." Emelia fumbled with her phone, suddenly unable to read her contact list. Kalico lifted it from her hands and scrolled down to Jankowsky. There he read: Elizabeth, Frank Jr., Donald.

"Would you like me to call them?" he asked.

"No. It's my duty."

Dr. Munjabi cleared his throat. "If an autopsy is not requested, you may call a funeral home to come and pick up the body. Do you happen to know if Susan made arrangements?"

Miss Winterjoy looked at him blankly. Of course they had discussed arrangements. But that talk had been hypothetical. Susan wished to be buried beside her husband at the Cook-Walden Memorial Park. Emelia and Nancy had signed as witnesses to her will. Frank, Jr. held a power of attorney.

"Doctor, do you think an autopsy is warranted?" Kalico asked.

"No. Susan died of natural causes."

There's nothing natural about a fit woman of only seventy dying alone from a heart attack. Aloud she said, "Susan positively glowed with good health. Goodness, she rarely ever caught a cold. She never spent a day in the hospital—except to deliver her children." Emelia shook her head.

An EMT appeared at the kitchen door, and Dr. Munjabi looked pointedly at Kalico.

"Miss Winterjoy? Emelia?" Kalico quietly directed her attention to the business at hand. "You need to call Frank Jr. to break the news about his mother and see if he wants an autopsy performed."

"Of course."

Somehow Susan's children were informed; travel arrangement, made. An autopsy denied, Cook-Walden transported the body to the funeral home. Emelia called friends, listening repeatedly to shocked voices and sobs and questions. Finally, the house was quiet and still. Emelia rinsed the coffee cups and placed them in Susan's dishwasher with the dessert bowl. She folded the pink sweater, still redolent with the scent of lavender, and placed it on the table. She paused in the living room, staring at Frank's eyesore of a chair that clashed horribly with the peach, cream, and brown tones of Susan's décor. But she had refused to reupholster it or replace it, saying that she could still feel Frank's presence when she sat there.

Kalico coughed behind her. "Let's lock up."

"Yes." But she did not move. *What was she forgetting?* "Delilah! We can't leave Delilah here. Susan's cat." Emelia rushed through the house calling for the cat. A sob escaped her, and she pressed a fist to her lips.

"Is this who you're looking for?" Kalico emerged from the kitchen, a compact black cat cradled in his arms. He transferred her to Emelia, who buried her face in the warm fur. Then they left the silent and empty house.

Chapter Seventeen

Kalico sprinted down the basketball court, stopped half way, and set up for a three pointer as Vic waved a hand in his face: he shot, the ball arched gracefully but missed the backboard altogether. Again. Vic retrieved the ball, dribbled in, swiveled right, and made an easy jump shot over his much taller friend. "Man," he said, breathing hard. "You're making this too easy."

"Sorry." Kalico couldn't focus. Ten days had passed since the death of Susan Jankowsky. He knelt to tie his shoelace.

He had stayed with Miss Winterjoy as she called her friends to tell them about Susan's passing. Gradually, a narrative formed. He listened as she repeated what most likely had occurred: Susan, a night owl with insomnia, had gone to bed, couldn't sleep, and gotten up sometime after midnight. She made herself a cup of tea and warmed a bowl of berry cobbler, topping it with a scoop of vanilla ice cream. Then she'd settled in Frank's chair with a novel and dessert. She'd either dozed off and died in her sleep or suffered a sudden fatal heart attack. She had looked peaceful. No, she had not suffered.

"What's up, Ben? A philandering poodle? A murderous mutt? An amorous Afghan hound?"

"I only wish." He laughed half-heartedly.

Vic pulled his friend to his feet and propelled him forward. "C'mon. Breakfast tacos are the universal cure for what ails you. On me."

Twenty minutes later, seated at a picnic table beside a large silver food truck, the men dug into brisket tacos with white cheese and avocado. Red sauce dripped down Vic's chin; he swiped at it with a napkin as he took another giant bite. "Heaven." Swallowing, he turned his dark gaze onto Kalico. "Okay, Dick Tracy. Give. What's up with you? Tell Uncle Victor everything."

Kalico found himself enumerating his financial difficulties, the problems attracting clients, and the disappointing response from the law offices he'd approached. He told Vic about the job offer to become an in-house investigator as well as the very real possibility that he needed to move in with his parents.

"What happened with that cold case you were so excited about? Did you solve it?"

"Ended up with a lot of false leads." He would not betray Miss Winterjoy's trust or trivialize her concerns. He did not want to talk about Nancy's near-fatal encounter with a bee or Susan's passing. He yanked at his hair. "And to top it all, I'm a joke: the Calico Cat Detective!"

As if on cue, a stray golden retriever, its coat caked with dirt and burrs, limped up to Kalico, sat down and placed a giant paw on his knee. Groaning, Kalico gazed down into gentle brown eyes. "Why me? Huh? Go away! Get! Go find your owner." He gestured at the empty lot. "Go over to Vic: he's got beef." The dog cocked its head and tentatively wagged its tail, but did not move from Kalico's side.

Vic fought back a grin, then turned serious. "Ben, you've always been the man with a plan. You set goals and march straight for them. It seems to me you need to recommit to a goal. Stick with the agency. Take the investigator job. Enter the Austin Police Academy. Just commit and go for it."

Kalico nodded. Vic was right. He needed to choose a direction and commit.

"And, for Pete's sake, ask the girl out!"

"How'd you know…?"

"I have my sources."

Kalico reached across the table and took a slice of brisket from Vic's plate and gave it to the Golden, who licked his fingers appreciatively. He disentangled his long legs from under the table. "I've got to take care of my furry friend here. And Vic, thanks. See you next Saturday?"

"Not if I see you first."

Fortunately, the dog was chipped, its owners were home, and a joyful reunion was realized in just over three hours. *Three unpaid hours*, Kalico noted ruefully, as he entered his office.

He leaned back in his chair, tracing the diagonal crack in the ceiling with his eyes. Patterns in the popcorn texture formed and reformed as he swiveled left and right, left and right. A question mark. A maze. Edvard Munch's, *The Scream*. Women dancing in a circle. If he could read them, perhaps they'd tell him what he should do. Close his agency? Join the police academy? Become an in-house investigator? His gaze shifted to the white board. Miss Winterjoy and Nancy, the ladies of the book circle, and Lynn gazed back at him. He stood up and began to take down the pictures and the bits of string that connected them.

He held Susan Jankowsky's picture. She was laughing into the camera as she struck a model's pose—hand on hip, head tilted, chin up, eyes bright. A question tugged and teased at the outer corner of his mind, then evaporated.

The photograph had been set up on an easel in front of her closed casket beside pictures of Susan as a bride, Susan as new mother, Susan as a writer and editor, glasses on the tip of her nose. Fragments from her funeral flooded his memory. Kalico had arrived late. The chapel was full, so he stood at the back. Clay pots of daffodils and crocuses, iris and sweet alyssum lined the stage behind the podium. Blushing peonies were mounded on the casket. Two middle-aged men and a woman sat in the front pew—the Jankowsky children. The book circle ladies and Lynn sat directly behind them, dressed in springtime colors—rose, lilac, butter-yellow, pale green, and peach. A shock of color in a sea of gray and black. Kalico learned later that Susan herself had chosen the music, Bible passages, and flowers, directing that her friends wear colors to celebrate her life, not mourn her death. All in attendance were to be given a flower to plant in her memory.

Susan had also orchestrated the speakers. Lynn, somber and lovely in pale peach, read a poem, something about a 'woman, lovely in her bone.' Frank Jankowsky used to recite it to his wife. When she finished, the book circle ladies rose and stood in front of the podium.

Miss Winterjoy cleared her throat and began: "Our dear friend was concerned that we would be long-winded, so she composed a few lines about how she wants us to remember her." She paused, checked to make sure her friends were ready, then stepped forward: "Remember me as one who laughed more than I cried." Nancy moved up: "Remember me as one who loved and strove to keep hate out of her heart." Margie, her voice unsteady, next read: "Remember me as a woman blessed with family and dear, dear friends." Jane, voice a watery whisper, concluded: "Remember me as one who found beauty in everyone and everything."

Miss Winterjoy turned to lead the ladies back to their pew, but Jane froze. Ignoring Margie's gentle hand on her arm, she exclaimed, "And Susan did. She did find beauty in everyone—even in me. She was my first friend in Texas and my best friend. She should never have died. Never!" She turned and rushed over to the coffin, babbling and crying. Margie and Nancy pulled her away, leading her back to her seat.

The ceremony concluded with Susan's eleven-year-old grandson singing *Somewhere Over the Rainbow*.

Kalico placed Susan's picture in a manila folder labeled "Winterjoy Case." He finished clearing the white board. He placed Lynn's photograph at the corner of his desk organizer. He checked that copies of his reports were labeled correctly and placed in the right desktop folder. Miss Winterjoy had sent him a check and acknowledged his final report—without so much as an inserted comma or a complaint about his use of the passive voice. Surely, that was a sign of her grief, not of his improved prose.

Three hours later, having reviewed for the hundredth time invoices from the last six months against the accounts payable, he was no closer to a decision. He picked up a red and a blue marker, drew columns on the board, and listed pros and cons, hoping to make a logical decision about his professional future. Two paths offered financial predictability. He added that under Police Academy and Investigator. Returning to his desk he gazed at Lynn's picture. He picked up his phone, then set it down again.

***

Kalico pushed his chair back from the kitchen's light teal Formica table. Little had changed in this room since he'd been a boy. The white cabinets had received a new coat of paint and the countertops were now comprised of a shiny granite, but his mother's white ceramic ducks still waddled across the windowsill, the 1960's big-faced wall clock still measured the minutes, and snapshots, children's drawings, old report cards, a faded blue ribbon, and a Big Ben magnet still defaced the refrigerator. The quiet, however, was new. He found himself missing the rapid-fire chatter of his three sisters, the laughter, the political debates, and the nightly reports on what had occurred during the day.

"Another piece of chicken, dear?" his mother asked.

"No, thanks. I'm stuffed. Great barbeque, Dad."

"Just felt like firing up the grill." His father pushed his glasses up on the bridge of his nose. He was a handsome man in his mid-sixties with red-hair that had receded and faded a bit and deep laugh lines around his eyes.

"Where's Katie tonight? I thought she relished Saturday night dinners to get away from dorm food."

Katherine Kalico smiled broadly. "You'll never guess!"

"A date? Okay, what's his name? I can do a criminal background check."

"Ease off, Big Brother. No, she does not have a date. She's having dinner this evening with…" she paused for effect, "Melissa!"

"M's? That's terrific." He pushed his hand through his hair, staring silently at the kitchen clock.

"C'mon, Ben. Give." His dad pushed his plate away and turned his full attention onto his son.

Kalico cleared his throat and filled his folks in on the status of his business. "Right now, I feel like its flat lined. Even the pet retrievals have dried up—except for weekly calls from Mrs. Buonanotte, and she pays in pasta." He smiled ruefully. "Great pasta," he added.

His parents exchanged a look but remained silent.

Kalico continued, laying out the financials and the other job possibilities. He took a deep breath. "I want to give my agency another year to begin breaking even or, better yet, to make a profit. I have enough in my operations budget to cover expenses for at least that amount of time, but not enough to pay myself a living wage." He looked down at his hands.

"Son, your mother and I are in a position to help you financially. We could give you a business loan...."

"No. No, thanks. I don't want you guys to take anything out of your retirement fund. What I wanted to ask is this: Would it be okay if I moved back home for a time?"

His parents enthusiastically agreed, his mother commenting on how difficult it was to cook for only two.

"I want to pay rent..."

"Let's defer that for a few months." His dad rose and beckoned Kalico to follow him down the stairway that led to the one time playroom, den, sewing room, exercise room, and—the last time he'd seen it—junk room. His mother placed a hand on his shoulder.

"Would this space do for a bachelor's pad?"

The space had been transformed. A deep blue love seat was centered in the room facing a small television. A lighter blue area rug covered the wood floor. A double bed with a nightstand stood against the far wall. Kalico's high school desk and chair were placed in from of a small window. A newly installed door opened onto a side lawn.

"What do you think, Benjy? See, you'll have your own entrance. There's no sink or bathroom, so you have to use the one at the top of the stairs. It would be almost like having your own place. And, of course, the refrigerator is open, and you can have meals with us whenever you're home—if you choose. It's so hard to cook for just the two of us. And I promise to give you your privacy...."

Kalico turned and hugged his mother, then shook his father's hand, pulling him into a bear hug. "When did you do all of this? How did you know…?"

"Just contingencies, Son."

It was agreed that Kalico would move in at the end of the month.

"Let's have dessert. Sara Lee and I have made a marvelous turtle cheesecake!" Katherine Kalico led the way back upstairs. She served generous slices to her husband and son, cutting out a sliver of the rich cake for herself. "I'm trying to stop eating sweets," she explained.

They discussed ways of marketing the detective agency, the possibility of bringing on a business partner, possible contacts….

Later as Kalico prepared to leave, Katherine suggested, "Why don't you try out your new pad? I'm making waffles in the morning."

"I will, but only if you stop calling it my 'pad.'" He grinned. "I prefer 'den' or even 'lair.'"

"So why don't you stay in your lair tonight?" Then, becoming more serious, she said, "Why not invite Lynn over for Friday's movie night? Your sisters are coming home…." She watched her son's face close. "Now, Benjy—Ben—don't look like that! I know what you're thinking, but Lynn did not strike me as a young woman who expects to be wined and dined every night."

"I'm in no position to date or to get involved with someone."

"Your dad and I didn't have two nickels to rub together when we started dating. We enjoyed long walks, and watching television in my parents' den, and just being together."

"Girls today are different, Mom."

"Shouldn't you let Lynn make that decision? She did not strike me as the kind of young woman who cares about material things. She told me that finding Stanley had been the most fun she'd had in a long time."

Kalico just shook his head, kissed her on the cheek, and went downstairs to his new place. Perhaps, he would call Lynn. After all, he still owed her a dinner. He slept well that night, pleased that he had settled again on a definitive direction. He would make a go of it as a private investigator—even if it meant taking on infidelity cases. As he fell asleep, Susan's voice echoed at the edge of his consciousness. Something that she had said was important. But he lost it as he sank into a deep and untroubled sleep.

Chapter Eighteen

Kalico awoke to the smell of bacon and coffee. He stretched, enjoying the soft blue down comforter his mother had placed on the new bed.

"Ben? Are you awake?" Katie peeked at him from over the stair railing, backlit by the open door.

"No."

Taking the reply as an invitation, she ran down the stairs and jumped on the bed. "Wake up! I want to discuss Ghost and M's and a plan."

Kalico groaned, but sat up. "Can't we have breakfast first? Or at least coffee?"

"Your stomach can wait. We have a plan to find Ghost." She rustled his covers. "Think of the big reward."

"Okay. I'm awake. What's your plan? A séance?" He frowned. "And since when have you become interested in my cases?"

"Since working to find Ghost is a safe way to connect with M's. She's almost her old self when we talk about the dog."

"Fair enough. What have you come up with?"

Katie, relieved that her brother was taking her seriously, hugged a pillow and began to speak rapidly. Last night the girls had gone over all of the reports and notes and sightings of the beautiful husky—with several breaks for hot fudge sundaes, of course. "We decided that the facts of this case are not getting us anywhere. We know that Ghost got spooked during a storm, somehow broke free from his kennel, and escaped through a small hole in the fence. We think that the important question is not 'Where is Ghost?' but 'Why?' Why does a well-trained and pampered dog keep running?"

"Perhaps he's heard the call of the wild," offered Kalico mid-yawn.

"How very Jack London of you."

"How English-nerdy of you to get the reference."

Katie stuck out her tongue at him. "M's has mapped the Ghost sightings, and," she paused for effect, "we found a pattern."

"No one has reported seeing him in thirteen days," Kalico reminded her.

"Look." Katie pulled up a map on her phone. She traced small red x's with her finger. "Ghost moved steadily east from Dripping Springs, until he got to Austin. Here he zigs and zags, but then heads south from Travis Country. We think he's traveling with purpose."

"Maybe. But where? It's almost impossible to find a dog after this much time. And his trail goes cold at Dick Nichols."

"Almost is the operative term, Ben. As I've heard you say, oh-brother-of-mine: when stumped, go back to the beginning. We need to interview Mr. Skifford and Ghost's trainers. Perhaps, if we can get to know Ghost, if we can probe his personality, we can figure out where he's heading."

"We?" Kalico nodded thoughtfully. "My initial interview with Skifford was cursory. I'll have M's set up an appointment and go out to the ranch next week."

"We want to come too. Finding Ghost is important to M's and reconnecting with her is important to me."

"As long as you don't miss classes. I'll text you the day and time. Now, let's go up to breakfast."

***

By 9 a.m. on Sunday morning, Emelia Winterjoy had accomplished more than most people achieved in a day. She'd eaten breakfast, walked the dogs, dusted and vacuumed the living room, reorganized the hall closet, watered the front flowerbeds, and pulled weeds in the back ones. Now she sat in a wrought iron chair on her deck, drinking her third cup of coffee and watching the yellow finches at her bird feeder. Grief over Susan's passing reawakened sadness over her mother's death, over the loss of friends, over the fatal shooting of a young man with laughing blue eyes.

The day was crisp and bright, but, if one could believe the meteorologists, a not so rare front would arrive later in the day bringing a chance of thunderstorms. She sighed.

"Snap out it!" she admonished herself. She knew better than to indulge grief. It was a heavy emotion that would stay with her for a long, long time. One just had to move through it until the burden gradually lightened. But her normal strategy of keeping busy and productive was not working. She felt "at sixes and sevens" as her mother would have said.

Nancy's house next door was quiet and still. A subdued and inordinately accommodating Connor had escorted his grandmother to church. Emelia had observed the young man mowing the lawn and even cleaning the gutters. She had been bowled over when he offered to mow her yard. Still, a nagging suspicion made her wonder if he were diverting suspicion by his good behavior. She shook the thought away. She'd have to trust Nancy's love for him or lose her friendship.

Catching commotion in her peripheral vision, she turned to see Trey and Snow busily digging in the mulch. "Gentlemen, leave it!" she commanded. Trey obediently raised a nose encrusted with dirt and trotted to her, tail wagging. Snow ignored the command.

"Snow. *I said leave it!*" The little corgi begrudgingly left the flowerbed and walked to her, head down. She brushed dirt off their muzzles, tisk-tisking and not unkindly asking her boys what they were thinking. Encouraged, Snow grabbed a blue tennis ball and dropped it at her feet. She tossed the ball until the dogs were panting and her arm was tired.

Wandering back inside, she grabbed *Atonement*, read a few pages, lost the story's thread, and closed it. She turned on the television, although she did not approve of watching shows during the day. She settled on a program about herb gardening. Perdita appeared and curled up on her lap. A few moments later she stood up, dumping the annoyed cat on the floor, and crossed over to her dining room table, where two leather-bound books rested beside Jane's clean glass baking dish. Lizzie Jankowsky had dropped off the books before she left for the airport with her mother's cat, Delilah, safely ensconced in her kitty carrier. The books were mementoes from Susan to be given to Margie and Jane. She'd selected a rare first edition of F. Scot Fitzgerald's *The Great Gatsby* for Margie and a lovely three-volume edition of Jane Austen's *Persuasion* for Jane. Nancy had received a beautifully illustrated copy of Lewis Carroll's *Alice in Wonderland*. She bequeathed a fine, early edition of Charles Dickens' *Great Expectations* bound in blue calf with a marbled front board to Emelia.

Miss Winterjoy decided to get out of the house. She'd deliver the books to Margie and Jane, then go to Central Market for fresh fruit and salmon for supper. Fifteen minutes later, she was behind the wheel, enjoying the gentle notes of Debussy's *Clair de Lune*. When she pulled into the long circular driveway in front of the Davis' ranch-style home in Shady Hollow, Margie, in worn blue jeans and a powder blue sweatshirt, was digging a new flowerbed around her mailbox. She exclaimed in delight at Susan's gift, removing her gloves and touching the embossed lettering, then her eyes filled with tears, and the two friends hugged for a long moment.

Fifteen minutes later, having refused Margie's invitation to stay for coffee, Miss Winterjoy studied Jane's address, printed in clear block letters on the tiny notepad she kept in her purse. How odd that she had never been to Jane's house. Perhaps she should call first, but as usual the phone Lynn had given her for Christmas was sitting by her bedside table. She directed her car north toward Riverside Drive. Jane would be pleased by Susan's gift. Perhaps it would bring her some comfort. She had not seen her since that unseemly outburst at the funeral. She shook her head at the memory.

Miss Winterjoy turned right onto Eastside Road and began scanning mailboxes for 6213A. Small side-by-side duplexes in various states of disrepair were backed by towering apartment building that had grown up on the hill. Her body jerked as her left front tire hit a deep pothole. She slowed and maneuvered her car carefully down the deeply rutted road, pausing in consternation as a potbellied pig casually crossed in front of her. Finally, she pulled up beside Jane's small brown and white house, noting the bedraggled pansies around the mailbox, the unmown St. Augustine lawn, more weeds than grass, and the tightly drawn blinds.

She picked up the baking dish and book, locked her car, and walked up to Jane's front door. The beige paint was flaking. She knocked. Rustling emanated from behind the door, followed by the sound of a deadbolt being turned.

"Emelia! What a surprise." Jane's smile did not quite reach her eyes, which were red and puffy. She was still in pajamas covered by a dirty blue nubby robe. Her thin brown hair, unwashed, hung in limp strands around her face.

"Good morning, Jane. I hope I didn't wake you. I was in the neighborhood and wanted to drop off your casserole dish and a gift from Susan." She held out the items, prepared to turn and leave.

"Not at all. I've been awake for hours and hours." Jane grabbed Emelia's arm with surprising strength and pulled her into the house. "Come in and visit for a while. I'll just put on some clothes and make us coffee."

It took Emelia's eyes several minutes to adjust to the deep gloom of the living room, but gradually she could make out a small gray loveseat decorated with floral pillows and wads of Kleenex. A bookshelf filled with knickknacks, pictures, and paperbacks leaned against one wall and a television on a wooden cart fronted the loveseat.

She placed *Persuasion* on Jane's dinette and set her casserole on a kitchen countertop cluttered with dirty dishes, a purple stained wine glass, magazines, and mail. Her fingers itched to clean and straighten, but she resisted, not wanting to offend her hostess. She compensated by returning to the living room, straightening the pillows and throwing the used tissues into the wastebasket.

"I'll be right with you," Jane called from the bedroom.

Miss Winterjoy turned her attention to the bookshelves. She longed to dust. Three photographs held a prominent place. The first picture in a lovely sterling silver frame showed a group of four UT students posing proudly behind a mound of trash bags. A sign read: *Plastic is the Scourge of the Oceans*. Two young men and two young women smiled into the camera. One girl, whom Emelia recognized as a young Jane, gazed up at the boy in a green plaid shirt beside her. His face was partially turned away from the camera, but something about him seemed familiar. The other pictures showed Jane and Susan standing in front of an iconic, tree-like cactus; the last showed the friends posing with the Golden Gate Bridge in the background.

On two prominent shelves she observed books her group had read over the years: *Gaudy Night* by Dorothy Sayers, *White Teeth* by Zadie Smith, *The Guernsey Literary and Potato Peel Pie Society*.... Each book, a dear friend. Had Jane been keeping up with the group all these year? Probably Susan had stayed in contact; had made time to discuss the books. Emelia swallowed an unaccustomed feeling of guilt. She should have reached out more to Jane. She should be more charitable and certainly, less judgmental.

Thus when Jane reentered the room, Emelia greeted her with unusual warmth. She'd never felt close to her; in fact, she reflected that this visit may be the only time that they had ever been alone together.

"Excuse the mess. I've been..." Jane swallowed hard. 'I've been distracted."

"Not at all, dear. Lizzie dropped off this gift for you from Susan, and I felt that it could be some comfort."

Jane gently lifted the three lovely volumes in turn. "*Persuasion*. It's my favorite book. Suse knew. She understood." She moved into the kitchen and began to fill the coffee maker.

"Really, Jane. I can't stay." Emelia felt an unreasonable desire to escape. She turned toward the front door.

"Suse knew. I was persuaded once. I stepped back. I lost him."

"Really, Jane...."

"Stay." Jane appeared suddenly in front of Emelia. Her dark brown eyes magnified behind her round glasses were commanding.

"May I help?"

"No. Take a seat on the back porch, and I'll serve us." The anger Emelia thought she had seen in her friend's eyes had vanished. Her voice was high-pitched and almost cheery.

Miss Winterjoy breathed deeply as she observed Jane's backyard. The wind had shifted to the north, lending crispness to the air. It was pleasant after the sense of suffocation she had felt in that cramped and messy house. *So much for being charitable*, she chided herself. The tiny backyard was largely unlandscaped, except for one terra cotta pot that held a large upright shrub with glossy green leaves. A few green berries darkening to an inky blue gleamed within the foliage. She leaned forward to look more closely at the fruit.

"Don't touch. The fruit is poison." Jane emerged from the house carrying a tray with coffee mugs, cream, sugar, and what looked like a lemon pound cake. A kitchen knife glinted in her right hand. "Cake?"

Slightly flustered, Emelia sat down at the small picnic table. "Yes, please."

Jane cut a generous slice. "I brought that shrub with me from my garden in Arizona. It's called Belladonna—Italian for beautiful lady. And she is." She looked admiringly at the plant. "But she's also deadly."

"Oh my." Emelia sipped the strong coffee and took a small bite of the pound cake. Her mind whirred as she sought something to say to Jane. The uncomfortable silence lengthened. She shivered and pulled in her cardigan. "It's getting chilly. We're expecting a cold front this afternoon. Should drop the temperature thirty or forty degrees."

Jane did not comment.

"I do hope we get a soaking rain—so good for the garden."

Jane sat still, her gaze on something beyond or behind Emelia. "And how is Nancy?" Her tone was oddly flat.

"Sad, of course. But she's back at work...keeping busy."

"Good for her." Jane seemed to watch something just over Emelia's shoulder. Her thin lips formed a slight smile.

"Lizzie asked me to say good-bye and to thank you for being such a special friend to her mother."

Her eyes snapped to Emelia's face and red blotches appeared on Jane's neck. "You know, I expect the phone to ring any minute. Susan and I spoke every Sunday. Sometimes we just touched base; other times we chatted for hours about books, about her kids, about my real estate business. I just keep expecting the phone to ring." Her voice broke and her hands formed into fists.

Impulsively, Emelia reached across the table to pat her shoulder. Jane flinched as though burned, rose quickly, and took the coffee cups. "More coffee?"

"No. No, thank you. I really need to go to the grocery store and get home to the dogs." She rose and moved purposefully toward the door, willing herself not to run.

"Thank you for bringing the book and my dish. So thoughtful."

"You're welcome. We must help one another get through this dreadful time. Let's have lunch soon."

Relief flooded Miss Winterjoy as she pointed her car toward home. She opened the windows and let the cold air wash away the mold and clutter and grief and something else—something disturbing—that seemed to cling to her clothes. The energy in that house had been all wrong. Discomfort had deepened into fear. *Afraid of stolid, rounded little Jane? Ridiculous.* Emelia glanced at her reflection in the rear view mirror. Worry lines were etched deeply between her brows. *It's just her grief. I must stop judging her and befriend her as Susan would want me to do.* She did her best to shake off her trepidation, skipped the grocery store, returned home to her dogs and her cat and her lovely, safe, well-kept home.

Later that night as she drifted into an uneasy sleep, her last thought was: *I must call Benjamin Kalico.*

Chapter Nineteen

Kalico picked up his phone, then set it down. He filled a box with loose papers, old mail, and books, sealed it, and placed it with the stack of boxes by the front door. He picked up his phone again, looked up Lynn's number, then turned the phone off—again. She probably didn't remember his promise to take her out to dinner. He was not in a position to date. Still…

"Hello, Lynn? It's Ben. Benjamin Kalico."

"Ben, how nice to hear from you. What have you been up to?"

"I've been packing." Better to tell her his situation immediately.

"You're moving?"

"Yes. I'm moving back in with my parents." He waited for her response.

"I bet your mom is pleased—to say nothing of Stanley! How is that beautiful boy?"

Encouraged by Lynn's tone, Kalico relaxed. He told her about Lois installing a "cat-cam" so that she could check on Stanley from work; he enjoyed her delighted laugh. "Say, I was wondering if you would like to go out to dinner this evening?"

"On a school night?"

"Oh, sorry. Sorry! I didn't think about…."

"Ben, I'm kidding. Teachers never quite grow up. We're always doing homework, trying not to stay up too late on school nights, and waiting for Christmas break, spring break, and summer holidays!" She laughed again. "I'd love to have dinner with you with one proviso: can we have an early one? Say, around 5?"

Kalico readily agreed. He found himself grinning after he switched off his phone. He'd take boxes to his folks' house, shower and change clothes there, and then pick up Lynn.

An hour later, he was adjusting his tie when Katie bounded into the room, hopped onto his bed, and sat cross-legged, appraising him with a critical eye.

"Hey, Kat! Ever hear of knocking?"

"Had to come in and see you in what Mom is now calling 'the bachelor pad.'" She surveyed the room. "Not bad. But I can't see you successfully seducing a bevy of beauties with that gallery gazing down at you!" She pointed at a bulletin board bursting with photographs of Kalico and his sisters at all ages.

"'Bevy of beauties?' What have you been reading? And don't worry about my seduction techniques." Kalico smoothed his hair.

"Does my big brother have game?" Katie looked at him with narrowed eyes. "Eighty-six the tie. And why not wear your forest green shirt? It makes your eyes pop."

"Who appointed you my fashion consultant?" He grumbled, but he removed the tie and found the shirt.

"So where are you taking her?"

"None of your business, kid."

"C'mon, Ben. Give. Mom is over the moon that you're dating Lynn. I can't wait to meet her."

"We're not dating. We're just going to dinner because she helped me find Stanley. I thought we'd go to Jack Allen's."

Katie nodded her approval. "And, for heaven's sake, talk about something other than work. Don't mention finances. And what ever you do, do not tell her that you've moved back in with Mom and Dad." She formed an "L" with her thumb and index finger and waved it in front of his face.

"Already did."

"And she still agreed to go out with you?" Katie shook her head in wonder.

"So what brings you here? Shouldn't you be at the dorm studying or something?"

"Dorm food sucks. I thought I'd grab leftovers from our fridge, then raid my old closet for something other than jeans or shorts. Any word from Mr. Skifford?"

"No. He's still in LA working on a movie."

"Don't forget that M's and I are going to interview him with you."

"I won't."

Katie bounded up the stairs, then skipped back down and engulfed her brother in a bear hug. "Remember, Benj: you're a catch!"

***

Nearly four hours later, Kalico peeled off his mud-streaked and torn forest green shirt and threw it in the trash. He examined the ripped knees of his dress slacks, then tossed them away too before stepping into the shower. How could it all have gone so very wrong? He let water pound on his head and shoulders. He relished how the spray stung his scraped knuckles and cut knees.

Scenes from his date played and replayed: Lynn, lovely in a powder blue skirt and blouse accented by black tights and high-heels. Lynn, a cobweb in her hair, her cheek bleeding, her blouse streaked with mud and her tights shredded. Lynn laughing at one of his stories, and taking his arm as they walked into Jack Allen's. Lynn shivering and silent as he drove her home.

He should never have answered the phone. When he saw Mrs. Buonanotte's name appear as the caller, he should have let it go to voice mail. But, no: he answered. And, of course, Zoe was missing. And, of course, Mrs. B. was frantic. And, of course, he had to find the little Boston. Lynn had nodded her acquiescence and said that she'd enjoy 'a ride along.' He reassured her that Zoe never ran far and that they'd be back at the restaurant in forty-five minutes or less.

But the Boston terrier was not within her normal four-block radius from home. He drove slowly, windows down and heat on full to abate a cold north wind. They scanned the sidewalk for a white-tipped tail, calling Zoe's name every few seconds. Thunder rumbled in the distance. He pulled up beside a neighborhood park that led down to a small creek. Although Zoe had never ventured out so far, Kalico decided to scan the area quickly on foot. Lynn, pointing ruefully at her heels, stayed behind in the warm car. If only she had remained there....

Kalico turned in the shower and let the water pound on his face. He'd felt rising panic as the temperature continued to drop and the skies threatened rain. He dreaded the idea of returning to Mrs. Buonanotte without Zoe. He jogged through the small park, whistling and calling for her. Then as he stood quietly on the edge of a small rise overlooking the creek, he heard a muffled bark from below. Skidding and sliding on rocks and mud, he searched the hillside and creek bank, pausing and calling, pausing and calling. The light was fading rapidly as the sun began to set and thunderclouds continued to build.

Then, he spotted the gaping mouth of a drainage pipe about four feet above the water on the other side of the creek. He crossed the shallow stream and pushed his way up to it, crouching to gaze into the concrete opening. The flashlight on his iPhone caught the shining eyes of an animal. Staccato, high-pitched barks echoed off the walls of the pipe. It was Zoe. He called her and heard scrambling but the terrier did not appear.

Getting down on his stomach, he maneuvered his head for a better look: Zoe was caught on some kind of wire lodged inside the tunnel. Kalico cursed. He'd have to get her.

He quickly called Lynn and filled her in on the good and the bad news, directing her to call 311. Then he set up his phone so the light shone into the pipe, and began to inch his way forward. His left shoulder grazed the concrete and his shirt ripped. Rocks and broken glass wedged themselves into his knees. He sucked in his breath, hunching his shoulders forward; he pushed with his feet. Zoe's bark changed to kind of howling whine. But Kalico could not budge; he was just too big. He tensed, afraid that he was stuck. Then he willed himself to relax, let out a breath, and inched his right shoulder back. His knuckles grazed the wall, but finally he emerged from the tunnel and sat back on his heels.

A cold drop of rain hit his forehead and lightning illuminated the creek and its narrow banks. In the flash Lynn materialized beside him. She calmly handed him her heels and the industrial flashlight he kept in his car.

Gleaning her intention, he protested: "Lynn, it's too dangerous. We need to wait for animal rescue." He grasped her arm.

"They won't get here for at least an hour." She narrowed her eyes and lifted her chin, looking remarkably like her aunt. "And, Ben, it's going to rain!" She took three steps to the pipe, dropped to her knees, then onto her stomach, and disappeared into the tunnel. Cursing, Kalico knelt by the opening and directed the flashlight into the darkness. He could just make out Lynn's body as she inched forward. Raindrops multiplied and thunder boomed.

Kalico stepped out of his shower and threw on his robe. The face that stared back at him from his mirror seemed older. The ten minutes or so that Lynn had been in that drainage pipe had seemed like a lifetime. She'd emerged, disheveled and bloody, clutching Zoe to her chest. She was crying. Kalico guided her down the hill, across the now rising creek, and back to the car where she sat silently and cradled the little dog.

Kalico slumped into his couch and leaned his head back against the pillow. At least Zoe, the little monster, was safe. She had not even had the decency to be ashamed of herself, but had trotted up to her owner with her head high and tail wagging. But he didn't expect to see Lynn again. He glanced at his phone, surprised that the time read just 9:20. Perhaps he should call to see if she were okay. On cue, the phone buzzed.

"Hey, you owe me dinner!" Lynn's voice was light and teasing.

"Hi! How are you? I am so sorry...."

"I'm starving. Kerby Lane in fifteen minutes." The phone went silent.

In eleven minutes Kalico, dressed in jeans, t-shirt, and tennis shoes, walked into the restaurant where Lynn, likewise in jeans and a tee, waved to him from a booth. Her hair, still damp, curled softly around her face. The only sign of their adventure was a cut on her left cheek.

"I've ordered banana nut pancakes with scrambled eggs and bacon for us. I hope decaf is okay?" She grinned at him.

"Yes. Great." Kalico slid onto the bench across from her. "I love breakfast for dinner."

"Me too."

He studied the top of the table for a moment. "I'm sorry about this evening. I should never have taken that call."

Lynn reached across the table and took his hand, giving it a warm squeeze. "Nonsense. Zoe would've drowned! Ben, I can't tell you how amazing it feels to save a life." She laughed delightedly. "I read about and teach about adventures, but rarely do I get to live one. I can't thank you enough, and if you apologize one more time for giving me one of the best times ever—I will punch you!"

Kalico relaxed. Between mouthfuls of softly scrambled eggs, they relived the evening's events, sharing details from their own perspectives. Lynn recalled the moment of panic when she reached Zoe and could not free her collar from a wire grill—until it dawned on her that she could simply unfasten it. Ben told her about his terror as the rain began to fall, and he imagined a flash flood.

"If we'd been ten minutes later...." He shook his head.

As they dug into rich, buttery pancakes, they discussed work and politics and the crazy Texas weather. They shared family stories. Lynn told him about her mother's death and how Aunt Emelia, her father's no-nonsense older sister, had marshaled them through their grief. "She let me cry or hit my pillow, then she'd say, 'Busy hands are happy hands,' and we'd plant a bulb garden or make chocolate chip pecan cookies or create a memory scrap book or read *Little Woman* aloud." Lynn smiled at the memory. "And you know, my hands were happy, so I learned that in time more of me would be happy too."

Kalico recalled how his two older sisters, Karen and Karla, begged his parents to allow them to go on a high school sponsored camping trip to Big Bend. After weeks of whining and negotiating, his folks agreed on the condition that Ben accompany them. "Now, I was a freshman and the twins were exalted seniors. They did not want their nerdy little brother with them—especially since several senior boys from the swim team were there." He chuckled at the memory. "I, of course, took my duties seriously and posted myself just outside their tent flap after lights out."

Their waiter appeared and asked if they'd like dessert.

"I shouldn't...." Lynn paused. "Oh what the heck! I'd like the apple cobbler, please, with the vanilla bean ice cream." She looked at Ben: "Two spoons?"

"No. I'll have a cobbler as well." A question that had been pulling at the edges of his consciousness suddenly formulated. "Say, Lynn, do you know how Susan got a dish of cobbler the night of our book circle dinner?"

"No. Margie or Jane was passing out leftovers to everyone. I assume she just accepted the containers with a little bit of everything. Why?"

"I remember hearing her refuse the dessert. Yet when we found her...." Kalico stopped.

"It's okay. Aunt Emelia described the scene for me. She won't admit it, but she's having a difficult time dealing with Susan's death. I think she keeps reliving the discovery of the her body."

Kalico tried to push the unbidden image of Susan so still in that old chair. "It was traumatic. But your aunt was a trooper."

"She says the same thing about you." She looked at the big redhead seriously. "I suppose as a detective, you've come across death often?"

Kalico shook his head. "No. I'm not a homicide detective. Cheating spouses, would-be insurance company defrauders, a bicycle thief, and lost pets, yes, but no murderers—yet."

"Why are you concerned about Susan having the cobbler?"

"I honestly don't know." He ran a hand through his hair. "I guess it's just the detective in me wanting to make sense of any loose ends."

They paused as their waiter set hot apple cobblers topped with scoops of already melting vanilla ice cream before them. They ate in silence for a few moments.

"Susan had a serious sweet tooth." Lynn dabbed at a trace of vanilla on her lips. "She was always trying to keep desserts out of her house, but she probably caved at the last minute."

"I suppose." Kalico pushed back from the table and sighed. "I'm stuffed."

"Me too." But Lynn kept eating her dessert. "Ben, tell me about how you found the Persian cat."

"Diva? My claim to fame?" He grinned crookedly at her. "I never tell that story until the fifth date."

"Fifth, hmmm?" Lynn raised an eyebrow, wondering just how many fifth dates Kalico had had. "We'd better get moving then—we've four dates to go before my curiosity is satisfied.."

"Just what I was thinking. How about dinner on Saturday night?"

"No. Let's not try another dinner. How about a picnic? The weather is supposed to be nice. Let's go to McKinney Falls."

"Great."

Lynn glanced at her phone. "I can't believe it's after 11! Ben, I really need to get home. It's a…."

"School night. I know."

Kalico walked Lynn to her car. The rain had stopped, leaving the air cool and crisp and fresh. Clouds played hide and seek with the stars. She looked up at him, then stepped forward, lifted up on her tiptoes, and kissed him gently on the mouth. Surprised, he tightened an arm around her and pulled her toward him, but she placed a hand firmly on his chest. "Not 'til the fifth date!" she whispered, then she was gone.

Chapter Twenty

Kalico whistled under his breath as he unlocked his office door, registering the newly emblazoned, *CAT*, now in bright orange, after his name. But nothing could bother him today. The move to his parents' basement has been painless and would free up money for the business. He had four meetings this week with potential clients, and a date with Lynn on Saturday. Yes, life was looking up.

He ran downstairs and out into the bright late March morning. At 7:15 a.m. M's and Katie pulled up in the yellow Beetle. His sister jumped out of the passenger seat and crawled into the back, leaving shotgun for her brother. Their appointment with Ghost's owner Mr. Skifford was at 8 o'clock, so they had plenty of time to get out to Dripping Springs since they would be going against traffic.

"Morning, Ben." M's handed him a coffee. She merged into traffic, pointing the car west.

"How was the big date?" Katie leaned forward between the front seats.

"Okay," said Kalico, but he could not hide his grin.

"Tell!"

Ignoring her, he asked M's for news about Ghost.

"I scanned rescue sites throughout the Texas Hill Country last night. Nothing. It's as if Ghost has dropped off the map: no one had spotted him since Dick Nichols Park. Even the inexhaustible Freddie has given up sending daily scouting reports."

"Perhaps someone has taken him in without searching for his owner," offered Katie.

"Or that beautiful husky is hurt or worse...."

They drove in silence.

Turning to look at his sister, Kalico asked, "What in the world are you wearing?" Katie was dressed in a cream-colored pants suit with a grey, high-collared blouse adorned with pearl buttons. Her mass of red hair was restrained in a tight bun at the nape of her neck, and a pair of clear, tortoise shell glasses dangled from a gold chain around her neck.

"You like?" Katie grinned and placed the glasses on the tip of her nose. "I found these in our old prop box at home. Remember when we did scenes from *How to Marry a Millionaire*?"

"Kat, you look more like a reject from *Mad Men*."

"That's where you're wrong. I've been thinking."

"That's always dangerous," commented Kalico, who received a punch in the arm. "I bet Ghost ran away from the Skifford kennels because he was abused. I bet they mistreated that dog, and we're going to need to get them to confess!" She pursed lips adorned with carefully applied cherry red lipstick.

M's glanced at her friend in the rearview mirror. "Katie, you forget that Ben interviewed Mr. Skifford and his staff when Ghost first disappeared."

"Ah! But Ben was not looking for nefarious deeds. He must have bought the gleaming façade. I bet beneath the surface there's an ugly underbelly of greed and abuse. Skifford may be even running a puppy mill." She nodded her head emphatically; the glasses dove from her nose.

"Nefarious deeds?" Kalico scoffed. "Skifford's operation is professional. Remember, he's the concerned owner, not a suspect."

"For now. I say that we grill him and uncover the dirty underbelly of his operation."

Amused and alarmed, Kalico intervened. "You're terrifying," he acknowledged, "but let me do the interviewing. I want you to observe, take notes, and remain silent." Noting the stubborn jut of his sister's jaw, he added, "Or you will stay in the car."

M's turned onto Fitzhugh Road and began looking for the Skifford Star Ranch and Kennels. A bright white and red sign directed them to turn left onto an unpaved road that dead-ended at a black wrought iron gate framed by large white rock pillars. M's rolled down her window, pushed a button on the intercom and waited.

"Yes?" a voice growled from speaker.

"Benjamin Kalico, M's Moon, and Katie Kalico from the Kalico Detective Agency to see Mr. Skifford."

"Mr. Skifford is in Los Angeles."

"We have an appointment. It's about his lost dog, Ghost."

"You can speak to Dick Crenshaw, our head trainer. Follow the drive to your right and park beside the main kennel. You'll spot him."

"Thanks." M's pulled the car forward as the great gates began to swing open and proceeded slowly down the drive. The Star Ranch was beautiful. All of the cedars had been cleared, making way for tall native grasses. Stands of live oak graced the meadow, where a small stream meandered. A sprawling, single story ranch house with a wrap-around deck stood lookout from a small hill on the left. The road angled right to reveal several fenced training pens with different agility courses set up. M's parked in front of a large white rectangular building with a sign that read Kennel One.

The trio knocked on the kennel door. Except for a random yap, the place was empty and silent. The front door to the kennel was locked, and their knock brought no human response. Barks, however, erupted.

"Let's look around the side," suggested Katie, who paced forward, not waiting for the others. Movement in a far off enclosure caught her attention. She pointed. "Look. I bet that's our Mr. Crenshaw. Prime suspect, *numero uno*."

"But there's been no crime," Kalico and M's called out in unison to Katie's back before following her across a grassy field.

They stopped beside a chain link fence. A trim, dark-haired man in his forties was putting a border collie through its paces on an agility course. With short whistles and hand signals, the trainer ran the course, directing the compact black and white dog to leap over fences, rush through pipes, zigzag around poles, climb a stairway, and slide down a ramp. As the obviously gleeful and panting dog sat down at his trainer's feet, the girls broke into applause. The man turned, commanded the dog to heel, and strolled over to his audience.

"That was awesome!" Katie danced from foot to foot, grinning. She bent down with hand extended toward the border, who looked up at his trainer. At the man's nod, the dog walked over to Katie and raised a paw.

So much for bad cop, thought Kalico, before introducing himself to the trainer. "Hello. This is Bess." He smiled proudly at the dog who was now being hugged.

Remembering her role, Katie stood up, adjusted her glasses, and frowned at the trainer. "Did you breed her here?" She was ready to spring at any hint of a puppy mill.

"No, she's a rescue. Bess was picked up by the Bastrop Humane Society. She'd been left on the side of the highway at seven weeks old. Mr. Skifford brought her here about a year ago now. She's going to be an agility course star. Aren't you, girl?" The border collie, nosed her trainer's hand and received a small treat.

"But you do breed dogs here, don't you?" Katie removed her glasses and pointed them at Mr. Crenshaw, who appeared slightly amused or flustered. Kalico elbowed her in her side, willing her to be quiet.

"Bess, is a beautiful dog and so well trained!" M's interrupted. "We're here to gather any information that may help us recover Ghost."

"Yes, of course. As you know, he bolted during a thunderstorm about a month ago now."

"Did he pull off his leash or get out of his kennel or…?"

"Our intern, Davis, was cleaning out Ghost's kennel. The dog bolted past him and disappeared." He shook his head. "I can't believe we lost him."

"Had Ghost ever tried to escape before?" Katie leaned in accusingly, as her brother unsuccessfully tried to signal her to be quiet.

"Escape? I assure you, Miss Kalico, that Star Ranch is not a dog prison. We practice affection training, have spotless kennels, and feed our animals only premium food. The husky was frightened by thunder and ran. Now, if you'll excuse me, Bess and I have work to do."

Katie made a noise that sounded like a stage *Ah-ha!* followed by a whispered, "Methinks he doth protest too much." As she opened her mouth to respond, Kalico stepped forward.

"No one is suggesting that Ghost was mistreated or had any reason to run away. What puzzles us is why he keeps evading capture. I assume he's been well socialized. Is there anything that you can tell us about his background or training that would help us understand him better?"

Crenshaw glanced at Katie who stayed quiet. He took a breath. "Ghost's behavior puzzles me too." He paused. "When he came to us, he knew the basic commands, socialized with the other dogs well, and was quick to train. He likes people and enjoys contact. Mr. Skifford recognized his potential for photo shoots, commercials, and even movies. Perhaps, you saw Ghost in the ad for River City Wilderness Supply Company?" Kalico and the girls nodded. "Anyway, I started training him to ignore any and all distractions—the first rule of order for a show biz dog—and to stay still for ever-increasing periods of time. When he ran away, Ghost was a finalist for a national dog food commercial."

"You said, 'when he came to you.' You didn't raise him from a puppy?"

"No. Ghost was almost two years old when Mr. Skifford bought him." He glanced pointedly at Katie. "We don't breed dogs here. Ninety percent of our dogs are rescues. The others, like Ghost, Mr. Skifford buys. He had high hopes for our husky."

"Did Ghost seem..." M's paused, searching for the right word. Out of the corner of her eye, she saw that Katie was once again petting and sweet-talking Bess. "Did he seem, I don't know, unhappy or unsettled in any way?"

Crenshaw shook his head again. "No." He signaled Bess, who heeled instantly. "Ghost seemed happy, and that boy loves to work. But every now and then, he would suddenly lose focus. We'd be running a course, or I would be training him to "go to mark" in preparation for a movie shoot, when Ghost would just stop. He'd raise his head, listening to—I don't know what. He'd ignore commands." He shrugged. "Then, he'd snap out of it and be fine."

"Thank you for your time." Kalico extended a hand and signaled Katie that it was time to leave. "We're going to continue to do our best to find him."

Katie repeated M's thank you, then she asked, "Do you happen to know the name of Ghost's first owner?"

"Not off hand, but I have it in my files. I'll text it to you when I go back to my office."

They watched the trainer and his border collie make their way back to the agility course. As they made their way back to M's bug, Katie was uncharacteristically silent.

"Okay, Kat. What's up?" asked Kalico as M's started the car.

"What if the husky was homesick? Maybe, just maybe, he ran away and keeps running because he's searching for his first owner. Maybe he wasn't running *away* from this place—I have to admit it's gorgeous and seems on the up and up—maybe, he's running *to* his old home."

M's looked skeptical. "Now you're replaying *Lassie, Come Home*?"

"It's not that far-fetched. Dogs are loyal." Kalico concentrated for a moment. "Remember the story of the little Scottish dog? What was its name? It searched for its owner or sat by its owner's grave or something for years and years!"

Katie nodded gratefully at her brother. "He was Greyfriar's Bobby! That terrier stayed by his master's grave for fourteen years."

"How in the world does that apply to Ghost?" M's said in exasperation. "Are you picturing him languishing beside a loved one's grave?"

"It's not that far-fetched." Katie grumbled.

"I'll follow up on Ghost's first owner," promised Kalico. "But let's not get our hopes up. The more time that passes, the less likely it is that we'll find him."

"And it's possible that he doesn't want to be found," asserted M's. She braked as a motorcycle cut in front of her. "Ben, don't forget your 10 o'clock with the auto insurance company." She paused to let a Subaru merge. "I need to drop Katie off at the dorm, drop you off at the office, and get to class. The professor is returning our *Jane Eyre* papers today."

"Can you drop me off at my folks' house?" asked Katie.

M's raised an eyebrow.

"Mom made lasagna, and I'm hungry."

"It's only 9:15!"

"Lasagna is good at any time." Katie began pulling hairpins from her bun, letting her red hair shower over her shoulders. "Besides, I'm thinking of moving back home."

M's frowned but refrained from commenting.

"The dorm is so..." she paused trying to find the right word. "So incommodious!"

"But to move back in with your parents! After having freedom..."

"To quote that poem we learned in AP English: I, too, am one who has *felt the weight of too much liberty*! Besides, I miss my old room, home cooked meals, Mom doing my laundry. And Ben is back!"

"Temporarily," he asserted, looking up from his phone.

M's shrugged. "I don't get it. The only thing I want is to get away from...." She stopped.

Silence stretched out between the friends. Katie studied M's profile, before she tentatively asked, "Missy, did your folks *do* something to you? I know they're strict, but...."

"Katie, stop! Bethany and Stephen Montgomery are picture perfect parents." She paused somewhere between exasperation and anger. "They just want me to be someone I'm not. They won't let me breathe."

"Raising parents is challenging," Katie said lightly. "But you know they love you, right? They're worried and just want to understand your, uh, transformation!"

M's grunted.

Ignoring her brother's warning look, Katie nodded her head twice, whispered *No guts—no glory*, and asked, "M's, what happened senior year? You know that you can tell me—and Ben—anything. I just want to understand."

Eyes fixed on the road and hands gripping the steering wheel, M's frowned deeply, her lips forming a straight line.

"Melissa Anne Montgomery!" Katie flashed with red-headed temper. "I am so tired of you shutting me out. I am tired of walking on egg shells around you! I am tired of biting my tongue, afraid that I'm going to say the wrong thing!"

"Then stop talking!"

On fire, Katie picked up her pace. "What am I supposed to think? One day you're blonde; the next, you've cut your hair, dyed it black and blue, and changed your name! I don't care if you change your name to Bambi and dye your hair lime green, but I can't stand it that you will not talk to me. We've been best friends forever. You stopped talking to me after that birthday party incident and...."

"That was in the *fourth* grade."

"And it took ages and ages for you to open up, and it was all about...I don't even remember what! This time you are...." Katie paused dramatically. "You are insufferable!"

"Get out."

"I will not. Not until you tell me what happened to you!" She glared at M's profile.

"Katie, get out. You're home." M's looked at her friend's flushed face.

"Oh."

"You went to Tiffany Court's princess birthday party, and I wasn't invited."

Katie shook her head, puzzled.

"In the fourth grade, you went to the party, and they posted pictures of you and Tiffany, arm and arm, with the tag, 'Besties.'"

"Mom made me go, and I couldn't stand Tiffany. She just wanted to play with Barbie, and I hated dolls."

"I know." M's faced her friend and grinned crookedly. "Bambi?"

"Don't change the subject!"

"Leave it be, Kat," she said quietly. "Leave me alone."

"All right, I will." Katie pushed against Kalico's seat, and leaped out of the car, the instant that he pulled the backseat forward. She stormed to her front door without a backward glance.

M's and Kalico rode to the office in silence. As he unfolded his tall frame to exit the Beetle, he leaned in and patted his assistant awkwardly on the shoulder. "You know, Katie means well. She loves you."

M's shrugged off his hand and drove away without comment.

Chapter Twenty-One

Kalico had just thirty minutes to prepare for his meeting with the auto insurance company, newly opened on the East side. He moved into his office and leaned back in his chair. Yes, he could envision a steady stream of important cases coming his way: insurance fraud, missing persons, cold murder cases, art theft....His phone vibrated—his ten o'clock cancelling. He sighed and decided to spend the next hour responding to emails, cold calling companies M's had compiled for him, and rechecking his accounts receivables, hoping that magically the bottom line had changed.

He turned finally to the Winterjoy file, preparing to write CLOSED in large block letters across its cover. He opened it one last time. Nancy's accidents had been just that—accidents. He opened the baggie containing her left gardening glove. The delicate scent of lavender swirled around him. He shook his head. Nancy was allergic to lavender, so why was her glove soaked in it? Had someone tried to attract bees? Had the bee sting been part of a murder plot? He shook his head ruefully. Most likely, Nancy had picked up one of Emelia's gloves by accident. *The simplest explanation is usually the best one*, he reminded himself.

He stared for a moment at Susan's picture, experiencing again the shock and sadness at her passing. But why had her skin retained that slight blush hours after her death? And who had given her that cobbler? He conjured the bustle of good-bye's at Miss

Winterjoy's front door: guests carrying containers of leftovers, laughing and calling out thank-you's and good-byes; Emelia hugging Susan and Margie and Nancy as the trio of friends departed; Susan laughingly declining dessert; Emelia encouraging her to take it....

Kalico scribbled on scratch paper: listing names and events, circling some, starring others, placing a huge question mark beside Susan's name. Under Nancy's name he wrote: fall, car accident, bee sting. Certainly Connor and the book circle ladies all had opportunity and means—if Nancy had been a target. In fact, Miss Winterjoy had been present at each "accident' except for Nancy's fender bender. But her decision not to attend the book circle had certainly facilitated the potential for disaster. Instantly, he imagined the retired English teacher as a white-haired criminal mastermind who had hired him to divert attention away from her. Perhaps she had played him for a fool. But what motive could she have? What motive could any of them have for wanting to harm Nancy? Money? She was not a rich woman, and, logically, her son would inherit if she died. Power? No. Sex? Revenge? He squinted at the crack in his ceiling, hoping it would reveal a reason.

He put a box around Susan's name as he tried to figure out what was bothering him about her death. What if Susan had not suffered a heart attack? What if she had been murdered? What if someone had poisoned her cobbler or her tea? He, again, conjured Miss Winterjoy carefully washing Susan's cup and dessert plate. What if?

Kalico resolutely shut the file, wrote CLOSED across the front, and placed it his file cabinet. Done.

His phone buzzed.

"Hello, Benjamin."

"Miss Winterjoy! Hello." Kalico stifled a groan. "I was just thinking about you."

"Call me Emelia, please. After all that we've been through...."

"Emelia, then. What can I do for you?"

Her voice was unusually soft and sounded a little tentative. "I was wondering if you could meet me for coffee?" She named a café around the corner from his office.

"You're welcome to come here. I can put a pot on."

"No." Her voice was stronger. "No. I'd like to meet you here. Now, please."

Five minutes later, Kalico entered the Capitol Café. Miss Winterjoy clad in light grey, sat alone at a window table and waved at him. He slid in across from her, watching her carefully as they exchanged the usual pleasantries, noting that she seemed to fidget and avoid his eyes. After their coffee arrived, he drank and let silence expand between them.

Miss Winterjoy glanced furtively around the room, checked over her shoulder, and perused the sidewalk outside of the window before fixing her blue eyes onto Kalico's face. "Thank you for meeting me here. As you know," she said pointedly, "I promised Nancy that our professional relationship has ended." She narrowed her eyes and waited.

Not quite sure what she expected, Kalico asked, "And how is Nancy? I trust there have been no more—accidents?"

"Nancy is fine. Back at work." She leaned forward, willing him to speak. But about what?

"And you're well?" he asked. "Lynn mentioned that you've been having trouble...."

"I'm fine. I miss Susan, but at my time of life, death is no stranger, after all." *Cold.*

Kalico searched for something to say. "And what is Connor up to?"

Colder. She shook her head but answered.

"Connor is being amazingly thoughtful and useful. He's studying hard, still working at the restaurant, but he made the time to mow both his grandmother's yard and mine!" She pursed her lips. "I think I was wrong to suspect him. He's just young and sometimes a bit reckless, but he loves his grandmother. I believe that." She frowned, adding ruefully, "I have to or Nancy will disown me."

Her eyes narrowed, and she tilted her head, like a hungry sparrow, willing him to speak again.

Kalico leaned back in the booth at a loss. He felt like he was failing a quiz on a subject that he had never studied.

"That was quite a temperature drop yesterday," Miss Winterjoy commented mildly.

"Yes. Heard there were wind gusts of over fifty miles an hour," he said. *Why are we talking about the weather?*

"I was lucky to get my errands done before the storm."

"Oh?"

"Yes. I dropped off bequests from Susan to Margie and Jane."

"How are they?"

Miss Winterjoy leaned forward, nodding. *Warm!* "Margie is doing as well as can be expected. She was transplanting the bulbs from Susan's funeral. We all are. They will be a beautiful memorial every spring." She raised an eyebrow and leaned forward.

"And Miss Roundtree?"

Hot.

Miss Winterjoy took a deep breath, and beamed at Kalico as though he were a slow student who had finally gotten a problem right. "I'm glad that you asked. Jane is naturally stricken by Susan's death. Understandable. They were very close. But her grief seems to me to be out of bounds. There's another emotion behind it. Anger, I think. Or guilt...."

In precise detail she related her visit to Jane's house, describing its clutter and disorder: a sign, she suggested, of a disordered mind. "Benjamin, honestly, at times I felt threatened." She rubbed her wrist where Jane had grabbed her, still feeling her icy grasp.

Kalico listened closely, nodded, and waited silently as the elderly woman gathered her thoughts.

"She looked at me for an instant with real hatred. When she appeared behind me holding a knife, I thought I'd faint! And when she asked after Nancy—the tone of her voice...." She shuddered. "And that plant of hers: deadly nightshade, Belladonna, as she called it. Menacing."

"A poisonous plant?"

"Yes. Now, I'm not a person who tilts at windmills." She squared her shoulders. "I believe that Jane is dangerous. She's not who she appears to be. There is anger, hatred, and, yes, I believe, something malevolent in her."

"Do you think that she harmed Susan?"

Miss Winterjoy frowned, shaking her head. "Suse? No. Jane sincerely loved Susan." She paused, selecting her next words carefully. "I think that it is entirely possible that she engineered Nancy's accidents. In fact, I think that she intended to kill Nancy on the night of our book circle dinner."

"The cobbler?" Kalico held his breath.

"Yes!" Miss Winterjoy smiled broadly at him. "Clever boy. The cobbler. Jane made the dessert and was dishing it out with the leftovers for our guests. She handed a container to Margie who gave it to Nancy."

"But Nancy gave her dessert away to Susan."

"Very good. Susan refused dessert initially, but on the way out to her car, Nancy offered her the cobbler, and poor, dear, sweet-addicted Susan could not refuse it a second time."

"And you surmise that the cobbler was poisoned?"

"Yes." She leaned back in the booth, suddenly exhausted. "I wanted to ask you to accompany me to the police department as a corroborating witness."

It took two hours, two turkey sandwiches, and four cups of coffee to convince Miss Winterjoy that they did not have any evidence that the police department would accept or act upon. They covered and recovered the details of Nancy's accidents, the events of the book circle dinner, and their suppositions about Susan's death until a convincing narrative formed.

"There's no motive," Kalico sighed.

"Jane is mentally ill, Benjamin. I sensed her rage. Isn't that motive enough?"

"No. Think about how she has proceeded so far, Emelia. She's been incredibly careful and patient. She has not acted impulsively or out of uncontrolled anger. Remember, she left the consequences of her actions up to chance."

"Or fate."

"If Nancy had died, her death would have been labeled an accident. Or, like Susan's, attributed to a heart attack." Kalico ran a hand through his hair. "Fate, we could say, has now turned on Jane."

"Yes. Susan's death was an accident—a horrible twist of fate." Miss Winterjoy studied her clasped hands. "Benjamin, we cannot know how she will react. After the shock of murdering her closest friend, she could just stop her plan to hurt Nancy."

"Or," he waited until his companion met his eyes, "be driven by guilt and anger to act again—more directly and more violently."

Ramrod straight, shoulders squared, and eyes bright, Emelia Winterjoy stated, "Mr. Kalico, I would like to hire you to solve a murder." She opened her purse and handed him a check. "And to prevent one!"

***

At one o'clock, Kalico returned to his office, his mind whirling. M's was not at her desk, so he checked his messages to find a reminder that she was in class. As he had expected, there were no new leads on Ghost. He settled down behind his desk. He could hear Lynn's voice, mocking him. What had she asked him at one of their first meetings? Oh yes: "Have you followed my aunt down the rabbit hole?" Had he? While sitting across from Miss Winterjoy, their story of what had happened to Susan and the danger facing Nancy seemed logically sound. Now, in the quiet of his office, it all seemed far-fetched. Still, they had developed an action plan: Miss Winterjoy would dine with Nancy this evening, guarding her against any surprise attacks. Moreover, she would tell Nancy of their suspicions and of her decision to rehire Kalico. There would be no more secrets between the two old friends. Lynn, too, would be brought up to speed on the investigation. Even Connor, over Emelia's mild protestations, would be told of their concerns and enlisted to guard his grandmother.

Kalico would dig more deeply into Jane Roundtree's background, research the effects of Belladonna, speak with Dr. Munjabi, and initiate 24 hour surveillance of the suspect. Two people were to be hired to each take eight hour shifts. Kalico would take the third. Miss Winterjoy had directed him to spare no expense.

Kalico turned on his computer and googled *belladonna*. The plant had a fascinating history. Women in the 18th century had used it to dilate their eyes, and it was still used medicinally today by ophthalmologists and by doctors to treat such conditions as irritable bowel syndrome and Parkinson's disease. Technical phrases like "anti-cholinergic taxidrome" and "Atropa" punctuated the screen. Then Kalico found what he was searching for:

The ingestion of ten berries is toxic to an adult, leading to cardiovascular collapse. A symptom of belladonna intoxication is dry, scarlet skin.

He saw again Susan's flushed skin, picked up his phone, and called Dr. Munjabi. The doctor was gracious but resisted any idea that Susan had died from an obscure poison. He reasserted that in his professional opinion she had suffered heart failure and rejected forcefully any suggestion of exhumation.

Kalico next returned to the brief background check he had initially completed on Jane Roundtree. Born in 1946 in Galveston, Texas, she was the only child of a store manager and a stay-at-home mom. A good student, she had received a scholarship to the University of Texas where she majored in biology with the intention of becoming a doctor. She left college unexpectedly in her junior year and moved to Phoenix, Arizona, where she acquired her real estate license. Her last employment was with Desert Realty. No husband. No children. No criminal record—not even a parking ticket. Nothing remarkable. She retired at age 67, sold her home in Phoenix, and returned to Austin.

"Why did you drop out of UT, Jane?" Kalico asked his computer screen. "What happened?" It was time to interview her. Were Miss Winterjoy's impressions sound? He needed to find out for himself.

He picked up his phone and called Mrs. Buonanotte. "May I have a plate of lasagna to go?" he asked. Then he mapped out a line of questioning.

Chapter Twenty-Two

As Kalico was about to turn onto Riverside Drive on his way to Jane Roundtree's house, his phone buzzed. M's voice crackled over the speakers: "Ben, I've found Ghost! Come quickly. Please." She gave him an address.

Kalico executed a U-turn, and pointed his Civic south toward Gallant Fox Road in Oak Hill, the address of Ghost's first owner. Thirty minutes later, he parked behind the Beetle in front of a white stone house. It appeared to be deserted. The front yard was overgrown with weeds, and a red and gold "For Sale" sign lay partially obscured on the curb. M's and Ghost were nowhere to be seen.

Kalico donned his leather jacket and gloves, grabbed the pet retrieval pole and strode up the walkway, knocking firmly on the front door. He listened. Barks erupted from around the neighborhood, but nothing in the house stirred. Cupping his face with his hands, he squinted through the beveled glass door. The house was empty. He silently said a thank you that M's had not broken in.

As he moved around the side of the house, his senses began to tingle. Turning the corner into the unfenced backyard, Kalico spotted movement on the cedar deck and heard a low and warning growl. Ghost stood poised by the back door, his hackles up and ears pressed flat against his head. M's sat frozen on the wet grass about ten paces from the husky.

Kalico set the pole down, lowered and angled his body, sidestepping slowly to his assistant. "M's?" he said softly. No answer. Taking care not to make eye contact, he surveyed the husky with his peripheral vision. The dog was hardly recognizable. His beautiful white coat was matted and caked with mud. Something—blood, perhaps—was crusted over his right eye. His ear was torn. Ben gently placed his hand on M's shoulder.

"No," she hissed. "No means 'No!'"

"Are you hurt? Did Ghost…?"

"No." Her hands gripped the wet grass, her thin body was tense, and her eyes fixed on a scene beyond the dog beside the door.

"Let's get you back to the car to where it's warm and dry."

M's pushed her weight more forcefully into the ground. "No."

"I'll be right back." Keeping an eye on the still growling husky, Kalico slowly angled away from the backyard. Once out of Ghost's sight, he ran to his car, grabbed a blanket. He called 311 to alert animal control, spoke briefly to his mother, and left a message for Dick Crenshaw at Star Ranch.

Neither Ghost nor M's had moved. He draped the blanket around the girl's shoulder to allay the cold and possible shock. He sat cross-legged beside her and began talking in a low and soothing tone.

"You found him, M's. Probably, saved his life. Kalico continued a stream of small talk. Eventually, the girl seemed to relax. A glance at Ghost revealed that the dog, too, was no longer standing aggressively at the back door. He now sat. His ears were up, listening, but so were his hackles.

M's took a deep, shuddering breath. "He's hurt," she began.

"Yes, the dog's hurt, but we're going to get him home and cared for."

"No. He hurt me. Mr. Jeffers, he...." Her small frame shook, but her eyes were dry and her face impassive. Suddenly, words began to tumble out. She relayed a fragmented and disjointed story: her delight when her AP Physics teacher had taken a special interest in her, signaling that he had chosen her to become his assistant after his college intern suddenly left; her shock when the teacher had returned her lab report with an angry red zero scrawled across it.

"He accused me of plagiarism, said it would be on my permanent record, said that I would be suspended or even expelled, and that my dreams of college were over."

Mr. Jeffers had picked up his phone to call her parents, before pulling a chair close to her desk. "There's a way we can get you out of this situation," he'd said, beginning to massage her shoulders. M's recounted an overwhelming sense of powerlessness, as the older man had removed the band from her ponytail, had run his hands through her long blonde hair.

"I said, 'No.' His breath smelled of peppermint." She stared dry-eyed at the wet grass. "He pinned me in my seat. I fought him. I fought him." Her hands struck the ground.

Kalico placed his arm around her shoulders. Fury, sadness, anxiety warred in his chest. He breathed deeply.

A small whine reminded him of the big dog's presence. Ghost stood now at the edge of the deck. His tail wagged slowly.

Kalico extended his free hand, palm up toward the husky. "It's okay, boy. No one here is going to hurt you. We're here to take you home."

"He is home," whispered M's. "Don't you see, Ben? All this time, Ghost hasn't been running away; he's been running home." She sniffed, "But his owner's moved away. He can never go home again."

"But you can, M's."

Kalico held his breath as the dog hesitantly limped toward them. Ghost sniffed his extended hand, then placed his nose under M's arm, burrowing his head into her lap. M's gasped and buried her face into his thick, muddy coat and sobbed.

After what felt like a lifetime later, Kalico placed a collar around Ghost's neck, helped M's to her feet, and led them back to the car. Initially, Ghost had resisted, but M's had said, "Your owner—Veronica, wasn't it?—isn't here, boy, and she's not coming back." Surprisingly, the husky had shifted his gaze to M's and allowed himself to be led to the front yard.

Katherine and Katie Kalico, accompanied by Bethany Montgomery, stood in the drive. Upon seeing them, M's ran forward. "Mom!" The women encircled the teen in a group hug. Kalico thought her heard his sister say, "M's, I'm so sorry I got angry," and that he heard M's reply, "Call me Melissa."

As the women drove away, Kalico cancelled his call to animal control and waited with Ghost at his side. The big dog allowed his chest to be petted and remained still as a soft wet cloth wiped away the crusted blood from his left eye. When Dick Crenshaw arrived, Ghost greeted the trainer enthusiastically and jumped readily into the SUV's back seat. The husky's blue eyes met Kalico's for a moment before he was driven off to the ranch.

Suddenly exhausted, Kalico climbed into his Civic. He registered surprise that it was light out. He glanced at the casserole of lasagna, now cold, perched on the passenger's seat. He longed to go home, shower, check on M's, but his gut nagged at him to get to Jane Roundtree's house and quickly.

***

Twenty minutes later, balancing a fragrant lasagna casserole in his left hand, Kalico rapped gently on Jane Roundtree's front door. Sensing eyes watching him from behind the blinds, he composed his face into pleasant and, he hoped, vacuous lines.

"Benjamin Kalico. This is a surprise." Her tone did not convey whether she thought the surprise to be agreeable or not.

"Hello, Miss Roundtree. My mother asked me to bring by this casserole for you." He hoped Mrs. Buonanotte would forgive his white lie.

"How kind." She opened the door and beckoned Kalico to enter.

Neither Jane nor her home was what he expected. Instead of the clutter, dust, and general disarray described by Miss Winterjoy, the living room was spotless with a lemony scent of furniture polish. No wads of used Kleenex decorated the couch or the floor, and the wastebasket was empty. Instead of a disheveled and grief-stricken madwoman, Miss Roundtree appeared calm, her dark brown eyes, framed by her round glasses, met his forthrightly. She was dressed neatly in black pants and a black turtleneck sweater adorned with a pearl cluster pin. Her make-up had been recently and carefully applied.

Kalico followed her through a small living room, lit only by the flickering of a muted television screen, into a bright kitchen where he placed the casserole on the counter. "Mom always says that friends bring food and comfort immediately after we lose a loved one, but forget that grief lasts a long, long time. She wanted you to know that she, that all of us, are thinking of you and your loss."

"Thank you." Jane's eyes grew misty. "I miss Susan terribly." She paused to compose herself. "She was stolen from me, from us, so suddenly. It wasn't right."

Kalico nodded and murmured in sympathy. *Why stolen?* "You were friends for a long time."

"For over forty years." She turned, seemingly ready to escort him out.

"You were college roommates, weren't you?"

"Yes. Susan took me under her wing." Her eyes took on a faraway look. "The other girls referred to us as the butterfly and the bullfrog. But I didn't mind. It was true. Susan was ethereal—all light and laughter. I was an awkward, unsophisticated country girl, bookish and shy, but, for some unknown reason, she claimed me as a sister."

"And that's when you met the other book circle women?"

"Yes. Suse brought me into her group."

"It must be some comfort that you have Emelia, Margie, and Nancy as support."

"Of course. Old friends." She turned to leave the kitchen.

Had he imagined a hardening of her tone? He wanted to interview Jane and to verify that she had the *Belladonna*, but she was not offering him the expected invitation for coffee. Kalico cleared his throat. "May I have a glass of water, please? I just finished a run," he prevaricated, "and am parched."

Jane returned and filled a glass from the tap. As he drank, she eyed him curiously. Then turned again to lead the way out. Instead of following her to the front door, Kalico swerved into the living room as though drawn to the photographs on her bookshelf.

"Great pictures!" He smiled and pointed to one showing a group in front of plastic bags. "Were you and Susan part of an environmental club?"

Jane appeared beside him and gently lifted the photograph. "Yes. We were pioneers at UT." She smiled proudly. "Susan was determined to save the planet; she inspired us all." She set the photograph firmly down on the shelf.

"I bet you have great stories about the beginnings of the environmental movement." He sank into the soft cushions of her couch.

Jane paused; he watched as she seemed to listen to something outside before she nodded her head once. Then she sat down beside him, her expression unreadable. She switched off the television. "Oh yes! Lots of stories. We were a small but devoted team." She launched into stories of initiating a recycling program, a disastrous composting effort that attracted rats, and hilarious strategizing sessions over plates of double chocolate, fudge brownies.

Kalico nodded and grunted occasionally, encouraging her narrations, happy to be able to observe her. Jane was a good storyteller, animated with a wry and, at times, self-deprecating sense of humor. But he judged that he was watching a performance—something else was beneath the surface.

As Jane paused in the middle of a story about a sit-in at the Dean's office over Styrofoam, he asked, "Did you and Susan stay in the club for all four college years?" He knew the answer, but waited to see if Jane would tell the truth.

Jane frowned. "Susan became president of the club and helped it grow throughout her four years. I, however, left the university just prior to our Junior year."

Trying to sound only mildly curious, he nudged her to expand. "Leaving must have been difficult," he sympathized. "May I ask why?"

"Oh, money troubles, a broken heart, a distaste for academic life...none or all of the above." She waved a hand in the air dismissively. "Take your pick."

Kalico stood as though ready to leave. "I really like your duplex. I've temporarily moved back in with my parents and...."

"I gather being a pet detective is not lucrative?"

Did her voice hold an undertone of derision? "I am *not* a pet detective," Kalico protested. "I investigate insurance fraud, marital infidelities, run background checks, and...."

Jane peered at him over the rims of her glasses. "Yes, of course, you detect more than puppies and kitties."

Kalico's neck reddened. "I am, as a matter of fact, investigating a murder. Quite a serious and complicated case."

"How exciting! Do tell." Jane leaned forward.

Kalico cursed himself and backtracked. "It's a cold case—unsolved for over twenty years. I am not at liberty right now to discuss it. Police matter, you know."

"Of course. Please thank your mother for the lasagna." She stood.

"I will." He walked to the front door. "Just text me when you finish it, and I'll come by and pick up the dish," He handed her his card. Then, as though struck with a new idea, he said, "Miss Winterjoy mentioned that you will be moving into a new home soon?"

"That's right. This little place is just a temporary *pied-a-terre*, until the work is finished on my new house."

Kalico registered the lie. "And when do you expect that to be, if you don't mind my asking?"

"Soon. But you know how contractors are."

"Would you mind showing me this place? If it suits me, I was thinking that I could sublet when you move into your new house." Kalico smiled innocently. "That is, if you have the time."

Jane studied him over the rims of her glasses. "I'm meeting an old friend for dinner, but I don't have to leave for a while." Kalico trotted after her as she showed him two bedrooms—one good sized, the other tiny—and a bathroom.

"This place would be perfect for me," he enthused. "But do you have a fenced yard?"

"Yes. Ben, why don't you check out the backyard? I have to make a quick call and then I'll be right with you."

Kalico stepped out onto her back porch—a small and, he noted, *bare* back porch. No large shrub, Belladonna or otherwise, adorned it. Could Miss Winterjoy have been mistaken? Jane seemed understandably sad, but composed and not unfriendly. He'd sensed an undertone of something off, but couldn't that be because he was looking for something disturbing? He shivered in the cold wind that was still blowing from the north, and gazed across the long and narrow yard with its patchy St. Augustine lawn rimmed by a chain link fence. Jane had sidestepped his question about why she'd left the university. And she had lied about buying a new home. But most likely she was embarrassed that her financial situation was so far below that of her friends.

His phone buzzed, but he ignored it. A faint, circular dirt ring on the edge of the porch caught his attention. He knelt down to look at it more closely, pulled out his phone took a quick picture. The ring was definitely the right size for a large potted plant. He ran his fingers over a small ridge of hardened soil, then stopped, sensing someone behind him. He untied and began tying his right shoe. Jane Roundtree cleared her throat.

"What do you think?" she asked.

Kalico sprang upright. "Of what?"

"The yard. Will it do?" she seemed amused.

"Yes. My dog, uh, Bruno, will love it." His face reddened.

"I will let you know when my new house is finished."

"Good. Great. Thanks." Kalico opened the sliding glass door...

"Wait, Ben." He turned to see Jane, head tilted like a small sparrow, smiling at him. "Would you mind doing me a little favor before you leave? I need a box of books that I've stored in the shed. They are up high and too heavy for me to get down. Would you mind?"

"Not at all. Happy to help."

He followed her across the sodden lawn to a red and white shed. She unlocked it and opened the double doors. "My boxes are on the left; the right side belongs to the other side of the duplex."

Kalico stepped into the gloom of the shed. He uttered an involuntary yelp as his face pushed into a clinging spider's web. The faint odors of gasoline, grass, mulch, and mildew mingled and made him crinkle his nose. He waited for his eyes to adjust. He made out the shape of a loveseat covered in thick plastic beside a wooden rocking chair. An overstuffed pillow, gray or green, lay discarded on the floor beside them. Two shelves on the back wall were stacked with cardboard boxes. And in the far corner he spotted what looked like a large shrub.

"I need the third box," Jane said behind him.

Kalico tore his glance away from the suspicious plant and grabbed a small ladder, opened it, and secured its hinges. He climbed three rungs and stretched until his right hand could grasp the corner of the far box. It wouldn't budge. He'd have to lower the other two boxes to the floor to get to Jane's books. He gripped the first box and inched it toward his chest.

Suddenly, a swift sharp blow knocked his legs out from under him. Kalico found himself launched into the air and falling sideways. He landed hard on his right side, his shoulder crunching under him, and his head bouncing once off the concrete. Stunned, he lay still, breathing hard. *What the hell?* He rolled onto his back, began to sit up, then sank back down, his head throbbing and spinning, his vision, blurred.

"Impudent young pet detectives should mind their own business."

Kalico turned toward the voice that spit out words with contempt. Jane's short, round figure was backlit against the open door. She leaned against a long-handled shovel.

The realization that she'd swung that shovel like a bat to knock him off the ladder slowly percolated into his brain. He suppressed a groan. From somewhere to his left, a phone buzzed. He lurched toward it, but a wave of nausea forced him to lie down again.

"We can't have that now, can we?" Jane picked up Kalico's cell phone and placed it in her pocket. She walked quickly to the open doors. "No use shouting for help, Ben. No one can hear you from back here." She placed the shovel against a wall and moved outside of the shed. The doors closed with an echoing clang, and he heard a chain being threaded through door handles.

Darkness and silence. He closed his eyes, willing the dizziness and nausea to stop. Vic was going to have a field day at his expense. He could just hear his friend now: "Bested by a septuagenarian! Felled by a female! Turned your back on a suspect, my boy. First thing they teach you *not* to do at the Academy. You best stick to tracking treacherous terriers." Yes, a field day....

Kalico jerked awake, eyes opening to impenetrable blackness. How could he doze at a time like this? *A time like what?* he thought. He knew he needed to move fast, to get out of this shed, but why? His brain was fuzzy, his head throbbed with each heartbeat, and his right shoulder, elbow, and knee ached. *Think.* He breathed in and out slowly and deeply. He forced himself to sit up. *Good. Now focus.*

"Jane Roundtree knocked me off a ladder with a shovel and locked me in her shed." He repeated these facts aloud to himself three times. His mind cleared suddenly: *Jane was going after Nancy. No more manufactured accidents; no more playacting as the good friend. She was out for blood.*

Adrenaline rushed through Kalico's body. He stood, ignoring his protesting knee and crushing headache. He looked left, then right: a long sliver of pale gray light marked the door's position, no more than five steps away. He clenched his teeth and shuffled forward. Instinctively, he reached out and rattled the door's handles. He braced his good left shoulder against the frame and pushed. He grabbed the shovel, inserted the blade between the doors and tried to lever it open or at least widen the gap. Finally, sweating profusely and breathing hard, he stopped, defeated, raised his head, and shouted for help.

He silenced himself and listened. Nothing. Not even barking dogs. He leaned his back against the doors. *What are your options, son?* Kalico recalled his dad's response whenever he was faced with a problem that seemed unsolvable.

"Okay, what are my options?" he said aloud. He held up an index finger. "One: break down the damn door." But with what? There was nothing that could help him on Jane's side of the shed, but what about her neighbor's side? He tried to recall what he had glimpsed when he'd entered. He closed his eyes, saw himself pausing in the doorway, waiting for his eyes to adjust. Yes, there on the left, he'd seen a lawn mower, rakes, loppers, and leaf bags. A bright red toolbox rested on a small table. Various paint containers were stacked against the back wall.

"One: I can use the lawn mower to break out of here." He held up a second finger. "Two: pick the lock or sever the chain." Although the gap between the doors was small—no more than half an inch—he could try to get shears or needle nose pliers through it. Perhaps he could cut or twist the chain or move the padlock into a position that would allow him to manipulate it. The red toolbox would hold tools to help him.

"Time to move!" He stepped reluctantly away from the small, lighted area, then stopped himself. His dad always insisted on a third option for every problem because it forced him to think "out of the box."

Kalico held up three fingers. "Three." He had nothing. His head ached. Two possibilities were good enough. *Patience, Ben. Think.* He ran his hand over the door. It was made of some kind of resin, most likely reinforced with steel. He reached up to the top of the doors—the seal was tight. He ran his hand down one side over two hinges and to the floor. The doors were flush with the floor. Two hinges!

"Three: take off the hinges and let the door fall!"

That was it! Grinning, Kalico forced himself away from the door and stepped slowly into the darkness, inching his way toward the small table with the toolbox. He kept his hands out in front of him, stopping when his shin nudged what he assumed was the lawn mower. He then sidestepped until his arm grazed a table. He found the toolbox, unlatched it, plunged his hand inside of it, and came out gripping a hammer. He placed it in his left hand continued and groped again, pulling out first a wrench, and then—bingo!—a screwdriver, and—yes!—it had a flat head.

Several solid blows later to the hinges with leveraging from the screwdriver to pull out the pins, followed by a strong shove, and one side of the shed's double door fell slightly forward. Kalico stepped out into the cold air—free. He ran to his car, opened the trunk and drank deeply from the bottle of water he kept for rescued animals. Then he poured the cold water over his head, cursing as it stung his scalp and cheek. But he felt alert again. He jumped behind the wheel, right knee protesting, and sped off to Nancy MacLeod's house.

Chapter Twenty-Three

Emelia Winterjoy stood at her kitchen sink, an open can of Fancy Feast Liver Paté in one hand, and stared at her image in the window. She looked pale and another night without sleep had formed dark smudges under her eyes. Blush and concealer had done little to amend her haggard appearance. She sighed deeply. It was five o'clock and time to walk next door for dinner. She had determined to tell Nancy about her suspicions of Jane and about her decision to rehire Benjamin Kalico. She'd even called Lynn at the last minute, inviting her to join them. *Might as well kill two birds with one stone.* She winced at the cliché. She was tired and worried. An annoyed "Meow" brought her attention back to the task at hand.

"Sorry, Perdita. Here's your dinner." The calico cat rubbed against her owner's leg once, then moved leisurely over to her dish and began to eat. Emelia picked up two dog dishes and filled them with dry food. "Trey! Snow! Doggie dinner time." Her corgis bounded into the kitchen, skidded across the tile, and buried their faces in their bowls, tails wagging furiously.

Emelia smiled at their enthusiasm, then she took a spinach salad from the refrigerator and, at the last moment, selected a bottle of chilled Pinot Grigio. She may need added courage. Nancy would be incredulous and would want to dismiss Emelia's suspicions. She may even be angry that her friend had resumed her sleuthing. Hopefully, Lynn would be on her aunt's side.

Never a coward or one to shirk responsibility, she squared her shoulders, lifted her chin, marched to Nancy's house, and rapped purposefully on her front door.

"Come in, Em. It's unlocked," Nancy's musical voice called out faintly from somewhere at the back of the house.

Emelia entered, locked and bolted the front door, shaking her head at the lax security, before walking into the kitchen and setting the salad and wine on the counter. "Where are you?"

"Cutting irises from the garden to adorn the table." Nancy swept into the room, her arms filled with pale lavender and deep purple flowers. Moody wiggled forward to greet the visitor and to demand pets. Emelia complied, as Nancy arranged the irises in a clear blue vase.

"They're beautiful!"

"Yes, indeed. And I have a pot of Chicken Tika Masala simmering on the stove, and I stopped at Phoenecia Bakery for *naan*. Tonight we are going to feast Indian style! I have even lit a fire in the fireplace!"

"Nance, how marvelous." Emelia breathed in the delicious spices. "Lynn is running a bit late because she had an after school conference with parents."

"Not a problem. I will wait to make the rice." She uncorked the wine and pulled two stemless wine glasses from a cupboard. "Let's go into the living room, drink the wine, and have cheese and crackers. Will you get the cheese plate from the refrigerator?"

The friends settled on the couch and poured the wine. Nancy raised her glass. "A toast: 'May those who love us love. And those who don't love us, may God turn their hearts!'" She laughed and sipped the cold wine. Emelia followed suit.

"That's an old Irish toast. Gareth used to say it at every special occasion. I can't recall the ending." She shook her head ruefully.

"Oh, I've heard him say it! Doesn't it include something about God turning ankles so that we may recognize those who don't love us?"

"Yes, that's right. 'So we'll know them by their limping.'" Nancy chuckled at the memory.

"If only it were that easy," murmured Emelia.

"What, Em?"

"Nothing. Nothing. You seem in bright spirits this evening."

"I am." Nancy spread her arms wide, showing off the delicate rose, mauve, pink, and tangerine swirls of color in her long-sleeved silk blouse. "It's been such a trying few months—what with my accidents and the loss of our Susan—I decided to do a little retail therapy, try a new recipe, and embrace my dearest friends. We must treasure each moment we have together."

"I agree." Should she tell Nancy now or wait for Lynn? "In the spirit of treasuring one another…," she began.

"We need to get you into some spring colors. New clothes will make a new woman of you." She studied her friend's face. "In fact, Em, you look exhausted."

"I haven't been sleeping."

"Is it grief over Suse?"

"Yes. And no," Emelia answered honestly. Where was Lynn, anyway? She glanced at the clock over the mantle. It was 5:20.

"At least you're not worrying about me anymore!" A teasing smile crossed Nancy's face. "I'm so glad that you gave up the absurd notion that I was in danger. We need to chalk that fantasy up to too many Jane Marple mysteries!"

Emelia's arm jerked at Nancy's assertions, and she dropped her wine glass, which rolled onto the carpet, luckily unbroken. "I'm sorry. So clumsy of me."

"Stay put. I'll get some paper towels and another glass." Nancy swept out of the room with Moody at her heels.

Emelia blotted drops of wine from her gray pants, then moved over to the fireplace. The gas flames were cheerful. She glanced at the pictures framed on the mantle: a young Gareth, wearing a green plaid shirt, and holding a "Save Our Planet" sign.

"Here's another glass of wine, Miss Butterfingers." Nancy looked over Emelia's shoulder at the picture she was holding. "I love that one. Look how serious he is—that was during Gareth's environmental warrior days."

"Nance, did Gareth know Jane in college?"

"What an odd question." She thought for a moment. "They may have had a class together, but, no, I don't think so."

"Oh, but we did know each other. We knew each other well." Jane Roundtree commented from behind them.

Emelia gasped. Moody growled deep in her throat. Nancy, however, turned with a smile. "Jane, what a lovely surprise. I didn't hear you knock."

"I let myself in. You really should lock you backdoor."

"True. You're just in time for dinner. I've been meaning to call." She shushed Moody, and motioned for the little terrier to sit.

"I didn't expect to find you here, Emelia." Jane ignored Nancy's invitation. "Is this a 'lovely surprise?'" She mimicked Nancy's soft tone.

Her mind racing, Emelia moved to the couch. She picked up a glass of wine with one hand while her other hand moved to the side pocket of her purse that held her phone. "Of course, it is, Jane. Wine?"

"No. And I'll take your phone." Jane moved forward, grabbed Emelia's purse, took out her phone, and pocketed it.

"Em? Jane? What's going on?" Puzzled, Nancy looked at each woman in turn. Then she saw the small gun in Jane's hand.

"Nancy, join your friend on the couch. Sit. Now." Jane moved leisurely, placing herself in front of the two women. "Do you want to tell her or should I?" she nodded toward Emelia who cleared her throat.

"Nancy, I believe that Jane is here tonight to kill you." She took her friend's hand in hers and squeezed it.

"Succinct as always, Miss Winterjoy. Would you care to expand?" Her words were mocking. She relished the fear on Nancy's face.

"Certainly. I believe that Jane tampered with your car, causing your accident. I also believe that she somehow engineered your bee sting."

"Emelia, that's ridiculous!" Nancy inserted, momentarily forgetting the gun pointed at them.

"Not so ridiculous. I did puncture your brake line and quite enjoyed seeing your bruises. Now, the bee sting was genius—if I say so myself. I simply took the EpiPens from your bathroom and your gardening bag and sprayed your gloves with lavender and sugar water. Then I let fate take charge. Fate always punishes the wicked."

"But why?" Nancy's voice was a whisper. "Why would you want to hurt me? I've never done anything to you. Jane. We're friends."

"Friends?" Jane growled. "You ruined my life. Stole the only man I ever loved. Enjoyed the life I should have lived." She paced the room, waving the gun erratically at the couch. She picked up a photograph of

Nancy and Gareth holding their newborn son. "Patrick was supposed to be my son; Connor should be my grandson."

"But, Jane, you never went out with Gareth, did you? He would have told me."

"Gareth and I worked together to save the planet. We shared a passion that would have grown into an abiding love. But you flounced into the library, flirted with him, seduced him away from me. My poor Gareth never knew what hit him once you got your claws into him."

Nancy gasped at the hatred in her voice and the virulent look in her eyes.

"Jane," Emelia said soothingly, "that's such old history. Isn't it time to let the past rest? Put the gun down, and, and join us for dinner."

"Yes. Please put that thing away. You haven't done any real harm. I forgive you for my...accidents."

"No real harm, huh? I think Miss Know-it-all Winterjoy knows better, don't you?" Jane glared a challenge.

"No. Certainly not." Emelia stared into her eyes, feigning ignorance. "Besides Connor is due home any moment, and you don't want to...."

Jane clicked her tongue. "Nice try, Emelia. But I called the restaurant to make sure that Connor was working late. I would never hurt my Gareth's grandson." She returned her attention to Nancy who was hugging Moody tightly against her chest. "No harm? I accuse you, Nancy MacLeod, of killing my best friend, Susan Jankowsky!"

"Killing? Are you insane?"

"Don't state the obvious, dear," Emelia whispered.

"Do you deny that you gave Susan your dessert after our last book circle meeting?"

"No. I gave her my cobbler. I had so many leftovers, and Susan loved her sweets."

"I rest my case."

"I don't understand." Nancy looked inquiringly at Emelia. "You don't mean...? You couldn't mean...?"

"Jane poisoned the cobbler. She meant it for you."

"But I had no idea. You can't blame me for her death!"

"You never accept responsibility, Nancy. You glide through life, running over anyone who stands in your way, stealing loved ones, murdering my best friend." Jane aimed the gun at Nancy's head. "It's time you paid for the harm you've done to me."

"No!" Emelia commanded in the tone she'd use to subdue teenagers for decades.

Jane imperceptibly lowered the gun and took a deep, shuddering breath. "A bullet is too quick for the years of suffering that you have caused me." She turned to Emelia. "And there's the question of what to do about you. I have never liked you, you know? Always so superior. You think your opinion of a book is the only one that counts."

"Jane," Emelia began.

"Quiet. I need to think." Jane circled the living room, never taking her eyes off the two women.

Emelia's mind raced. She prayed that Lynn would not arrive and be put in harm's way. She looked at Nancy who was pale and seemed to be frozen in disbelief. *No help there. Snap out of it!* She stared pointedly at her friend. They couldn't just sit on the couch and let Jane shoot them. She caught Nancy's eye and nodded toward the wine bottle that sat in the middle of the coffee table.

"Ladies, I am going to present you with Sophie's choice." Jane's voice was cheerful, almost giddy. She pulled a Ziploc bag from her coat pocket, wiggled it in the air, before tossing it to Nancy. Then she pointed her gun at Emelia's head. "Either you eat that bag of peanuts right now, or I will shoot Emelia. Your choice."

Nancy slowly opened the bag.

"Nance, don't do it. She'll shoot me anyway!" Emelia's hands dug into the cushions of the couch. She bit her lip to keep from screaming. Peanuts were toxic to someone as allergic as Nancy.

"Your choice, bitch. Not that you've ever done a selfless thing in your life."

Nancy's eyes filled with tears as she looked at Emelia. She shrugged, delicately lifted a single nut from the bag, and placed it in her mouth.

"The whole bag full!" Jane focused on her victim, although her gun did not waiver from its target.

Moody suddenly stood up and barked, her tail wagging.

"Shut that mutt up or I will! Eat!"

Nancy complied, cramming a handful of peanuts into her mouth. As she chewed, her eyes locked on Emelia's and she nodded once, twice….

***

Kalico pulled up in front of Nancy MacLeod's house and jumped out of his car. His vision blurred, and his head spun. For a moment, he thought that he might throw up. He leaned against the Civic, gulping fresh air.

"Young man? Young man, are you okay?" A middle-aged woman, her voice filled with concern, stood before him, yellow lab panting at her side.

"Yes. I'm fine."

"Your head is bleeding. Do you want me to call an ambulance?" She took out a cell phone. .

"Yes. I mean, no." He fished a card out of his wallet. "But I'd appreciate it if you'd call this number and ask for Victor Carrillo. Tell him that Kalico is reporting a B

& E in progress at this address. Tell him to send a squad car asap."

The woman looked at the card. "Kalico. Victor Carrillo. B & E. Now. Got it."

Kalico nodded a thank you and walked quickly up to the MacLeod's front door. He had no doubt that Jane was in there with Nancy, and that she meant to harm her. He gently tried to turn the doorknob: locked. He raised his hand to knock, then paused and peered through the beveled glass of the door. He could just make out a small, white-haired figure sitting at the edge of the couch—Miss Winterjoy. For a second he felt relieved. The friends were probably just visiting. He frowned. Even from a distance he could tell that the elderly woman's posture, always perfect, was unusually stiff. Her attention was fixed on someone out of his sight. He lowered his hand.

Kalico moved around the side of the house to the back yard. His heart pounded with urgency as he tried the back door. It opened easily. He entered quietly, holding his breath and inched down the short hallway and into Nancy's kitchen. As he crouched behind her breakfast bar to peer into the living room, Moody barked a warning.

"Shut that mutt up, or I'll," Jane threatened. "Eat!"

Jane's back was to Kalico, but he could see the gun in her hand, pointed at Emelia. Nancy was putting something into her mouth and nodding her head as she chewed.

Suddenly, Moody jumped off the couch and sped toward Jane. Growling, the little terrier bit into her ankle. She yelped, trying to shake the dog off. In that instant, Emelia launched herself at Jane's knees, Nancy picked up a wine bottle and threw it at Jane's head, and Kalico took two running steps and lunged for her gun hand. A shot reverberated in the room.

"Is everyone okay?" Kalico, his knee in the small of Jane's back, pressed her head into the carpet as he pulled her hands behind her back. Moody, hackles raised, growled beside the prostrate woman, who sputtered obscenities.

"Yes." Emelia released Jane's legs and stood, a bit shaky, but fine. Later, she would say that when she leaped at Jane, she felt just like Brett Favre sacking a quarterback. "Nancy?"

"Yes, for the moment." The old friends hugged. "But my poor carpet!" She pointed to the broken bottle of wine and large wet spot that had formed on her rug.

"You need to improve your aim."

"Next time." They laughed. "But my mouth is tingling. Better get the epinephrine for me." She sank back onto the couch.

Sirens could be heard in the distance. In minutes, the house was filled with officers and paramedics. Lynn appeared at Kalico's side, exclaiming at his bloodied face and demanding answers. Victor grinned at him and handcuffed Jane, pulling her none too gently to her feet. As Jane was hauled off, Nancy and Kalico were loaded into an ambulance.

Left alone for a moment, Emelia picked up Moody and scratched her behind the ears. "You got the bad lady, girl. We all did." Then she got the little dog a special treat from the pantry, collected her purse, locked the back and front doors, and joined Lynn so that they could follow their friends to the hospital.

Chapter Twenty-Four

"Man, you never, and I mean never, turn your back on a perp!" Victor shook his head at Kalico who was propped in a hospital bed, with his head in bandages, his right arm in a sling, and a brace over his right knee.

"Hey, a little sympathy for the wounded."

"And to be taken out by a little old lady. Ben, it's bad enough that you are the retriever of retrievers, the finder of felines, the catcher of...."

"Officer!" Emelia Winterjoy's voice demanded silence. "I'll have you know that this fine detective prevented two murders tonight and solved a third. He is not to be trifled with!"

"Yes, ma'am. I mean, no, ma'am."

Kalico grinned as Victor stood at attention. He had not seen that particular look on his friend's face since Mr. Gordon's American Literature class junior year of high school.

"Benjamin is in no condition to give his statement. You may return in the morning. I, however, will be free to speak with you in a few minutes—if you will be so good as to step outside."

"Of course, ma'am." For a moment Kalico thought he was going to salute. "Benj, I will see you mañana." Then, Officer Carrillo practically ran from the room.

Emelia stared gravely at her young detective. "How are you feeling?"

"Not too bad considering."

The elderly woman moved to his bedside and surprised him by reaching out for his good hand. She squeezed it warmly. "Benjamin, there are no words. Thank you seems inadequate for the service you have done for me and for Nancy."

"You are welcome. How is Nancy?"

"Fine. They're going to keep her under observation for a few more hours. She had taken a Benadryl earlier in the day which delayed the onset of symptoms." She shuddered at the memory of her best friend calmly chewing peanuts. "I cannot believe Jane's maleficence. Nance sends her love and will be in to see you tomorrow."

"Aunt Emelia?" Lynn stood in the hospital room's doorway. "Your three minutes are up. There's a line out here."

Over the next hour a steady stream of people appeared to commiserate over Kalico's wounds and to wish him well. M's and Katie entered to share "before" and "after" pictures of Ghost, who had been bathed and groomed and was safely back at Star Ranch. Mrs. Buonanotte smuggled in Zoe and cannoli, making him laugh until his aching head ached some more. His parents arrived, anxious but proud, followed by his older sisters, Karen and Karla. Finally, only Lynn remained.

"You look exhausted," she murmured. "I should go too."

Kalico patted the bedside, grinning at her crookedly. What? No succor for a wounded man?"

Lynn laughed and gently eased in beside him, resting her head on his good shoulder.

"That's better."

"Ben, I don't know how to thank you. If anything had happened to Aunt Em...."

"Just doin' my job," he drawled. "But seriously, I think your aunt and Nancy would have been fine. If you could have seen Emelia tackling Jane and Nancy hurling that wine bottle—they were not going down without a fight!"

"Still, I'm grateful that you believed Aunt Emelia—that you took her seriously."

Kalico chuckled. "She didn't give me much choice."

Lynn sighed and lifted her face, kissing him slowly and sweetly.

"Hold on!" Kalico teased after a moment. "It's not our fifth date yet"

"I'm an English teacher, Ben. And English teachers can't count!" She brushed her lips over his again before snuggling into his shoulder.

"At least we've broken the Kalico curse!"

"What curse?"

"It's just something my dad always says—that Kalico men are destined for women whose names begin with 'K'."

Lynn laughed. "But, Ben, I thought you knew: Lynn is short for Kaitlyn—with a K!"

Kalico groaned, but tightened his arm around her. "Did I say, 'curse?' I meant blessing."

THE END

ABOUT THE AUTHOR

Penny S. Weibly is a lifelong educator who earned her masters and doctorate in English literature from the University of Texas at Austin. She has taught English at the university level, directed a non-profit designed to assist students who have dropped out of school, and been a freelance writer for multi-media companies. Currently, she teaches English literature and creative writing at a private Catholic high school. She loves to read, travel, exercise, and spend time with friends. Her students inspire her daily. She resides in Austin, Texas, with her beloved dogs Zoe and Riley.

Made in the USA
Coppell, TX
03 January 2023

10300150R10146